D1059718

Revolt of the Moles

Revolt of the Moles

Alan Tongret

For Jo Ann

3rd edition, May 11, 2023
1st edition 24 Nov 2021; 2nd edition 2022

ISBN 978-0-578-99780-3
Imprint: This is a DBA Tongret*ARTS* publication.
alantongret@gmail.com
Twitter — @AlanTongret
Also on Linkedin

MOLE END

YOU CAN BE DEAD CERTAIN that the cabin and its three wooded acres are Mole End, because a hand carved, pinewood sign *tells* you so. The cabin is tucked behind a split-rail fence—a rest stop for a charm of finches—and is backed up by a fieldstone fence that's grizzled with lichen. Fruit trees sway in the breeze, entertaining a vegetable garden and a lawn that are lush from a recent rainstorm, and fir trees intoxicate the air with their resin scent. A brook and waterfall feed a pond that's deep enough in summer for skinny-dipping and broad enough in winter for ice-skating, a pond that's permanently leased out to a frog quartet who belt out a nightly cabaret. A fox and her kits frequent the pond to drink, and are greeted by a barn owl, some mourning doves and cardinals, and a mockingbird—who auditions all year round for a guest spot on the animals' cabaret.

But the moles for whom this homestead is named are rarely heard or seen, except for their tunnels that meander beneath the lawn like the runs in a schoolgirl's tights. The cabin itself is silent as can be, though quaint enough that motorists hit their brakes to gaze at its hand-shaved clapboards and well-seasoned cedar shakes, while its second-floor dormer windows gaze fondly back beneath half-lowered shades.

Nearby Mole End are several other homesteads on Orchard Lane, a bucolic road situated on the edge of the Village of Wildrose. But you may wonder what hints there are of Mole End's human inhabitants. If you look behind the cabin you'll find a vintage Volkswagen camper and two bicycles with wicker baskets, leaning against a shed that's piled high with well-kept tools. A terra cotta chiminea fire pit graces the cabin's roofed-in back porch, accompanied by a trio of Adirondack chairs that whisper of elderberry wine and old slippers.

But what if you've stumbled upon Mole End on your e-device and don't believe this idyllic portrait of it? How's it possible, you ask, that somewhere so altogether *out-of-it* can be the fuse and fan of the Noise War that's embroiling planet Earth? To answer that we must go to Sunday evening—June 1st of this very year—when a pair of hammered-brass lamps are chasing the shadows from the cabin's front-door stoop. Then Mole End is suddenly awakened by a sound that's borne on a wind gust from the teakwood deck of a mansion a half-mile up Orchard Lane. The mansion boasts a five-car garage and an arboretum stocked with Old World trees, a Swiss chalet style maintenance building, and an airstrip with its hangar. Go closer and you'll find walls of Ponderosa pine logs as stout as warship canons, and bullet-proof windows that stare brazenly down at you from a turret that crowns the mansion's four princely stories. It's a dwelling you'd expect to find at Lake Tahoe or Newport, Rhode Island, and rumor says Disneyland is about to open a replica of it, only much smaller.

The sound wafting onto Mole End suddenly grows louder, but it isn't what you'd expect from such eye-popping battlements. It's *music*—and we aren't talking steel guitars or 1,000-watt keyboards with speakers the size of bathtubs. Nor are there crack-cocaine high-hats or meth-amphetamine-powered tom-toms. We aren't even talking the Marine Band, serving up a Sousa march. It's *string* music, bowed by conservatory-trained musicians on custom-made instruments. The music is in fact coming from a pair of cellos—on which the musicians are playing *Mozart!*

~ VILLAGE OF WILDROSE ~

UPPER ORCHARD LANE

>Mont-Obiston Manor. Thaïs, Zebulon & Raffia Mont-Obiston

MIDDLE ORCHARD LANE

>Middlemarsh Manse B&B. Silt, Wanda, Henna & twin boys

>The Whingers. Clovis, Madge & beloved swimming pool

>The Plinketts. Po, Pru & their Chihuahuas

>Mole End. Sam, Jenny, Leah & Moleen Ashlar

>The Offmans. Honus & Winney's auto-rehab business

>The Silvertongs. Sol, Figgie & their sportplatz

ORCHARD LANE BOTTOMS.

(West Side of the U-bend)

>Dinsmore Farm. Dewey, Mynah, son Sparrow & numerous sibling dirt bikers

ORCHARD LANE BOTTOMS

(East Side of the U-bend)

>The Elms' Cosmic Sonic Sisterhood. Calliope, Pavana, et al

PART ONE

-1-

TO BEGIN, WE FIND SAM ASHLAR, tucked in a cushioned armchair at the knees of the two cellists, and he's happier than a hound dog with its own burger stand. Sam is holding hands with Jenny—his wife of 42 years—and they drink in the music as the two cellists end the duet. Then the coals in a barbecue pit behind Sam and Jenny *hiss* to reassert their hold on all of the guests lounging on the teakwood deck at Mont-Obiston Manor, a deck so vast it could double as a basketball court. The cellists—Pierre and Marie Pasquin, husband-and-wife music faculty at nearby All Souls College—bow gratefully to the applause.

"Bravo!" says Sam, taking an unlit pipe from his mouth.

"Bra*va!*" says Jenny.

Pierre and Marie beam over their cellos, and Leah—Sam and Jenny's auburn-haired granddaughter—pans her movie camera from Pierre and Marie to Sam as he pockets his pipe and bounds up to congratulate them on their performance. The movement was over-zealous and he winces in pain.

Jenny turns to him in alarm, but he says it's nothing, although he probes his back with his fingers.

Leah sees it's not serious and turns her camera to the other guests as they cloak Pierre and Marie in *Oos!* and *Ahs!*

"What nifty music!" says Clovis Whinger, one of the Ashlars' neighbors on Orchard Lane. Clovis slaps Pierre on the shoulder so hard it rattles his cello, and Clovis's wife Madge gushes to Marie, "Both of you are so talented! I hope your little duet just grows and grows until it's an *orchestra!*"

The evening's hostess—Thaïs Mont-Obiston—strides over and slips Pierre and Marie a fat envelope. Former European Union CEO-of-the-Year and current Wildrose mayor, Thaïs mesmerizes her guests with an indigo silk gown, a Bruges lace choker, and an ePendant suspended from her neck, set with a five-carat ruby above its tiny screen. She moves on to the Ashlars and lowers a platinum-ringed hand onto Sam's shoulder, peering down at him from her seven feet, nine inches.

"Well, Sam," she booms, "what did you think of the recital?"

He throws back his head to meet her eyes. "It was remarkable! And such a skilled orchestration of Mozart's 'Duet for Violin and Viola in G Major'!"

Then Thaïs lowers her other hand with its own load of platinum on Jenny, who exclaims, "And a lovely finale to our first weekend in Wildrose!"

Across the deck, one of the Ashlars' other neighbors—Silt Middlemarsh—shakes his head in wonder at Leah (moving deftly about with her camera) and exclaims to his wife Wanda, "What an enchanting young woman!"

"And gifted!" says Wanda. "Remember that documentary we saw about the vanishing American farm? *She* produced and directed it!"

The party lights heighten the lime green of Wanda's chiffon dress that she'd bought upon graduating art school 17 years ago and fitted with yellow tansy trimmings for the barbecue—the first outing that she, Silt, and the dress have had in months.

Silt grabs her hand. "As soon as Thaïs is done with her Katherine-the-Great act let's get the jump on the rest of Orchard Lane and ask the Ashlars to dinner!" He gets a card from his wallet:

Middlemarsh Manse, B&B
Victorian Ambiance ~ Modern Comforts.

"And don't forget to give them one of *your* cards!"

"I'm out of cards!"

"Wanda!" He pinches her arm. "Then make sure they see *that*." He jerks his head at a glazed dish on the buffet table, sculpted with seashell contours and driftwood handles. "Mention the commission Thaïs gave you, for God's sake, and don't forget to tell them you're a Village council member!"

Leah, meanwhile, focuses her movie camera on Thaïs, whose every strand of platinum hair remains perfectly in place as she once again leans down to Sam and Jenny—a derrick at a worksite.

"Didn't both of you teach the humanities?"

"Sam taught English literature," says Jenny.

Clovis Whinger springs forward. "Hey, Sam! We get all the best novels at Knokdown Drugs. You oughta come by for a look!"

Thaïs silences Clovis with a flash of her black eyes, and he backpedals a yard or two as Jenny adds, "And Sam played horn in the Emerson University Orchestra."

"And Jenny taught dance and botany!" says Sam.

"Dance and *botany!?*" says Thaïs, wrinkling her forehead at Jenny. She looks back at Sam. "Well. I hear you're writing a book. The *Wildrose Voyeur* must do a story, and I'll ask our Village Clerk to interview you."

"His book is about Thoreau," says Jenny, "whom he can talk about forever!"

Thaïs jerks as if she'd been slapped. "*Thoreau…?*"

She starts to protest when a throng of pickup trucks, retro rods, e-cycles, and Lectro SUV's roars by—some of them sowing black clouds of fumes—while blasting their horns and blaring a cacophonous brew of puke-Rok, Gregorian rant, rap^3, jazzBach, and other noises impossible to describe, causing Thaïs's guests to cover their ears and flock to the deck railing in alarm.

"It's ICEE!" cries Po Plinkett, swatting at the fumes.

Po, his wife Pru, and their beloved pair of Chihuahuas live just north of the Ashlars, and they stare in shock as the vehicles disappear down Orchard Lane.

Marie Pasquin was shaken in the act of retiring her cello to its case by the vehicles' ear drubbing, and she turns to Po in alarm. "ICE?"

"With two EEs, rhymes with *spice!* Internal Combustion Engine Enthusiasts," says Honus Offman, butting into the conversation and hooking his oil-stained thumbs in his denim jumpsuit. "Hellv'a fine group! Winney and me joined up years ago!" Honus lives directly across Orchard Lane from the Ashlars in a ramshackle bungalow with a matching carriage-house, where he and his wife Winney tinker endlessly with broken-down cars.

Pierre's face darkens. "Those bikes and Lectro SUVs have been so loud this spring that we had to cancel the College Wind Band's Fresh Air Practice Series!"

Having captured this exchange and finding it alarming, Leah turns her camera on Thaïs and her grandparents—but Thaïs seems not to have heard the vehicles. Instead, she shoves Thoreau to the back of her mind and gestures at a group of Lombardy poplars beyond her lawn as she smiles down at Jenny.

"As you're a botanist, I'd be honored to have your opinion of my arboretum. And I imagine you're itching to get your hands on the greenery at Mole Retreat."

"Mole *End*," says Jenny.

"I beg your pardon!" says Thaïs, putting a hand to her cheek and dropping her sleeve enough to reveal a forearm that would frighten an NFL lineman.

"Though Mole End *is* a retreat," says Sam. "And we're relieved to have left the city, with the noises worsening every year. Wildrose is so calming I'm certain to get loads of writing done!"

Thaïs turns to Jenny. "Wasn't Mole End your family homestead?"

"It was my late uncle's, but until now I don't think we'd been there for five or six years. Still, I find Wildrose as lovely as ever. Except for that new freeway—and that sprawling housing development on the river where those small farms used to be. What's it called? Condo Estates…?"

Thaïs's eyes narrow. "*Condor* Estates."

"Oh, of course!" says Jenny, taking Sam's arm. "Named after Wildrose's glorious mountain, *Condor Lookout.* We went by it when we drove in Friday night."

"Well," he says. "It was past midnight and raining like mad!"

A movement at an upper-story window catches his eye, and he sees Thaïs staring down at him from between the shutters! He blinks and she's gone! Then after a moment of confusion (and feeling he's drunk too much) he returns to Thaïs, towering over him.

"Anyway, your Manor is certainly impressive!"

Leah moves in with her camera and Thaïs takes hold of her. "Have you gotten some good footage in the can, my dear?"

Leah is sobered by a hand that smothers her shoulder like a saddle, but laughs as she removes her earbud. "I tried to avoid everyone who's camera shy, and got the Pasquins' blessing to film their recital."

Pierre and Marie blow kisses from the deck railing.

"Heavens!" says Thaïs. "I'd think anyone would kill to be in your film. I'm certainly yearning for *my* debut on the silver screen!" She chortles and the deck chortles with her. "Have you chosen a title?"

"It's a documentary about the ups and downs of retirement—though my grandparents are *very* far from retired!" Thaïs lifts an eyebrow in amusement and releases Leah to hug her grandparents and declare, "I'm calling it, *Sam and Jenny Meet Henry David at Mole End*."

-2-

THAÏS AND HER BUTLER—Gallifent—bid their guests goodnight, and as the servants hose down the deck under Gallifent's search-light gaze, Thaïs checks the messages on her ePendant's tiny screen while taking an elevator to the Manor's third-floor sitting room to confer with her ancient housekeeper—Petra—then alights at her own bedroom suite on the fourth floor.

"Hello, my pet! I'm back!"

Thaïs awakens the computer on her dressing table as her sister—Raffia—clomps in from the shadows to help remove Thaïs's party gown.

Raffia's already in her Snow White robe and slippers. Her own elevator (her mental one) was frozen on the floor of her seventh year by a childhood illness, and ever since she's been privately tutored in the several Mont-Obiston establishments since Thaïs got her MBA in Brand Management at the Sorbonne 18 years earlier. If Thaïs has dreams she shares them with Raffia, who presses them like forget-me-nots between the pages of her innocent mind.

A blurb flits across Thaïs's computer screen, showing that the family enterprise—Platinum LLC—has reaped a profit of 47% over the previous month.

"How delicious!" Thaïs thunders, and Raffia runs her banana-size forefinger over the graphs and squiggles on the screen.

"Delicious?"

"Financially nutritious!"

"Then I'm very glad!"

Raffia had suffered from a tummy ache that morning and Thaïs is happy to see that Petra's ginger tea relieved it. She watches with growing affection as Raffia stows the jewelry in a drawer, and Thaïs's gown and size 19 party pumps in a cedar-forest vault, then Raffia returns to the vanity table.

"Was the barbecue fun? I heard the big violins from my window and thought they were magical!"

Although Raffia's as tall and big-boned as Thaïs, she's as carefree and airy as a schoolgirl at a sleepover.

"They were cellos," says Thaïs. "And you might've joined us for a few minutes."

Raffia shudders. "But I hadn't anyone to play with!"

Thaïs studies herself in the vanity mirror, then draws her hand over her cheek and its emergent sandpaper texture. In a burst of angst she rubs in cold cream while Raffia gets facial tissues, and working together in a well-practiced routine they remove the opal foundation, ashes-of-rose rouge, russet-dawn lipstick, midnight eyeshadow, and the crescent beauty mark on Thaïs's left cheek.

Thaïs leans in to the mirror and probes her features as her voice grows husky. "…a superb barbecue…and the Ashlars! …smart, artsy, and so terribly eager to please!"

Then suddenly, "But what's this about *Thoreau*…?!"

* * *

"Zebulon…? Didn't you hear me?"

It's Raffia, moments later. She's cleared away the soiled tissues and neatened up the dressing table. The mammoth bra and slip are gone, freeing a torso more angular than curvy. Thaïs's platinum curls have been brushed back from the forehead and ears, and all adornment's gone but the ePendant and its glinting ruby.

Raffia watches the final transformation, then pulls the stopper from a cutglass bottle in the shape of a rampant stag and pours its umber liquid onto her sibling's outstretched palms, which splash it onto the rugged cheeks and anvil jaw above the Adam's apple—set free when the lace choker was removed. A bunkhouse aroma whips around the room.

"How'd you spend your evening?" Zebulon booms, rousing himself from the dressing table.

"I colored in my book!" says Raffia.

She follows him to a silent valet and helps him change into his lampblack eveningwear. Trousers and shirt, trench coat, and leather boots, blacker than a pair of rooks. With Thoreau nipping at his vitals, Zebulon drafts and prints a letter on the computer, then slips on a pair of riding gauntlets, snug as oil slicks. He takes a pair of $100 bills from a desk, folds them in the letter and seals it in a blank envelope.

"I must go out," he says, "and you must go to bed."

"And will you bring some stories back?"

Raffia is especially radiant tonight, reminding Zebulon of the tummy ache she'd had at breakfast time. His head spins, and he wonders if it's possible? Has it been a month already?! An electric thrill shoots up his spine.

"I always bring you stories back, my dove!"

He takes her hand and leads her to her room where she stretches out on her bed—a bed that suddenly portends a resurgent Mont-Obiston line. She snuggles against her toy stuffed giraffe as Zebulon pulls the quilt up to her chin, then shivering with joy he dims the lights and slips away.

* * *

Sam and Jenny stroll down Orchard Lane below the June 1st sliver of a moon and a smorgasbord of stars.

"What a night!" says Jenny.

They've been well fed on grilled sturgeon, Cheshire cheese asparagus, Potatoes Toulouse, strawberry parfait, and a prize-winning Riesling, and are mellower than a couple of kittens with a pet milk cow.

"What do you suppose that convoy of SUVs and trucks was all about?" says Sam.

"Maybe they took a wrong exit off the new freeway."

"And Thaïs? Does she have a sister? I swear I saw her double, staring down at me from an upper-story window!"

"She's one of triplets."

"*Triplets…?*"

"Madge Whinger mentioned it in the powder room. There's a sister and a brother. And such a powder room you've never seen!"

He laughs. "I'm sure! But I wonder why they weren't at the barbeque. It's hard to imagine *three* such giants in one family!"

"Madge said they're diehard recluses. The sister has a developmental problem and the brother's notoriously anti-social."

"For which Thaïs more than makes up! And speaking of things social, I guess we're dining with Silt and Wanda Middlemarsh on Saturday?"

"Silt gave us their card, remember? Apparently a posh bed and breakfast, just below here on Orchard Lane. He was the Wildrose High School Business Ed teacher, recently appointed Superintendent, and Wanda's an art potter and Wildrose councilmember. So it'll be fun getting to know them!"

Sam fishes the card from his sportcoat. "Ah, yes. Middlemarsh Manse, B&B."

"And we're lunching with the Whingers on Sunday, one house down from the Middlemarshes. Madge and Clovis—beside their swimming pool—of which they're *extra*ordinarily proud."

"And he owns a bookshop?"

"He runs the drugstore. I think he meant their rack of bodice-rippers."

"Oops! And weren't there other invitations? The Silverthongs and the—"

Jenny elbows him. "Silver*tongs*." They laugh and she goes on. "I finally lost track, but they all promised to send reminders!"

Their footfalls murmur on Orchard Lane's pine-needle carpet, with the occasional *crackle crunch* of a walnut hull. Sam has had several glasses of the world-beating Riesling offered up by the tanker car by Thaïs's caterer, and sways like a sailor on shore leave. He's blissfully happy and loves everyone on the planet—most of all Jenny—and he's certain that Thaïs and her guests love them. He and Jenny have found a haven from the brutal din that marred their final year in the city, and are free to spend their last years launching a counterattack!

* * *

In raptures over Raffia's condition, Zebulon leaps downstairs three steps at a time to the library on Mont-Obiston Manor's second floor, where wall sconces pour waterfalls of light over palisades of buckram, calfskin, and gold-gilt vellum. At the feet and eddies of these keepsake tomes are sealanes of Persian rugs amid islands of museum-quality mahogany armchairs, divans, and side tables. An aquarium bubbles with piranhas and other snapping fish, large enough to frighten a Navy SEAL, and beyond the aquarium a chandelier at the cathedral ceiling shines down upon a billiards-size table with an architect's model of townvillas, twinkling shops, and a river with a marina, topped off by a 12-story, bejeweled monolith with a sign that glitters:

CONDOR ESTATES *TURQUOISE TOWER*
GRANDE OPENING GALA — SEPTEMBER 6

Zebulon makes a conference call on his ePendant and his two generalissimos answer from their staterooms aboard the Tugboat Inn on Wildrose River. Marine Colonel Billy Umbo, Retired, and Chef Engineer Geoffrey Murgwynd.

"Gentlemen, I'm moving up the Gala!"

A ghastly silence, then Billy Umbo gasps. "Moving *up* the Gala?"

"A matter of five weeks," says Zebulon, and he gives the precise day.

Geoffrey Murgwynd stammers. "*F-five weeks?!*"

"Five weeks!" says Zebulon.

Murgwynd gulps. "Of course!"

And Billy Umbo stammers, "Yes, Sir! I'll get right on it!"

Zebulon ends the call and goes to a cabinet for a chunk of emerald-impregnated ore he'd collected three years ago during an exploratory visit to Wildrose. Its facets break the chandelier into a constellation of mini suns that illuminate the image of Thaïs in an immense triple-portrait oil canvas, hanging above the fireplace. It's Zebulon's greatest treasure, which the artist finished a few days before the dénouement of Thaïs's illness.

"Just 10 weeks off, my dearest! Our greatest birthday ever!"

He returns the ore to the cabinet, then touches a keypad and the date on the huge model with its terraced townvillas changes from SEPTEMBER 6 to AUGUST 9. He runs his eye over the blank envelope—sealed around the letter he'd just printed up and wrapped around the pair of $100 bills—and tucks it deep inside his trench coat pocket.

"And now for *Thoreau!*"

He plummets to the garage where a 1934 Duesenberg S J Roadster beckons with its platinum sheen. As much as he delights in its Yankee swank and brawn, he passes it by for a black van. Its rear door opens and he climbs in, awaited by something much darker than the van.

Zebulon whispers, "Nightshade!"

It purrs and Zebulon pulls on a nonreflective helmet and mounts Nightshade as its dials glow and infrared headlight awakens. He twists the handgrip and Nightshade pads silently from the van, then the garage door snaps open and Nightshade lopes invisibly down the driveway.

-3-

LATE THOUGH IT IS, Wanda Middlemarsh pulls a smock over her lime-green party dress and starts work in her studio. Her teenage daughter and two teenage sons are in their bedrooms, doing God only knows what on unfathomable socio-digital gadgets, and her husband Silt is stretched out in the parlor, sucked up by a James Bond film on their ancient TV's only working channel.

"O God," Wanda mutters.

They have guests coming soon and Middlemarsh Manse B&B is a mess, but at the moment she doesn't give a damn. She's weeks behind in starting the second of 13 sculptures commissioned by Thaïs, and she begins coiling a rope of wet clay with the idea of molding it into a wine jug in the likeness of a fish or mammal. Thaïs had asked for wildlife-themed somethings-or-other—13 "objets d'art" for her Camelot-size banquet table, and left the rest to Wanda. Each piece is to be glazed and fired and Thaïs is paying $15,000 for the lot. Wanda and Silt have already spent Thaïs's $3,000 deposit on new mattresses for their two B&B guestrooms, as the old ones were gamier than a presidential campaign, belying the Manse's promise of "modern comforts."

A sudden movement outside Wanda's window pulls her eyes to Sam and Jenny, their white hair and his white beard glowing in the starlight as they stroll down Orchard Lane.

"Thank God!" Wanda thinks. "A couple with whom I can discuss the arts!"

Then her daughter Henna bursts in, her teeth gleaming with the braces for which Wanda and Silt are still paying.

"Mom! I need a bath and the stupid water heater's gone blinkety again!"

* * *

A breeze ruffles Sam's tie as he and Jenny round the final curve above Mole End, while Zebulon follows on Nightshade. Jenny shivers in the breeze's chill, and Sam removes his fedora and plops it on her head.

"Nice touch!" Leah thinks, steadying her camera's telephoto lens on a pear tree limb beside the road.

Zebulon sees her, and intrigued by this third Ashlar he stops Nightshade.

Leah keeps her grandparents in the crosshairs of her shotgun mic, which can detect a ladybug belching at 200 yards. Then they move on—as does Zebulon, a wraith at their very heels—and moments later Mole End's porch lights appear out of the evening mist like the gaze of an enormous owl. Water splashes down the falls of Mole End's brook, crickets strum their tiny banjos, and the bullfrog croons a lullaby, luring Sam and Jenny to drink their fill of the moment.

Zebulon throws a toggle and Nightshade's headlight goes halogen as a meat-cleaver roar from its airhorn hacks the nighttime flesh.

"Watch out!" Leah shouts.

The soundwaves fling Sam and Jenny into the ditch as Nightshade tears by, choking them with the stench of burnt rubber.

-4-

It's 5:00 A.M. AND THE MANTELPIECE CLOCK in Mole End's living room strikes the hour. Sam is jolted awake in the bedroom down the hall, where the dawn light reveals the plasterer's trowel marks in the ceiling.

Then Sam remembers where he is and turns to Jenny—sleeping calmly beside him with her head resting on her arm above the bandaged wrist.

Sam normally rises at 6:00 a.m. sharp, his favorite time to read or study before breakfasting with Jenny and strolling with her to campus to meet their students. An afternoon nap on his office throw rug always recharged him sufficiently to conduct an evening seminar, grade student work, or enjoy a concert or a play with Jenny. Occasionally *he* was in the concert, playing horn.

The previous evening's incident hovers over him like a waking nightmare. At first he'd feared that Jenny had broken her wrist, but it was just a nasty scrape from the gravel in the ditch. Leah reviewed her footage of them strolling down Orchard Lane, but couldn't make out their assailant.

"Whoever it was got swallowed up, as if by a black hole!" she said with a toss of her auburn hair.

First it was the souped-up trucks and 'Lectro SUVs disrupting the mayor's barbecue, then that invisible thing! Sam had hoped they'd have the summer to soak up some peace and harmony, but in the five years since they last visited Wildrose it seems that the pall of noises that stalked them in the city had already spread to Orchard Lane!

He pulls himself from bed and feels the bruise on his shoulder from landing in the ditch, plus the arthritis in his knees and sciatica in his back. The cost of his 76 years, and very much like the Tin Man without his oil can.

He changes from his PJs to a sweatsuit and goes to the bathroom for a pee, then to the living room by the mantelpiece with the calm ticking of Jenny's heirloom clock to do his stretches, pushups, and chinups. He usually takes his time, focusing on his breathing and form, but now he rushes as though it were a contest. Rather than jogging in place for 20 minutes, he jogs up and down the hallway, burning up angst as much as calories. Now looser than Roger Federer, he showers, dresses, and slips to the kitchen. Instead of his usual hot oatmeal, milk, and banana, he downs a donut and some coffee. Instant rather than brewed.

Soon afterward Sam is snug in one of the Adirondack chairs on the cabin's back porch that opens upon Mole End's pond and genial variety of trees. The chill air nips at him, but he's warmed by his fedora, an old tweed sportcoat, and a thermos of coffee. He's further warmed with a loaded pipe, a loaded fountain pen and notepad, and one of the several volumes of his much-annotated copy of Thoreau's *Journal*, loaded with two million words. The terra cotta fire pit and box of willowwood kindling catch his eye, and he thinks it'll be fun to have a fire one evening, when he's sitting around with Jenny and Leah over a glass of wine. But now there's work to do and he plunges into the *Journal*.

Leah's already filming him. Wakened by the loose board beneath Sam's foot while he jogged up and down the cabin's hallway (squeaking like a mouse on an Inquisition rack), she'd slipped from her upstairs bedroom and hid behind the trunk of a massive black willow tree—felled by a winter storm, and the mother of the box of kindling beside the fire pit.

There's a sudden sharp splash as a great blue heron claims a sunfish and takes it from the pond to a cedar tree. Leah captures this in her lens and pans back to Sam, who's lost in Thoreau.

"My God!" she thinks. "He's on a tear!"

* * *

Tread on Us Retreads is a long-ago whitewashed concrete block structure of twin-bay changing stations and a Quonset hut warehouse—squatting on the junction of Salamander Ridge and the brand new Sky Vue Freeway, a five-mile stretch of blinding concrete that leans against Wildrose like the blade of an immense scythe.

It's 8:53 a.m. and the two owners plod from their bachelor quarters at the rear of the Quonset hut and clomp through the stanchions of reborn roadwear. The taller man unbolts the front door and sees an envelope on the concrete floor below the mail slot.

"Hey! It's another 'un!"

His muscular partner grabs the envelope and rips it open to find an unsigned, computer-generated letter, folded around a pair of $100 bills.

"Who ya think's payin us all this money?" says the taller one.

It's the third such windfall they've had and he grabs at one of the bills, but Muscles smacks his hand.

"Holt on, till we see wut hit says!"

The Quonset hut with its towers of black tires and insect-smudged florescent light fixtures is murkier than a barroom on Sunday morning, and Muscles cracks the door enough to let some sunbeams slash across the letter. He reads haltingly, as if he'd never gotten past Dick and Jane's first adventure—further instructions for the walkie-talkie left off at the Quonset hut a week earlier and a terse directive.

"Hit says we gotta take some noisy hog rides on Orchard Lane!"

-5-

THE SUN IS CRESTING MOLE END'S treetops when Sam puts Thoreau's *Journal* aside to mow the lawn, tall and vigorous from the rainstorm when they arrived in Wildrose the previous Friday night. He straps on a back-brace and rescues an old manual push-mower from the toolshed that he oils and sharpens with his farmboy skills, then trims the lawn as neatly as a barber trims a sideburn.

Leah is filming him and puts down her camera to help Jenny prepare the garden.

"What seeds do you have?"

"We'll run by the Cucumber Patch in Wildrose Village Center. A gardener's paradise!"

Perspiration loosens the bandage on Jenny's wrist and she smooths it back in place. The previous night's incident still clouds her mind, but the mild morning breeze is purging it, and she is thrilled to see Sam beguile the mower as its helix blades *swoosh* across the lawn. He wears a sombrero he'd gotten at an educators' retreat in Santa Fe, and wrangles the mower over a mole hummock while whistling the *presto* movement from a horn concerto—and she knows he's troubled by something.

He nudges the hummock with his toe, then discovers several others around the yard. "It's the New York subway system!"

A diesel truck scrapes to a stop a few houses up Orchard Lane and its doors squeak as machinery clashes and men swear. One of Po and Pru Plinketts' beloved Chihuahuas responds by barking from the bay window of their house immediately north of Mole End, then its sibling joins in with the worst kind of yapping.

Then a man hops from the diesel truck and brays out orders as other men bray back in Spanish.

"Must be a road maintenance crew," says Sam, and Leah puts down her mattock. "Why don't we take a breather!"

They settle in the Adirondack chairs on the back porch to enjoy her lemonade and Jenny's fresh-baked shortbread cookies—then the diesel truck clangs its way down the lane, one house closer to Mole End.

"Maybe it's a lawn-care crew," says Leah.

Jenny fans herself with her straw hat. "In Wildrose? I'm amazed that the neighbors allow it! But I guess most of them are away at their jobs. Clovis and Madge Whinger said they work in the Village Center, and Silt Middlemarsh runs the summer school." She frowns at the dovecotes beneath the toolshed eaves. "I wonder why some of those are empty. And there used to be a lot more wrens, and more waterfowl by the pond!"

The Chihuahuas at the Plinketts' bay window just north of them are barking louder and Jenny turns to Sam, who's stuffing the last of the tobacco into his pipe, as if trying to plug up the noises.

"And didn't Po Plinkett say he manages one of the shops that's opening this summer at the Turquoise Tower on Wildrose River?"

Sam lights up and blows a smoke ring. "I'm stunned that our neighbors *pay* to have their lawns done. They're missing out on fresh air and exercise!"

Up the lane, Wanda is hard at work in her studio, shaping a raccoon from the clay of the wine jug she'd begun the night before. She steps back to appraise it and realizes it wouldn't pass muster in an art therapy class for the metaphorically bewildered. And the lawn crew noises are driving her nuts. She slams down the windows—locking out the clanging and banging (as well as the heliotrope fragrance from her garden!), then rips apart the clay raccoon.

Leah pours more lemonade and the Ashlars sit patiently for some minutes, trusting that the lawn mercenaries will soon depart for another battlefront. And they do depart—to a battlefront one house nearer.

Sam grabs his sombrero. "I've gotta find out why mowing has to be so *loud!*"

He goes to the front gate at Mole End's split-rail fence and sees the diesel truck up the lane, droning on like the busy signal on a US Gov.com helpline. Then a riding mower shoots out the back of the truck. Its operator works levers and pedals that make the mower accelerate, reverse, and go into tighter spins than a salesman's pitch, while its vat inhales bushels of grass trimmings while snarling like a fighter jet on nosedive.

"God almighty!" says Sam.

Another worker darts from the truck with a fume-spewing hedger that guillotines any grass blades foolish enough to poke their heads *beyond* the lawn, and the Chihuahuas bark all the louder. A third man aims the nozzle of his high-octane backpack at the AWOL trimmings with a windburst that returns a few of them to the lawn, while the rest escape to the Plinketts' yard below the Chihuahuas' very muzzles. They've morphed into the Chihuahuas of the Baskervilles, and Sam retreats to the split-rail fence.

"I've gotta film this!" says Leah.

By the time she gets her camera the mower op unleashes his ravenous device onto Clovis and Madge Whinger's yard—another door closer to Mole End—rattling like a food processor with a mouthful of ball bearings.

"That does it!" Sam exclaims, and he makes his way through the petroleum haze to the Whingers' yard and taps the blower op on the shoulder. "Hey! That's an awfully loud gadget you got there!"

"Si!" says the man, and delighted that he has an admirer, he treats Sam to a complimentary nozzle blast.

Sam clings to the sombrero. "I think you're making a lot more noise than necessary!"

The man's boss sees Sam and tromps over. "Somp'n wrong?"

"I live across the way, and all of this seems a bit over the top!" The boss stares quizzically at the Whingers' roof and Sam tries again. "I mean, look at all the grass clippings he's scattering around!"

"We ain't done. He'll clean up every last scrap!"

"But you could do a lot better with a broom. Just think what you'd save on equipment and maintenance!"

The boss stares as if Sam were a madman. "Ya mean a *hand* broom?"

Sam points at the hedger op. "And that's louder than a morning talk show. Why don't you try one of those *electric* ones?"

The boss gets something on his earbud and roars into his chin mic. "If you're done with Buzzard Lane, I wan'cha to do Pokeberry Alley before ya break for your friggin lunch!"

He lowers his eyebrows at Sam. "Those battery things ain't worth diddlyshit!"

He gets an earbud call from another of his far-flung crews and stalks off, shouting instructions into his chin mic.

Sam throws up his hands and returns to Jenny on their side of Orchard Lane, who suggests they head off to Wildrose Village Center for an early lunch.

"We have to go there anyway, to sign the papers at Whitlow Insurance."

"Whitlow Insurance?"

Then Sam remembers—insurance for Mole End—the agency that Jenny's aunt and uncle used for decades. He loosens the strap on his sombrero.

"Good idea. And maybe we'll run across some of our neighbors who use these lawn marauders and give *them* an earful!"

-6-

INSURANCE TYCOON BUFORD WHITLOW trembles with joy as he stares across his desk at Billy Umbo, Platinum LLC's Chief of Customer Persuasion. "Joy" because Umbo just announced that Buford won the bid to provide coverage for the Condor Estates Expansion, which—*if it's approved*—will increase Wildrose's tax base by 35% and *double* Whitlow Insurance's income.

Since Buford is also a Wildrose councilmember he's glad that the Village will get an unexpected jackpot, but he's damned ecstatic that *he* will get some cash to save his agency from extinction. For months it's been foundering in red ink—due to the recent arrival of the predatory Worldwide Insurance on the new Sky Vue Freeway. Buford's agency was founded by his Great-Great Grandfather Plenteous Whitlow in his feedstore, and is being kept afloat on that red river of debt like an embattled innertube—inflated with the oxygen siphoned off from Buford's two employees' pension fund.

"This is pretty darn amazing!" he gasps to Umbo.

What most amazes Buford is how easy it had been to make the bid. Why, it was just a month earlier when—during his first visit to Whitlow Insurance—Billy Umbo tossed out a figure he thought Worldwide Insurance and other giant underwriters *might* bid, and said that if a *local* agency with longtime experience in the ways and wherefores of Wildrose were to make a bid in the *same ballpark*, it would weigh favorably in Platinum LLC's decision. That's all there was to it!

"If—it's—*approved!*" Umbo repeats, thumping Buford's desk with the flat of his hand. "You see. No rezoning, no Expansion. No Expansion, no insurance!"

Umbo is natty and super-buff in a charcoal sportcoat and cranberry bowtie. The creases in his grey slacks are sharp enough to slice a Stilton cheese, and his shoes are glossier than plums, recalling his days as a Marine Corps colonel, serving his final tour at Guantanamo Bay. At the start of their meeting he'd shoved his chair smack against Buford's desk, with his 200-pushups-a-day arms planted on it as if it were *his* desk.

"Well," says Buford, "as far as the rezoning goes, I can assure you that the Village Council will—"

Umbo scythes the air with his hand, causing Buford to slam back in his chair.

"Village councils aren't our concern!"

"But, as a councilmember *myself*—"

Umbo scythes another sheaf of air. "My friend. Platinum LLC never messes with politics. It builds dream resorts, and Whitlow Insurance provides seamless underwriting. We must let village councils do whatever they will!"

The morning is warming up and a trickle of sweat skis down Buford's neck and wipes out on the collar of the dress shirt. He no longer sends his shirts to the cleaner (being at the cleaner's himself) and the sweat makes him itch to turn on the AC. But he's praying that a cartload of cool air will roll in from the tree-lined Village Commons across the street so he can keep his God-awful electric bill under control.

Billy Umbo is so unruffled by the warmth that he might well have refrigerant in his veins, and he coolly hands over a check. "Your bidder's fee!"

Buford was surprised to have been offered a bidder's fee in the first place, and the figure they'd agreed on was $500. But the check is made out for *$5,000!*

Buford looks up at Umbo. "But—"

"Yes?"

"I thought—"

"Yes?"

Buford peers into Umbo's eyes, which mirror the office's fly-specked wallpaper, then he looks closer at the check. $5,000! Enough to cover the overdue interest on the second mortgage on his house—and add a few patches to that pension-sucking innertube! Another sweat bomb splats onto Buford's collar, but he doesn't give a fig.

"Right, Mr. Umbo. And thanks for being so… business-like!"

Umbo shoots to his feet, rifling back his chair that smashes the glass tank in Buford's great-great grandfather's water cooler, and gives Buford a no-turning-back hand squeeze.

"Thank *you*, my friend. And don't forget to let village councils do whatever they must!"

-7-

SAM AND JENNY ARE COASTING THEIR bicycles down Chipmunk Run toward their escape-the-noises lunch. His seat is set high to ease things for his arthritic knees and he rings his bell—for the fun of hearing its *b'ring-a-ling* as it chases the leaf blowers from his thoughts. Chipmunk Run is canopied with beeches that turn the Ashlars jadeite, making a great shot for Leah, trailing in her VW camper. Her camera is suction-clamped to the dashboard and she checks to make sure the composition is right on the mark.

"Gorgeous day!" she sings out the window to Sam and Jenny.

Sam has made a good start outlining ideas for his Thoreau book and is buoyed up by the abundant nature embracing them. Then the plaintive strains of flutes drift from the All Souls College Music Practice Room, next to the bandshell where folding chairs will be set up in six weeks for the Fourth of July Concert, free to one and all.

"How delightful!" says Leah.

Then some cars honk impatiently from behind her VW and race ahead of her, Sam, and Jenny.

"Good Lord!" says Sam. He shakes his head and turns to Jenny. "That reminds me. At the barbecue last night Pierre Pasquin said the traffic here on Chipmunk Run was getting too loud for the College Wind Band to practice outdoors!"

"Fueled by that Sky Vue Freeway," she says. "But don't forget to sign up for the band!"

"I won't!" he says, making his bell go *b'ring-a-ling.*

Several more cars hit their horns and rocket by in both directions, and farther along the Ashlars come to a hardhat crew by a semi-truck, whose gigantic praying mantis arm just settled an immense sign onto a steel pylon beside the road, where a worker fingers a keyboard to animate a message:

COMING AUGUST 9
CONDOR ESTATES *TURQUOISE TOWER*
GRANDE OPENING GALA!

"Holy cat!" says Sam.

They peddle through a thickening gruel of traffic to find that Condor Estates has swallowed scores of farms, which the Ashlars barely glimpsed through the rain as they arrived in Wildrose the night before last. They stare aghast as they bike along the Wildrose River bank, where Townvillas with party-size saunas and multi-SUV garages blind them with glaring metallic colors, sunburnt balconies, and money-back-guaranteed hominess.

"Thank God I brought my shades!" says Jenny.

They follow Chipmunk Run farther north, where Wildrose Marina stretches a quarter mile along the river and harbors the Tugboat Inn, replica Venetian gondolas, and 1830s-style keelboats that rent out by the day, week, or lifetime. Docks jut into the river and powerboats churn its channel into frothing wakes, and far above is the nearly finished Turquoise Tower, a soaring beacon that recalls the region's mining days. The Tower's innards prickle with scaffolding and building cranes, and trucks groan with construction materials as they trundle in from the Sky Vue Freeway. Embedded in the Tower's skin are 90 billion LEDs, the world's largest e-billboard and the only four-sided one. The stellar Turquoise Tower *QuadBoard.*

"I'd no idea!" says Jenny.

They lift their chins and follow Chipmunk Run another half mile north to Wildrose Forest, a remnant of the 23-million acre Great Forest and its defunct gemstone mine, plugged with a rusted iron door. On the edge of the Forest, Moonlight Knob broods down from its dizzying cliff-face, and higher still shimmers the celebrated Condor Lookout, perched among the clouds.

They pull over and Jenny's eyes moisten. "When I was a little girl my uncle took me hiking up to Condor Lookout, where you can see *everything!*"

Leah focuses her lens on Jenny, then a sudden clamor causes her to pan back to Condor Estates, where some asphalting trucks are befouling the air.

Sam sinks onto his seat. "Not a good day for biking!"

Jenny cuffs him on the shoulder. "I'll race you the rest of the way!"

* * *

Thaïs is touring Lapis Lazuli Concourse—the Turquoise Tower's aorta—and she's guided by the Tower's General Manager, Geoffrey Murgwynd, and Chief Engineer, Cornelius Flug. A pantsuit of fine mauve wool accentuates Thaïs's extension-ladder frame and a hardhat bears her name and title, asserting a self-assurance to equal a four-star general, goosing his troops across a battlefield. She and her two flunkies are spot-checking a few of the 1,007 shops, restaurants, and body-burnishing, pumicing, massaging, exfoliating, and depilating services, where armies of electricians, plumbers, and HVAC workers scramble like iron filings among magnets, infusing the air with the stench of acetylene torch fumes, PVC sealant, and Great Lakes of spray paint.

Some minutes later, Geoffrey Murgwynd leads Thaïs to the Lily Pad Lotions & Notions on the Tower's 14th floor, and Cornelius Flug brings it up on his Wristpad as Thaïs ducks through the doorway where Store Manager Po Plinkett is supervising the setup.

"Po! How's progress?"

Po's face is creased from the many weeks of 17-hour days he's poured into the Lily Pad's displays and furnishings, but he irons those creases into a grin.

"Couldn't be better, Your Honor!" He gestures at his underlings, searching for missing parts and puzzling over Mandarin instruction sheets. "We're thrilled about the new Grande Opening Gala date!"

One of Po's staff is cradling some cartons on an escalator that's letting her do all the climbing.

"What's going on there?" says Thaïs.

A muscle twitches in Po's face. "It's been like this for days, Your Honor. We've left a dozen maintenance requests!"

Thaïs drops her eyes to Murgwynd. "I can't speak for Platinum LLC, but it seems to me they'd want this repaired!"

"Absolutely!" says Murgwynd, dropping his eyes to Flug, who drops a quavering finger to his Wristpad. "I'll drop in another work order!"

-8-

JENNY'S IN THE LEAD ON HER BICYCLE as Leah films her grandparents' arrival at Wildrose Village Center, its many bustling businesses arrayed like daubs of paint on an artist's palette: The Save & Spend Bank, Boutique Gas & Lube, Food Bin, $2 Duz It, and Knokdown Drugs. Various shops in Toulouse-Lautrec blues and oranges grin down at the Village Commons' windswept turf where dogs snatch frisbees on the wing, and standing guard nearby is the Village Hall—a three-story Colonial monolith that houses the mayor's and clerk's offices, police HQ and tax office, and Wildrose Council Chamber. Farther along is the Happy Family Clinic, backed by a few lanes of wood-framed dwellings that boast bronze plaques, awarded because those dwellings escaped dry rot or the wrecker's ball for 183 years, or witnessed the birth of Millard Fillmore's aunt.

There's a *jingle-jingle* as the ManShot Trolley disgorges some middle-aged men on a daytrip to Wildrose, as other men clamber aboard to sink onto a stool and order a beer or whisky from the bar that runs the Trolley's full length—fleeing their wives or mistresses who rifle the thrift stores and giftshops. The ManShot *jingles* again and resumes its 25-minute circuit of the Village Center.

Sam and Jenny watch with amusement, then pull up to a gaggle of restaurants and lean their bikes against a bench on a herringbone-pattern brick sidewalk; then Jenny nods across the street at the Cucumber Patch.

"A gardener's paradise!"

Beside it is the Woodsculptors Loft, its display windows alive with handmade birdhouses and dovecotes, and a side yard that's dominated by a life-size moose carving below a chiseled sign:

CHAINSAW ART! CRAFTED LOCALLY!

Leah hops from the VW. "Wildrose has it all!"

The perky melody of Scott Joplin's "Gladiolus Rag" pours from the Green Goose Café a few yards away and the Ashlars decide *that's* where they want to eat. Then a motorcycle and its sidecar appear and brake to a stop.

"Oh Lord!" says Jenny. "I thought we'd escaped the noisemakers!"

But the motorcycle rolled in quietly, and the biker—sporting a daisy in his vest lapel—hefts a full-size carving of a grizzly bear from the sidecar and carries it in the Woodsculptors Loft.

The Ashlars smile with relief and enter the Green Goose Café, where the lean and youthful Giles McDrake is playing the Joplin rag on an old upright piano with a shillelagh resting on it.

He tosses them a friendly nod. "Top of the mornin to ya!"

Floorboards yield beneath the Ashlars' feet and lamps flare above booths and tables, rocking with grinning diners who hum along with the music. A sign invites the Ashlars to SEAT YOURSELF TO SUIT YOURSELF, so they claim a booth near Giles and his piano as a young woman in a green cap and apron zings over with menus.

"I'm Rita, yous guys' server. Welcome to the Green Goose!"

Jenny looks over the beverage list and tugs Sam's sleeve.

"They've got locally made wine and beer! Why don't we toast the start of your book, our first day's gardening, and Leah's film!"

She orders a glass of Green Goose Merlot and Leah (a conscientious driver) asks for a ginger ale.

"You oughta try the lager." The Ashlars turn to see the motorcyclist with the daisy in his vest. "When you finish one, you'll want two more!"

"Thanks!" says Sam. "I'll try it!"

The man offers his daisy to Rita, who socks his burly shoulder and runs off to get the drinks with the daisy tucked in her hair.

"Did you carve that grizzly bear with a chainsaw?" Sam asks. "It's stunning!"

The man gives him a woodchip with a seared image of a beaver that's inscribed, *Woodsculptors Loft — Lars Andersen, Woodcarver.* "I use an electric chainsaw at my farm. Far from the madding crowd! Feel free to stop by the Loft, where apple cider's always on tap—if the music hereabouts doesn't drive you out of town!"

Giles chuckles from his piano, and a woman of 40 or so in a chef's toque hoots from the serving window. "You're in big trouble now!"

Lars puts a hand to his heart. "Your cooking conquers all, Mabel!" He sits at the counter as Mabel hoots again and disappears into the kitchen's fragrant reaches.

Giles wrings the final bars from "Gladiolus Rag" and goes to the Ashlars as Sam says, "That was fun!" And Leah asks Giles if he takes requests.

"I most certainly do!" he proclaims, in a brogue thicker than the head on a pint of Guinness stout. Rita brings the drinks and Giles points to an easel with the daily special. "You oughta try the fried trout. Fresh this very mornin from Wildrose River and prepared by our very own Mabel, the best cook in ten counties!"

He winks at Leah, who asks if he'll play "Two O'clock Jump."

He dives into it and Sam rocks with the beat. "Between the Pasquins with their cellos, the All Souls College Wind Band and Giles, Wildrose is turning out to be a musical treasure!" He takes Jenny and Leah by the hand. "And I'm sorry for ranting at the lawn crew this morning."

"Hardly!" says Leah. "I thought you were too easy on them!"

"Darn right!" says Jenny. She brings the merlot to her nose and lifts an eyebrow, then takes a sip and lifts the other eyebrow. "Hey! This is *good!"*

Sam takes a swallow of Green Goose lager that foams his moustache. "So is this!"

Then Leah downs some ginger ale. "Make that unanimous!"

-9-

THE SAVE & SPEND BANK'S HEAD CASHIER—Figgie Silvertongs—hands Buford Whitlow a deposit receipt, the date stamped on it more genuinely than the smile is stamped on her mouth.

Until last week Figgie and her husband Sol patronized two generations of Buford's forebears at Whitlow Insurance—before yielding to the cutthroat premiums handed out by Worldwide Insurance like peppermint hearts at Valentine's Day. Worse still, Save & Spend Bank *itself* jilted Buford only last month in favor of those peppermint hearts—and ever since he's been grinding off tooth enamel as he dreams up ways to stave off the rising tide of blood-red ink.

But the $5,000 deposit receipt hints that business is on the uptick, and after tossing the traitorous Figgie a terse "Thank you so much!" Buford stuffs the receipt in his jacket like a tuxedo pocket square and scoots over to the bullet-proof cubicle of Bank Manager and fellow council-member Tabitha Tannenbach. Fifty but looking barely 49, Tabitha is Wildrose's most singularly dressed female, now appearing in a fashion-sideways ensemble inspired by a flak jacket and McGregor clan kilt—created by her couturier wife, Undine (Diploma in Fashion, LL Bean). Tabitha was just reviewing a list of delinquent mortgagers to whom the bank is about to send another round of THIS IS YOUR FINAL WARNING letters, and she runs a crimson highlighter over Buford's name. She puts down the highlighter and nods, suffering him to enter her counting house without offering him a chair.

"Nifty outfit," he says. "Did Undine make it?"

"World War Two Scottish Highlands revival. Keeps out the chill."

And there *is* a chill, Buford realizes, besides the one in her voice. The bank is hyper-airconditioned and is turning his sweaty neck into the north face of the Matterhorn. Frostbitten!—by the electricity paid for by his very own late-payment fees!

Tabitha narrows her eyes with impatience and Buford puts a hand to the receipt in his pocket.

"Lotta people moving to Wildrose, so we councilmembers oughta get our eggs in a row on the Condor Estates Rezoning Proposal!"

"It's on the next meeting's agenda."

"Two and a half months from now! I thought you, me, and Cecil oughta have lunch to brood over what's best for Wildrose!"

"Give me a few days to check my calendar."

She wonders if he's spotted his name on her list, highlighted in Day-glo crimson, then she folds her arms across her flak-jacket like a British WAAF—daring Reichsmarschall Goering to make another air raid over London—and eyeballs Buford until he says "So long!" and leaves.

It's all too clear to Tabitha that he's praying on bended knees that the Condor Estates' rezoning will *pass*, which would give him a shot at scooping up the flotsam of policies from the flood of Condor Estates townvilla buyers—after Worldwide Insurance devours the king crab share. She sure as hell doesn't want Buford to go belly up. What in God's name would the bank do with his tin can office across the Commons, or his depressing, cookie-cutter abode on Hathaway Hollow? She, too, favors the rezoning—for the increased banking it'll bring—and is certain that fellow councilmember and CPA Cecil Flinn favors it as well. Smalltown accountants must cast a wide net, and with a hightide of homebuyers swimming the shoals in search of tax dodges, Cecil could make a mighty haul. That would assure three of the five councilmembers *in favor*, enough to approve the rezoning of Wildrose's Pioneer Meadows from family farms and vineyards to a high-density, residential-commercial development.

As Buford leaves the bank he collides with Billy Umbo, who's charging in.

"Whitlow, my friend!"

Buford stumbles from the impact with this man of iron, and the artic windblast from the bank clashes with the inrushing June thermal, spawning an imp cyclone that plucks the deposit receipt from Buford's pocket and sends it spiraling toward the sidewalk. Before it can land in some pigeon-do, Umbo snags it and holds it out with the ***** $5,000.00 ***** in plain view.

"Yours, I believe!"

"Goodness!" says Buford, stuffing the receipt into his jacket's inner pocket.

"Soldier on!" says Umbo, then soldiers into the bank.

The door shuts behind him, and through his own reflection in the plate glass Buford sees Umbo enter Tabitha's ice cave and embrace her—cranberry bowtie to flak jacket. If Buford were a lipreader he'd have learned that Umbo is opening a Platinum LLC account, and will expand it by an amount that would make Scrooge leap up and kick his heels, *if* the rezoning is approved for the Condor Estates' Expansion!

* * *

Sam's and Jenny's fried trout and Leah's spinach salad are as delectable as Giles McDrake's piano playing, and the tension from their morning ear-drubbing vanishes like dirty undies down a laundry chute. They buy bottles of Green Goose wine for themselves and as gifts for their several dinner hosts, then stroll around the Commons to Whitlow Insurance to sign the policy for Mole End.

When Buford sees them out a few minutes later with their premium payment check tucked securely in his inner jacket pocket, Cecil Flinn comes from his CPA office next door, a thoughtful looking man in his 40s in a well-tailored pinstripe suit. Billy Umbo also emerges and shakes Cecil's hand before marching off. Cecil sees Buford and the Ashlars and comes over to wish them good afternoon.

"My wife Mabel and I woulda met you at the mayor's last night, but we had a church dinner to attend with our two boys. Buncha people from the barbecue sent LoveMes and Splats, so I feel as if I'd *already* met you!"

"Mabel?" says Jenny. "The chef at the Green Goose Café? We just ate there!"

"She's my wife!"

"Great spinach salad!" says Leah.

"Awful good of you to say so!" He excuses himself and returns to his office.

"Plenty of nice people in town!" says Sam.

Buford puffs out his chest. "Friendliness is our middle initial!"

He says a quick goodbye and hurries to the bank to deposit the Ashlars' check as they go to Knokdown Drugs, where Sam gets pipe tobacco and Jenny a thank-you card to send Thaïs for having them at the barbecue. Stock Manager Clovis Whinger rushes over and welcomes them like the Beatles reborn, and shows off the store's many wonders, featuring the book carousel with its boob-flashing paperbacks.

"Lemme know if your favorite authors aren't here and I'll special-order 'em! And don't forget to pile on the sunscreen this Sunday. We're dining poolside alfresco!"

"I'll bring my sombrero," says Sam. "And by the way, we noticed your lawn crew this morning and—"

"Aren't they somethin!"

"They're *loud!*" says Leah.

Clovis beams. "State of the industry! Madge and I been using them four or five years and never found a single blade of grass outta where it ought'n be! Here!" He gets his phone and brings up the number. "They only charge $450 a month!"

The Ashlars reel at this disclosure, and Jenny takes Sam's arm. "Here's *our* lawn crew, with Leah and yours truly the gardeners!"

Clovis pockets his phone. "Oh, that's right. You guys are *retired*—and got all the time in the world!"

-10-

THE INSTANT CECIL FLINN RETURNED to his office he held the check Billy Umbo just gave him under a bright light. Like the one made out to Buford it's for $5,000, but it's not payment for a bidding fee. Platinum LLC prefers its own CPAs with their Spandex consciences for trolling the orca-infested waters of taxes and investments, and this one's made out to the All Souls College Wind Band Boosters, where Cecil is Treasurer.

"Platinum LLC wants the arts to thrive in Wildrose!" Umbo had declared.

Cecil decides that before depositing the check in the Boosters' account he'll get the other officers' take on the donation. Prior to earning his business degree from All Souls College, Cecil was a Marine who got along quite well with the other enlistees and officers. But among them was a Billy Umbo or two—ultra gung-hoers with the scruples of scud missiles.

The Ashlars escape from Clovis to the Food Bin where Jenny loads up on eggs, flour, cocoa, raisins, and butter to turn into cookies, then they go to the Cucumber Patch for enough seeds to give hernias to their bicycle baskets. Clovis's wife Madge is Assistant Nursery Coordinator, and

Sam asks if she could recommend a way to discourage moles from making quite so many tunnels in their yard.

Her eyelashes flutter beneath a thick frosting of mascara. "Clovis and I won that battle when we put in the pool, settin out strychnine spikes. Evra'body says our lawn's as smooth as travertine!"

The Ashlars blanch, then Jenny says, "We noticed the lawn crew this morning, and thought they had quite a presence."

"They were quite *loud!*" says Leah.

"Aren't they!" says Madge. "I couldn't stand it if I was just sittin around the house all day, so thank God I'm a working girl. But next week Clovis and I will be on *vacation*, so we switched the lawn people to Thursday, when we'll be doing our salsa class at the Folkston Y!"

* * *

Back at Mole End, Jenny and Leah plant string beans and sweetcorn, and Sam unearths a one-man crosscut saw from the toolshed and tops off the kindling box from the fallen willow tree. His sciatica is behaving itself and the saw croons pleasantly with his even strokes. Then a sound rattles the clapboards on the shed—an electronic hissing, infused with ear-warping vocals and a head-snapping *thumpa, thumpa* beat.

Leah twists a finger in her ear. "I think it's someone's idea of post-rap rap!"

"It's coming from over there!" says Jenny, pointing her trowel at the back of their property.

They put down their tools and she leads the way through the mountain laurel to the fieldstone fence at the back of Mole End, where hammer-blows of sound are resounding from a Federal period house beyond a meadow that's knee-high with burdock.

"The Elms!" says Jenny. "My aunt and uncle used to know the family there—back when it still had elms!"

"They must be deaf!" says Leah, tossing her auburn hair as she runs for her camera.

The Chihuahuas at the Plinkett's bay window retaliate against the *thumping*, and Sam climbs over the stone fence and braves his way through the burdock, whose thistles cling to his corduroys like Velcro balls. By the time he reaches the Elms' back porch the virtual music has grown into a tsunami and he pounds at the door.

"Hello! Is anyone there?!"

He knocks again, and the door is suddenly pulled open by a young man in his early 20s, in a sort of swami outfit and hair like porcupine quills. Blown that way, Sam guesses, because he tripped over a loudspeaker on his way to the door.

Sam leans in and raises his voice. "Excuse me! Would ya mind turning it down?"

"Say what…?"

Sam presses his face as close to the guy as he dares to a stranger. "My family is working in our yard next door and can barely hear ourselves shout. Would you mind *turning it down a little!?"*

"Oh!" says the guy, and shuts the door in Sam's face.

Nothing happens for a moment or two, and figuring the guy's doing some eDumping or Splating before heading to his amplifier, Sam and Leah retreat to Jenny at the field-stone fence. The Elms' noises continue, and the needle in Leah's volume meter pole-vaults into the red.

"That *really* does it!" says Sam, and he makes another leap over the stone fence, pulling a muscle in his back.

Then the noises drop a notch and Jenny uncovers her ears. "That's better…. I think!"

Sam rubs his aching spine. "It hardly went down at all!"

Leah points out that her volume meter does in fact show a slight decrease. "Grandpa. You asked him to lower it *a little!*"

-11-

THE ASHLARS RETREAT TO THEIR living room with its fieldstone fireplace and floor-to-ceiling bookshelves—bulging with Sam's and Jennie's 4,371 works of literature, history, botany, ballet and other areas of human genius and folly, trailered to Mole End with Leah's VW camper two days before. Sam picks the burdock thistles from his corduroys and takes three aspirins for his throbbing back.

"I don't understand! Even if most of our neighbors are gone all day, why aren't the others spitting out nails?"

"Did you plan to work on Thoreau this afternoon?" Jenny asks.

"I must! The manuscript's due in four months!"

"Let's see what we can do!"

She shuts the windows and pulls the drapes—dampening the Chihuahuas' barking and the electronic rapping—but darkening the room so much they have to turn on the chandelier. Sam sighs and settles in a wing chair with Thoreau's *Journal.* He gets his pipe and new tin of tobacco, then remembers where he is.

"I don't mind if you smoke," says Jenny.

"Me, either!" says Leah, who begins offloading the day's filming onto her ePal.

"I'll just *chaw* on it," Sam says, "like the pacifier it is!"

That morning he'd uncovered some beguiling harmonies between Mole End and Walden Pond, and with the pipe clamped between his teeth and furious at the neighbors' thoughtlessness, fresh ideas stampede into his brain.

"Good!" Jenny thinks, and goes about organizing her botany books.

Sam writes furiously for some minutes, then wonders whether a honeybee is reconnoitering the Virginia bluebells beside the shed. But despite the closed windows and pulled curtains, the Elms' *thumpa, thumpa* is still scrambling his thoughts, and the barking of the Chihuahuas is really eating at him.

He jumps up, getting another jab in the spine. "Those dogs must have cast iron lungs!"

"Try these!" says Leah, hauling out her noise-canceling earphones.

He puts them on and is suddenly on another planet, free of thumping and barking. "Amazing! I'll never sneer at technology again!"

Leah laughs and Sam returns to Thoreau's *Journal.* But isolated from the least little sound, he finds it hard to concentrate, and feels he might as well be inside a diving bell at the bottom of the sea.

"I've got it!" says Jenny, turning on their venerable record player.

The turntable spins and the speaker hums behind its cloth arras as the tubes stretch and yawn, and Jenny puts on one of Sam's beloved records, Hovhaness's *Mysterious Mountain.* Ennobled with the crackling of the record's many outings, the music turns the living room into a grove of sighing aspens.

"You did it!" says Sam.

He hugs Jenny and hops in the wing chair to gather his thoughts, and as the minutes jog by images fill his mind like shimmering spun glass. He's in rapture and realizes this is it! The very soul of my book!

Then a new kind of noise shatters his dream and he jumps up. "Damn it to hell!"

With his back throbbing he hobbles down the hallway and out the front door with Jenny and Leah at his heels. The new onslaught is a mishmash of metallic gnashing and country-western music from Honus and Winney Offmans' carriage-house—*right across Orchard Lane!*

The Ashlars run over and find a jumble of machinery surrounding a rusted hulk on wooden blocks. Car innards are strewn about like a highway pileup, and a boombox the size of a sofa roars from the rafters with such rockabilly bathos that the dust bunnies on those rafters hop like mice on marijuana.

Amid all this are Honus and Winney in oil-stained overalls, safety goggles, and possum skin earmuffs. Honus is sledge-hammering a dent from a fender, and Sam picks his way through the car guts and taps him on the shoulder. Honus spins around and glowers through his goggles, then recalls that he'd met Sam at Thaïs's barbecue the night before.

"M'God!"

He goes to Winney, who's grinding crusts of old paint from another fender. She turns off the grinder and they lower their goggles.

"We just wandered by," says Sam, "and thought we'd say hi!"

They haven't the foggiest idea what he's saying, as the boombox is still roaring from the rafters, and Leah cups a hand to her mouth.

"Would you mind turning that *off!*"

Winney unplugs the boombox and the carriage-house goes still, just as Honus sees the camera slung from Leah's shoulder.

"Hey! We *love* being in movies!" She hits the button and he poses with his foot on the bumper. "Ain't she a beauty? Nineteen fifty-four Hudson Hornet!"

With its many parts heaped about the floor and a headlight dangling from its wires, the Hudson gawps like a Halloween fright of the worst kind.

Winney pats it on the roof. "In six months she'll be a gold-ribbon wonder!"

"More like eight months," says Honus, thumping the bumper with his boot and sending it crashing to the stone floor.

"Is this a hobby of yours?" Jenny asks.

"Hobby and perfession," he says. "A flatbed truck delivered this jewel jis about lunchtime, all the way from Valparaiso, Indianer!"

"Oh!" says Winney, pressing a greasy hand to her greasy cheek. "That flatbed was kinda loud, now I think on it, and it pra'ly disturbed yer lunch!"

"We ate at the Green Goose Café in the Village Center," says Jenny.

Honus wheezes with relief. "Thank the Lord! We always try to do our rehabbin on the QT, and would be worried sick if we was causin the least bit of ruckus fer the neighbors. Now me and Winney kin rest easy when we take our afternoon nap!"

"Maybe not!" says Winney. "The Plinketts' dawgs are barkin agin!"

"I think they're upset by the Elms' music," says Jenny.

"Music?! It's Pubic Nuisance Number One! Someone oughta ast 'em to turn it down!"

"We did ast 'em," says Sam. "But it did no good."

"Well, we jis hav'ta stand up for our rights!" Winney hikes over the Hudson's transmission to Honus. "Sticky bun? We're gonna take a break at the picanick table, where we'll be away from the Elms and those dawgs, and ast the Ashmars to join us fer some of my hominy squares. And when we git back to work we're gonna roll up our sleeves and *shut these doors ag'inst those dawgs!"*

-12-

SAM IS BACK IN THE WING CHAIR, *chawing* on his pipe, and Jenny is mulling over ways to shore up their windows' noise resistance. Concrete blocks or sandbags. Then Leah leaps from the sofa.

"Grandpa! I've got it!" She patches a pair of speakers to her ePal and dishes out the restorative sound of a Rocky Mountain stream. "Atmosphere for my films. I've got heaps of them!"

She switches to North Carolina Woodland in Spring, and southern birdsong roams the living room, as sweet as key lime pie. This is *it,* the Ashlars realize. They can bring the outdoors *in*doors, with super-audio panache!

Sam flops into the wing chair, and relieved that the aspirins are finally soothing his back, he grabs his notebook and starts rebuilding the spun-glass image in his brain—slain by the Offmans' auto rehabbing. But as the minutes pass he finds the birdsong *too* real. And something's missing, he thinks, fidgeting in the chair.

Jenny has the same thought and turns to Leah. "The sounds aren't quite the same without the smells!"

Before she can utter another syllable Leah puts out some sandalwood incense.

"And the breeze!" says Sam.

Leah pulls the chain on the chandelier, and a refreshing zephyr romps around the room. Sam and Jenny are content and Leah hops on the sofa to enjoy her handiwork. They revel in this paradise while Sam scrawls Waldenish ideas and Jenny wrestles with her herby tomes. There's no AC, and with the windows shut it's getting sultry, despite the ceiling fan. The increasing warmth doesn't bother them very much, but something else does—especially Sam.

He takes the pipe from his mouth and runs his fingers over its briar grooves, then shoves it back, as if corking up a cask of amontillado.

Leah watches with mounting regret, knowing that he's the best Grandpa in the world. She snuffs the incense and silences the North Carolina Woodland.

She jumps up. "It's a buncha horseshit!"

Jenny puts down her books. "But Leah, you've conquered the noises!"

Leah shakes her head. "You didn't come to Wildrose to barricade yourselves indoors with incense and sound effects. You came to get your hands dirty in the lettuce patch, and Grandpa came to spar with Thoreau and smoke his pipe. You could smoke it in here, Grandpa, and we'd really, truly enjoy the aroma, but you're too considerate to do that. So you chew your pipe instead. Getting the gristle and missing all the gravy!"

"I don't have to smoke indoors!"

"But this is your *home!*" She throws back the drapes. "And you and Grandma have a right to enjoy yourselves in the yard. To smoke your pipe there, too, and write your book, without being *shat* upon by leaf blowers and hammering and barking and music that's bad enough to make a maggot puke!"

Sam's sobered by Leah's outburst and she tears up.

"I didn't mean to say all that, Grandpa, but you're not gonna be happy in Wildrose unless you can make it more respectful. And I'm afraid you're too much of a gentleman to do that!"

She chokes back a sob and runs out. A moment later the VW door opens and slams shut, and they expect her to drive off in a cloud of disgust. But apparently she's just sitting there, stewing over the notion that her grandpa is the world's kindest wimp.

Then the Elms' thumping suddenly stops, prompting the Chihuahuas to quit barking.

"At last!" says Jenny, opening the windows.

And it's all quiet on the auto-rehab front. Either the Offmans are indeed having a nap after serving their hominy squares, Jenny reasons, or they're back at work on the Hudson Hornet and shut the carriage-house doors as Winney had threatened.

Jenny slips behind the wing chair and massages Sam's shoulders. "Don't mind Leah too much. Now! I'm gonna put that flour, eggs, and dark chocolate to use!"

Left alone in the living room, Sam is amazed at how palpable silence can be—as though his head were an empty concert hall—and the ticking of the mantelpiece clock seems louder than Big Ben. He mulls over what Leah said and knows he's been there before, a bruising incident at Emerson University that all but destroyed his teaching career. But the problem isn't just the city; it's the bloated Condor Estates on Wildrose River, and the babel of noises on Orchard Lane. Mole End is under siege and Sam knows he's gotta get his backside into gear.

And he gets his backside out of the wing chair and into the kitchen to take the first step of the most daring journey of his life before Jenny can break those eggs.

-13-

LEAH BURNS RUBBER IN HER VW to Wildrose Village Hall, where she and her grandparents enter a foyer leading to a cubbyhole office behind a nameplate, DUFFY NICKLEBOB, VILLAGE CLERK. Before they can ring the bell, a diminutive, slightly built woman with a pen dangling from a neck ribbon pops up from a desk.

"May I be of help?" They introduce themselves, and the young woman—Duffy Nicklebob herself—wrings her pink hands. "Glory! I was about to contact *you*, about Henry David Throw!"

"That's very kind of you," says Sam, having forgotten Thaïs's pledge at the barbecue to arrange an interview with Duffy. "But we need to speak with the police."

Duffy extends a pink finger from her cubbyhole. "Down there!"

Sam tips his fedora. "I'll get back to you for the interview."

They follow a corridor that passes a huge door lettered in gold leaf, HONORABLE THAïS MONT-OBISTON, MAYOR. Opposite is the TAX OFFICE, lettered in bright carmine, and father down is a door labeled in sober blue,

POLICE, partly open to a large room of desks and filing cabinets, nicked and scraped from long use. A nameplate on the nearest desk identifies LIEUT. REEVAS F. CONKLIN, and curled behind it is a man of about 30 with a gangling, Ichabod Crane physique in an unkempt teal uniform, polishing the brass rivets of a holster with an old sock and staring with a nervous face at the Ashlars.

"Yeah…?"

Sam removes the fedora and goes to a large desk across the room with the nameplate CHIEF OF POLICE VIVIAN TRUMAN, where a solid-built man in his 50s in a smart uniform gets to his feet.

"You must be the Ashlars. Word's all over town about you, because of the shindig at the mayor's last night!" He turns to Jenny. "You have the same sparkling smile as your aunt. Wildrose sure isn't as fine a place without her and your uncle!"

"That's very good of you!"

Then Truman sets his gray eyes on Leah and her camera.

"I've heard that half the Village is in the scenes you shot at the mayor's barbecue. You're welcome to do some filming among these old walls—though I doubt you'll want *my* ugly mug in your documentary!"

"I'll be glad to include your pleasant features as well!"

Sam clears his throat. "We came about the local noise ordinance."

Lieut. Conklin bristles at being passed by and rubs his nose with the sock, smudging it with brass polish.

"Well," says Truman, "it's pretty straightforward. It says there shall be no disruptive noises after ten p.m."

"Ten p.m.? That's it…?"

"Ten p.m. to six a.m. I'll get it for you."

Thaïs suddenly ducks through the doorway and straightens to her full height—the Eiffel Tower astride Paris. "I *thought* I heard cultured voices!" She sees the bandage on Jenny's wrist. "Been tussling with Mother Earth?"

"So to speak!"

"Please be careful. We don't want our newest residents on the disabled list, even for the greenest of causes!" She notices Conklin—who jumped to attention on her arrival. "Wipe your nose, Lieutenant." He obeys, smearing the brass polish all the more as Thaïs cranes her neck to Leah. "Doing more filming, are we?"

Leah sees that Thaïs's beauty mark is slightly adrift of where it had been at the barbecue, and realizes it's *painted* on.

"Inquiry about the Noise Ordinance," says Truman, pulling a folder from a cabinet and turning to the Ashlars. "I should've asked. Any disruptive noises going on by Mole End?"

"Gobs!" says Jenny.

"Tons!" says Leah.

"Truckloads!" says Sam.

They recount the day's events and Thaïs's black eyes flash.

"I'm shocked that Orchard Lane would be so boorish! In the two years since I came to Wildrose I don't recall any such nonsense, and certainly not in the five months I've been in office!"

"Here it is," says Truman, extracting a stained and yellowed document from the folder, as carefully as though it were a relic from a tomb. "'All Persons are prohibited from causing or abetting noises that are bothersome to individuals or the common weal, between Ten O'clock post meridiem and Six O'clock ante meridian.' " He hands it to Sam. "As you can see, it dates from April 1865."

Sam looks it over and surmises that it was probably dreamt up during a distill-your-own-hooch rally after Robert E. Lee surrendered to Ulysses S. Grant. He returns it to Truman.

"Well… thanks for looking it up."

"I'll be happy to have a little talk with the Offmans and Plinketts," says Truman. "And the Elms, although I don't know the people who live there now. But mind, I can't do anything *official* until ten p.m."

"What if the noises go on *after* ten and someone does complain?" Leah asks.

"If I consider the noises too loud for the circumstances, I'd ask the noisemaker to desist. I've never had much trouble."

"What if you do have trouble?" says Jenny. "Or if they ignore the warning?"

"If I feel the neighbors might take the law into their own hands, I'd issue a citation and take the noisemaker into custody, then fingerprint them and hold them in there." He gestures at a swayback log structure outside the window that would've given Abe Lincoln the willies. "If the judge rules against them, it'd be the fine plus the court costs."

"It seems awfully messy," says Leah. "Whether you feel the noise breaches the Ordinance, or if you think the neighbors might lynch the offender!"

Truman chuckles and puts away the folder. "So much of the law *is* messy!"

"Well, that's not good enough!" says Thaïs, pivoting on her heel and calling out. "Duffy! The *calendar!*" After a moment, footsteps echo from the hallway and Duffy scoots in—a tome in hand and dwarfed by Thaïs as a bonsai is by a Giant Sequoia. "The next Council meeting is…?"

"August 13, Your Honor."

"And the agenda?" Thaïs stoops to read where Duffy points, but it's a stoop too far and Duffy reads it for her.

"The proposal to rezone Pioneer Meadows, north of Wildrose River above Condor Estates. And the Final Reading of the proposal to subsidize the Middle School's Pumpkin Poetry Contest."

"Put this *atop* the agenda," Thaïs commands, and Duffy grasps the pen that dangles from her neck. "RE the Village Noise Ordinance: Whether it should be made more specific; whether it should cover more hours; and whether larger fines should be imposed."

"The next meeting isn't until *August 13?"* says Jenny.

"The Council meets monthly," says Thaïs. "Except June and July—due to the press of summer vacations."

The Ashlars follow Duffy to her cubbyhole for Sam's interview, and Thaïs returns to her office and types SAM ASHLAR on her computer. She's thrilled to have the Ashlars in Wildrose, but intuits that they're a breed she's not dealt with before. Not quite.

The computer unreels bits and pieces about Sam, showing fewer wrinkles and darker hair, a longer beard, a shorter beard, and no beard. Often there's a pipe and fedora, and a tweed or corduroy sportcoat, dress shirt, and tie. Now and then he wears a black suit and bow tie, playing Principal Horn in the Emerson University Symphony Orchestra.

"Must've been conceived under a suit rack!" Thaïs murmurs.

She finds rhapsodic reviews of Sam's books on Flannery O'Connor and Charles Brockden Brown, and warnings from former students against using disruptive e-gadgets in his classes, while calling him the hardest grader and best lecturer on campus. She moves the cursor again and Sam stares out with dark circles under his eyes from an Emerson University webletter that's captioned, DOOMED PROFESSOR!

-14-

THE ASHLARS GO TO THE WILDROSE library for cards, then to the All Souls College registrar, where Sam's admitted to the Symphonic Wind Band and gets the summer schedule. Practices Tuesdays and Thursdays, with concerts the Fourth of July and Wildrose Founders Day in September. They go by the Music Department Practice Room for a glimpse as Pierre Pasquin emerges from a session with his clarinetists.

"Welcome aboard, Sam! We lost a couple of good horn players at graduation and really need you!"

The clarinetists stare whimsically at Sam's tweed jacket and Walt Whitman beard as he introduces himself, Jenny, and Leah, while learning the clarinetists' names on the spot, a skill he mastered during his 45 years of teaching. They head off—glancing back in bemusement—and Sam asks Pierre about auditioning.

"Come 15 minutes early tomorrow and bring something with you. And thank goodness you've come! We've got fewer summer students in *all* of our instrumental sections, due in part from having to cancel the Fresh Air Practice Series. Fewer opportunities for young musicians and less music for all Wildroseians!"

"That's dreadful!" says Jenny.

Sam mentions that Thaïs put the Noise Ordinance atop the next meeting's agenda, and Pierre drops his shoulders.

"Three whole months from now…? We'll, I suppose it's a start!"

* * *

Duffy Nicklebob also interviewed Jenny and Leah at her cubbyhole, and the Ashlars are aglow with her praise for their passions for botany, filmmaking, and Henry David Thoreau that'll be expressed in her profile of them on the *Wildrose Voyeur* website later in the day. But the glow fades as they return home to find the Elms' unloading louder noises than ever across the burdock meadow, and the Plinketts' Chihuahuas *yap yapping* in defense.

"Looks like it's back indoors with us!" says Jenny.

Sol Silvertongs—one house down from them—is the rare Orchardlaner who mows his own lawn, and is giving it the sartorial works with a TendrTokus Riding Mower with enough horsepower to scalp the Great Plains.

"A one-man annihilation crew!" says Sam, shutting the windows.

Clovis and Madge Whinger's shifts are still dragging on at Knockdown Drugs and Cucumber Patch, but they donate some sound bites in absentia with an automated, shrill-voiced pump that's injecting their heart-shaped swimming pool with a highball of nautical nutrients, while an aqua hygienist uses an even shriller compressed-air scrubber to scour the cocktail spills, sunblock driblets, and other gaucheries from the poolside tiles.

"I can't believe it!" says Leah, closing the drapes and turning on the ceiling fan—just as the two Middlemarsh boys return from their summer-school purgatory to begin a few hours' virtual bongo drumming from their wide-open, second-story bedroom windows.

Sam escapes to the bedroom to run through the piece he intends to play for Pierre next morning—then hurries back.

"I think we should *practice* for the Village Council meeting!"

Jenny's doing ballet stretches with one foot poised on the mantelpiece and cotton in her ears. She removes the cotton and Sam explains.

"Why don't we host an *advance* meeting here at Mole End, to exchange views with our neighbors. With most of them doing the nine-to-five, they probably don't realize how jarring the noises are!"

"Great idea!" says Leah, and they put their heads together to print up a leaflet.

June 2

Mole End

Dear Neighbor,

You might have seen on the *Wildrose Voyeur* web-letter that in response to some unsettling sounds on Orchard Lane, Mayor Mont-Obiston has scheduled a review of the Noise Ordinance for the Village Council's August 13th meeting.

We feel it would be helpful if we Orchard Lane residents met beforehand to share how these noises impact all of us, so we invite you to Mole End for this coming Sunday, June 8, 6:00 p.m. to 7:30 p.m.

If you cannot join us, please share your thoughts via our address below. Beverages and Jenny's fresh-baked apple-crumb cookies will be served!

Please RSVP by Thursday night, so we know how many cookies to bake.

Sincerely,

(signed) Sam, Jenny, and Leah

They fan out along Orchard Lane to deliver the leaflets with Leah starting at the Offmans' carriage-house, where Winney's bearing down on the Hudson Hornet's roof with her trusty sander. She shuts it off and Honus shoots out from under the Hudson on an auto-creeper. Some backwoods wash-boarders are strumming up a storm from the giant boombox in the rafters, so Leah gives the Offmans the leaflet to read for themselves.

Honus slaps his knee. "Dang! It says yer meetin's on Sund'y. That's our monthly *hotrod* night, in our little Indianapolis 500 out back. We were gonna invite you and yer folks so's you could make movies of it!"

"Sorry!" says Leah. "As it says at the bottom of the leaflet, just send your thoughts to us, about the Plinketts' Chihuahuas or any *other* noises!"

Jenny takes on Middlemarsh Manse B&B—where the twin boys' eBongo drumming is pouring from their second-floor windows like the contents of a broken dam. Then Wanda pulls up in a station wagon, piled with groceries, cleaning supplies, and her teenage daughter.

Jenny waves. "Hello!"

Wanda shouts for the boys to turn it down, then returns Jenny's smile. "This is my daughter Henna."

"What a lovely name!" says Jenny. She sees a slender leather case in Henna's hand. "Is that a piccolo?"

Henna grins around her costly braces. "I just had my lesson with Ms. Pasquin at the College. She said your husband has joined the Wind Band! I think that's wonderful!"

She gets a couple of grocery bags and goes inside as Jenny turns to Wanda.

"She seems so young for college!"

"She's on scholarship for advanced high school sophomores." The eBongo drumming is growing louder. "Those boys! I've told them countless times!"

Jenny knows a cue when she hears one and hands over a leaflet. "Being a councilwoman, you probably already know that the mayor added the Noise Ordinance to the August Council meeting."

Wanda shoves the hair from her eyes. "I haven't had two minutes all day, between running the kids and shopping for the weekend."

"I hope you're not going to a lot of trouble for *us*."

"Heavens, no! I meant our B&B guests. Two couples on Sunday." She looks over the leaflet. "What a generous idea, Jenny! I'm sorry to say we'll be all tied up with our guests, but I'll be darn sure to send you some suggestions!"

Sam meanwhile arrives at the Silvertongs' place, where Sol is sound asleep inside his TendrTokus riding mower's airconditioned cabin with a milkshake driveling in his lap. The AutoMo feature made a good meal of Sol's lawn, and now is making a delicious dessert of his artificial putting turf.

Sam doesn't know that Sol's wife Figgie is Head Cashier at Save & Spend Bank, and he hunts fruitlessly for her among the skeet-shooting and pistol-firing range, the batting practice machine and party trampoline, and the three-story bungee tower. He has no better luck knocking at the door, and supposes Figgie can't hear him because an AutoMaid is steam-cleaning the carpets. He stuffs a leaflet in the mailbox and returns to Orchard Lane to find Jenny and Leah.

"Onward to the Elms!" he says.

Instead of repeating their morning trek across the burdock minefield behind Mole End, they hike down the west side of the U-bend to Orchard Lane Bottoms and come to a rusted mailbox marked DINSMORE, where a bumpy dirt driveway cuts through a rutted cornfield to a Li'l Abner barn and farmhouse.

Jenny sighs. "How terribly rundown it's gotten! My aunt and uncle used to come here for such delicious peaches and watermelons!"

She tucks a leaflet behind the mailbox flag, then they round the Bottoms and hike up the east side of the U-bend to the front of the Elms—a scene right out of "The Fall of the House of Usher." A wrought-iron fence imprisons a weedy frontyard below the Elms that's venting a fresh supply of surreal sounds, where a mailbox is labeled, C. S. S. UNLIMITED.

"That's not half cryptic!" says Leah.

Sam's about to drop a leaflet in the mailbox when he sees the half-opened gate, where a pile of Armageddon.com parcels are moored to a spiderweb in progress. He looks at Jenny and Leah, who nod assent.

They apologize to the spider before clearing away its website, then scoop up the parcels and follow the flagstones to a massive door that bears a violet-tinted plasma sign:

COSMIC SONIC SISTERS, UNLIMITED
Vibratory Quiddities & Apotheosisies
Appointments, Drop-Ins, or Dropouts
Any Day — Any Hour—Any How

"That clears it up!" says Jenny.

Sam slams the doorknocker and echoes abound, and after a few moments the door is opened by a young woman with particolored hair who greets them with a grin a yard wide.

"Salutations!"

She's framed by a darkly varnished entry hall and the archway of a drawing room—the incubator of the noises and reeking of peyote-scented candles. Several young women are drooped over divans and cushions and run their fingers over keyboards and more exotic devices. Among them is the young man with the porcupine hairdo who greeted Sam so cordially at the back door that morning.

The particolored-hair woman glances at the parcels the Ashlars are holding and waves her hand at a table.

"Please put 'em there!"

She skips to the drawing room and returns with some dollar bills.

Sam waves them away. "We're your *neighbors*, at Mole End. I knocked at your back door earlier on and spoke to the young man on the blue cushion." He nods at the drawing room.

"Pavana. It's a she. That's right! She mentioned it at Noon Mantra. Something about modulation…?"

"Loud noises," says Leah. "It was about loud noises. Like right now!"

"I asked if he'd mind turning it down," says Sam. "And he did. *She* did, I mean. A little."

"Hardly at all!" says Jenny.

The woman's eyes widen like eggs on a griddle. "Ah! That's sooo contra our Supreme Tenet!"

Jenny blinks. "Beg pardon?"

"To heal. The Sonic Sisterhood was spawned to succor this tired and drag-ass world. I'll bring forth your concerns at Evening Mantra, and I'm certain the Sisters will mend any rents we've made in the Fabric!"

A gaping pause, then Sam says, "I'm sure it was unintentional. Anyway, it's good to meet you, as we're such close neighbors!"

She introduces herself as "Calliope" and undulates her hands. "Music is our ship and shore of healing!"

Leah thrusts out a leaflet. "Please join us!"

Calliope looks it over and her eyeballs nearly pop from their sockets.

"This is soooo healing!"

-15-

JENNY'S CHOCOLATE CHIP COOKIES ARE a hit, baked just the way the Ashlars like them, with 92% cocoa and nutritionally appalling butter. In fact they're gone, fond memories and warm lumps in their stomachs, and the Ashlars are further warmed by the terra cotta fire pit on the back porch, whose willowwood flames make shadow puppets of their long faces against the cabin. Long faces because it's Thursday night—three days after they distributed the leaflets—and their plan for the neighborhood noise chat is stillborn. Of the dozens of Orchard-laners with whom they spoke, or at whose door they left a leaflet, not one responded.

The bandage is gone from Jenny's wrist and she rubs pensively at the scar. "I don't understand why the Plinketts or Silvertongs didn't reply. Sol seems a bit gaga with all that sports equipment and *Star Trek* riding mower, but he and Figgie were very friendly at the barbecue!"

"And the Elms," says Sam. "Calliope seemed so earnest!"

Despite Calliope's promise that the Sonic Sisters would repair any "rents" they'd made in the cosmos, the retro-rap *thumping* went on and on—in addition to the Chihuahuas' yapping and Offmans' ear-grinding auto rehabbing. Other lawncare crews poured on the noise, onto which Clovis and Madge Whinger piled a nightly dose of splashing and diving-board banging at their heart-shaped swimming pool.

Sam started rising at 5:00 a. m. instead of 6:00 a. m. each day to have more time with Thoreau before Orchard Lane began its daily clamor, and he auditioned well enough for Pierre Pasquin at All Souls College to make Principal Horn. At the Tuesday and Thursday practices he listened carefully, played fervently, and peddled home whistling like a schoolboy.

As it is late evening, Orchard Lane is finally quiet and Leah slips into the yard to get some wide shots of her grandparents, hoping to capture an apt tableau for her documentary as they round out their first week at Mole End. She tightens the frame on Sam, lost in his thoughts as a log snaps in the fire pit and showers his shoes with sparks.

Jenny pats his knee. "At this rate, you'll have to cut another box load of wood!"

The waterfall gurgles; the bullfrog competes with a tenor toad for the best mordents, glissandos, and hemidemisemiquavers; and the barn owl grumbles, proving once again that everyone's a critic.

Then two motorcycles chase up the lane with enough horsepower for a rocket launch. It's the owners of Tread On Us Retreads—the tall man and the beefy one—following the instructions on the anonymous letter they'd found Monday morning, which causes something to wrench inside Sam and make him laugh out loud.

He's tired, Jenny thinks. Then he laughs harder and she knows he's onto something special.

"What is it?" she pleads, beginning to laugh herself.

He brushes the tears from his eyes. "We'll need *lots and lots* of wood! You see, I was thinking about those ballistic-missile bulldozers, or whatever those contraptions were that just blasted their way up the lane!"

"I'm certain the Wildrose Council will do something," says Jenny, "placing it at the top of the agenda like that. And I don't believe Thaïs is someone to fool with!"

Leah agrees, but means something else by it. There's something about Thaïs that evokes Serena Williams and André the Giant.

She lowers her camera and says to Sam. "I'm really sorry for what I said to you on Monday!"

"What you said was right on target, Leah. But it's two and a half months till the Council meeting, and if things go as usual in democratic bodies it could be doomsday before the Ordnance is improved!"

He tosses another log on the fire, raising more sparks.

"I was also thinking about Thoreau. You know, when you get right down to it he could be a bit of a grouch." Jenny's aghast, but Sam goes on. "He got on with people well enough, but I for one could never have lived with him. We'd have been at each other's throat in no time—worse than Van Gogh and Gauguin. And that's partly why we pay heed to him. His best ideas affect us like a body rub in a briar patch, and he's not always a gentleman!"

Leah's ears burn, but she resumes filming as Jenny rests a hand on Sam's knee. "I think you're being too hard on him. And on yourself!"

He takes her hand. "Thoreau rang the town bell to wake Concord up to its moral duty, and was jailed for refusing to pay the poll tax, because he was furious that Massachusetts upheld the Fugitive Slave Law. He was *un*civilly disobedient, as *we* must be!"

"But it's not like you to get into fights!"

"Then it's time I changed!"

Then Jenny recalls the ugly struggle he'd had at Emerson University 10 years before, and Leah zooms in until Sam's eyes fill her monitor.

"Let's open a bottle of Green Goose wine, and I'll tell you what I have in mind!"

They share a magnum of Moscato and confer till long after the mantelpiece clock strikes midnight. Now and then a car with an absentee muffler ravages Orchard Lane, piling more fuel on Sam's outrage—but Jenny and Leah are swept up in his vision and toss out ideas of their own. They hone them razor sharp and engrave them with a PRIME DIRECTIVE.

Their brainstorming ends and Leah throws her arms around Sam. "This'll be stupendous, Grandpa!"

She runs up to bed, and as Sam and Jenny go in he asks about her mammal books.

"Squirrels and raccoons? You want them this time of night!?"

He nods cryptically and she leads him to a shelf.

* * *

Zebulon pulls Nightshade onto Mole End. Sobered by what he'd learned on the web about Sam's fateful year at Emerson University, Zebulon knows he must act decisively, or his dream for the Condor Estate's expansion might be imperiled. The monument to his beloved triplet!

He studies the cabin a moment and infers from the lamplight feathering between the living room drapes that one or more Ashlars are staying up *very* late.

"All right!" he mutters.

He plies Nightshade's infrared beam over Mole End's toolshed, pond, and trees. The barn owl blinks, and other nightbirds are caught amid their canoodling. Then he opens Nightshade's panniers and removes a hoard of pinecones, wood knots, and abandoned birds' nests (gleaned from the Manor's arboretum), and conceals them in crevices along the split-rail fence and toolshed eaves, and numerous niches around the frontyard, backyard, and porch.

He pauses a moment to study the arrangement of the trees, then hoists himself up a cypress with the ease of an Olympian gymnast and tucks a pinecone in the crotch of a branch, then drops to the ground and touches his ePendant.

He brings up spycam number six on its screen—a chestnut wedged in a knothole in the shed—and the ePendant gives a 58° view of the porch as its pinhead-mic sups on cricketsong. He switches to number 11, a walnut with a low-angle perspective of the pond and its bullfrog, troubadouring on a log.

One by one Zebulon adjusts all of the devices so Mole End's every twig and nail-head is covered, with power packs rated for two years. He takes out an object the size of a matchbook—magnetized and patinated with rust—and presses it to the VW's steel undercarriage. He touches his ePendant and it gives a GPS reading of the VW, shown with a pulsing blue star.

Then he vanishes on Nightshade.

Wanda is in her studio and supposes that the faint whisper of Nightshade's tires racing up Orchard Lane might be a hawk, gliding for a meal. She's torn her clay wine jug apart (for the eighth or ninth time) and is shaping it into a weasel.

An hour later Sam is in the wing chair, buried under a mountain of Jenny's mammal books while musing over a passage here and there, but mostly pouring over photos and illustrations. He turns another page and his heart summersaults.

"*That's it!*" he exclaims.

-16-

THE BOUTIQUE GAS & LUBE ATTENDANT is unlocking his pumps for the day as Leah and Jenny arrive in the VW to fill a couple of five-gallon cans with gas. He recognizes them from Duffy Nicklebob's *Wildrose Voyeur* interview and smiles as he hands over their receipt.

"Clearing out some hornets?"

"Yep!" says Jenny, and they return home to find Sam in the toolshed, wrestling the sparkplug from an ancient chainsaw.

"We got the goods!" says Leah, and with a bounce to his step Sam helps unload their purchases, as Leah and Jenny had also hit up Home Deposit on the new Sky Vue Freeway for hardhats with safety visors and swivel-down ear-protectors, and work lights on tripods with enough lumens to scorch an airport runway.

Drawing on his farmboy days, Sam scrapes the carbon buildup from the sparkplug, adjusts the gap, and screws it back in the chainsaw. And the women work up a lather on a grindstone, which Leah turns while Jenny whets a chisel, and Jenny turns as Leah sharpens a hatchet.

Leah asks what's next and Sam says whatever serves their PRIME DIRECTIVE. She glances at the chainsaw and her face lights up. "The muffler!"

Truth be told, most chainsaws haven't much of a muffler to begin with, which could no more blunt a chainsaw's grunts and growls than Henry VIII's jousting helmet could stop a cruise missile. And the muffler in question—on a 1917 two-stroke chainsaw—is smaller than a cupcake. But Leah leaves nothing to chance—the Prime Directive being *small effort! BIG NOISE!*—and she squirts some rust-off fluid and tosses the muffler aside. Then with her film-maker's eye she arranges the tripod lights around the frontyard and runs power cables to the cabin.

They find sheets of corrugated tin behind the toolshed—leftovers from when it was reroofed 33 years earlier—which make a rip-snorting echo with every sound that comes their way. They tuck in the sheets around the willow, zeroed-in on their neighbors and away from Mole End's wildlife. The world's orneriest backstop.

Meantime, their many Orchard Lane neighbors drag themselves from their beds to swallow their InstaWaffs, leftover pizza, or titanium-cut oatmeal bars, then discover Duffy's interview of the Ashlars on their e-whatnots and punch in a reminder to themselves to remind the Ashlars about the dinner, cocktail hour, or rib roast they'd mentioned at Thaïs's barbecue.

"If only they'd join the 21st century!" Sol says to Figgie. "At the barbecue on Sunday Sam and Jenny said they've *never had cellphones!*"

"Can you believe it?" Silt says to Wanda at Middlemarsh Manor B&B. She's woozy from lack of sleep and is mopping the basement where their 1930s water heater has sprung another leak. She wipes her brow as Silt gushes on.

"They're minor celebrities and *we're* having them to dinner. They might attract upscale overnight guests from Sam's publisher!"

Next door, Clovis and Madge Whinger are devouring super-sugar StaAwakes while heading off for their eight-hour internments at Knokdown Drugs and Cucumber Patch, and they glance longingly at their swimming pool.

"Gotta remind the Ashlars about the sunscreen!" says Clovis.

Honus and Winney Offman start work in their carriage-house by descaling the Hudson's valves, and the Sonic Sisters begin healing the neighborhood with deconstructionist bebop—which is double-decker dognip to the Plinketts' Chihuahuas, who deconstruct their windpipes with frenzied barking from their bay window.

Undeterred, the Ashlars insert earplugs and go about their scheme, and by early afternoon Sam is done tinkering with the chainsaw and gasses it up. He makes sure his earplugs are secure and puts on his back-brace, then Jenny and Leah give hopeful glances as he wraps the rope around the chainsaw's shaft and gives it a yank.

It coughs up a ball of smoke where the muffler used to be. A black poodle on a stroll.

"It's been ages since it was used!" Sam shouts.

They nod support—pressing their fingers to their own earplugs—and he wraps the rope around the shaft and yanks again. The chainsaw makes a couple of peevish revolutions and coughs up a couple of black poodles.

"Almost!" Jenny shouts back.

The mockingbird is singing *shoyerstuff, shoyerstuff*, and Sam knows his farmboy reputation is on the line. He again wraps the rope around the shaft and heaves for all he's worth, and this time there are no poodles or peevishness. The chainsaw vomits an angry smoke cloud and snarls like a hungover wolverine whose tail just got pulled.

Jenny and Leah cheer, but Sam can't hear them. He can't hear *anything*, other than the chainsaw, clawing at his earplugs. He replaces his sombrero with a hardhat, lowers its ear protectors and visor, and grasps the chainsaw. It's heavy but well balanced, and vibrates less roughly than he'd have guessed, given the noise it's barfing out, and he sets the blade against one of the willow's smaller limbs.

The chainsaw sniffs, bites, and gets a taste of willow; then eager for revenge at being shaken from its lengthy slumber, it goes at it with a vengeance.

Jenny and Leah press harder at their earplugs and retreat a few more paces, as squirrels take cover and a cloud swerves to avoid Orchard Lane. The memory of sawing trees for fenceposts and firewood on the family farm floods Sam's neurons, and he's intoxicated with the feeling of power. Real power! He knows he's getting but a fragment of the sound, and that anyone nearby *without* ear protectors would be heading for the madhouse.

The chainsaw finishes off the limb and it falls to earth. It's passed the test and so has Sam. He grips it like a smoking bazooka, a man who's shed his gentlemanly mantle and thinks, *My God! This is a blast!*

PART TWO

-1-

THE CHAINSAW WARMUP EXCEEDS THE Ashlars' loudest hopes, but they have more to do before unleashing their scheme. And the Sonic Sisters' hip hop blitzkrieg is on hiatus at the Elms. Probably, Leah says, because they fainted at their keyboards from the chainsaw's tryout. So with minimal interference the Ashlars conceal a pair of Leah's all-weather loudspeakers at the fieldstone fence (aimed *directly* at the Elms) and wire them to an amplifier linked to the record player.

Sam runs his eye over his rows of record albums and selects one that's revered for its muscular brass and slips it on the record player.

"Ready!" says Leah.

Jenny and Sam go to an attic window as Leah sets the needle on the record—Schumann's *Concert Piece for Four Horns and Orchestra*—and an instant later the burdock meadow convulses like Krakatau losing its temper. Better still, slates fall from the Elms' roof, a gutter tears loose, and dozens of bricks wiggle from the chimney and smash onto the backyard's stone patio.

"Wow!" says Sam. "It's topple music!"

Leah joins them in the attic as an Elms' third-story windowpane rips from its ancient frame and shatters on the patio. Pavana pokes her head out the gaping hole and clings with both hands to the sill against the typhoon of sound—which forces her porcupine hairdo straight back in the 1950s duck's-ass style.

"My, my!" says Jenny. "We got her attention!"

The horn music run-through gives the Ashlars a bonus by causing an alert from the National Weather Service about a freak occurrence in Wildrose, and at Village Hall Duffy Nicklebob gets frantic texts and phone complaints about a "Hatfield-and-McCoy gunfight goin on som'eres," and rushes the news to Thaïs, who orders Lieut. Conklin to cruise the Village to see what's up.

Thaïs's discovery of Sam's crisis at Emerson University warned her that his Harris tweed facade might conceal a granite core, and she found that the University's chancellor had tried to use the campus's new Lyceum as a personal moneymaker. But Sam had dug deep and discovered that since the Lyceum was created *strictly* as a learning facility—and because the chancellor's plotting violated university policy—the chancellor had acted illegally and was promptly fired.

Thaïs logs onto the pinecones, bird nests, and other covert eyes tucked in about Mole End, which reveal the freshly cut willow limb, the chainsaw, and the tripod lights. Then she sees the Ashlars at the attic window—grinning like the *Our Gang Little Rascals* at a bakery-van wreck—and her eyes glint with love and hate.

More bricks topple from the Elms, and feeling they have things on target, the Ashlars go downstairs and shut off the record player. The fieldstone fence speakers fall silent and Orchard Lane shudders with relief.

"We're all set!" says Sam.

They hunker down in the living room to enjoy a late lunch while keeping an eye on the mantelpiece clock, and the Offmans continue their own noises in the carriage-house—then three hours later they shut down for the day—inducing the Chihuahuas to collapse in a quivering mass at Po and Pru Plinketts' bay window.

Then Ashlars hear Thaïs's Duesenberg rumble up Orchard Lane as she returns from the Village Hall, and they see Honus and Winney Offman throw an oilcloth over their outdoor table and put out dinnerware.

"It's *picanick* time!" says Jenny.

The instant Clovis and Madge Whinger get home they rush to their swimming pool and are joined by their regular weekend guests—the Wildrose Aquanauts—suited up for their time-honored Friday Night Swim 'n Beer Bash.

Next door to them at Middlemarsh Manse B&B, Wanda and Silt return in their station wagon with Henna and her two brothers (lusting for a round of poke-your-ears computer gaming), while just north of the Ashlars Po and Pru Plinkett drag themselves from their drudgery at the Lily Pad Lotions & Notions and $2 Does It to find the quaking mound of their Chihuahuas—whose palates they stiffen with Viagra chewies.

Shortly afterward at Mont-Obiston Manor the resilient butler, Gallifent, is serving glasses of Beaujolais 1066 to some A+ list bankers on the teakwood deck—assembled to consider Thaïs's request for a 700-million dollar loan to finance the Condor Estates Expansion. Billy Umbo—in ultramarine blue civies—moves among these movers-and-squeezers, squeezing them for gold nuggets to drop in

Thaïs's ear, and Geoffrey Murgwynd circulates e-prospectuses on the Turquoise Tower's heady earnings' projections. But the evening's highpoint is a preview of the uniforms designed for the Tower's 598 employees by Tabitha Tannenbach's wife, Undine. The models' promenade among the bankers was choreographed by a Fashion Institute luminary, and Undine observes demurely from the side, wearing what appears to be an oversized tube sock. But her uniforms would astound the staff at the Palace of Versailles.

GlobBank's VP drools to Thaïs. "Sensational, Your Honor. Absolutely *sensational!*"

Back at Mole End, Jenny's heirloom clock strikes six p.m. and she puts her arms around Sam and Leah.

"Let's do it!"

They insert fresh earplugs and Leah gets her camera as Sam puts on his hardhat and back-brace, then with a single pull the chainsaw's roaring like a badass badger, ravenous for a meal that's rich in fiber. Sam picks a spot at the base of the fallen willow—just above the jungle of roots where the tree's girth is greatest—and Jenny stands by to help as Leah aims her camera.

Sam grips the throttle and intones, "*small effort! BIG NOISE!*" The chainsaw showers the ground with sawdust as its blurred teeth fill Leah's monitor.

Across Orchard Lane, Honus and Winney Offman lift their bulging cheeks from their picnic table. They can't see anything unusually vibratory going on just south of them at the Silvertongs' backyard *sportplatz*, and they look toward the U-bend at Orchard Lane Bottoms, where the numerous Dinsmore sons and daughters are known to take their dirt-bikes onto their cornfield for a few hours of dirt-road rage.

"Nothin doin there!" says Honus.

He can't see anything unusual at the Silvertongs' because all 23 Wildrose Silver Hair Softballers are crammed into Sol's and Figgie's basement multiplex for an evening of Major League Baseball on their SurroundEye TV. The chainsaw's soundwaves bludgeon the basement's earthen berm, then pistol-whip the electronics to flush out the Silver Hair Softballers and Silvertongs—who check to see if the satellite disc is being infiltrated by a repeat of *This Old Lumberyard.*

The Whingers' first sign that something is amiss is the jingling ice in their poolside margaritas; then a cherry tries to drown itself in Clovis's daiquiri and he freaks out.

"God! It's an earthquake!"

Sam's an inch into the willow with 900 inches to go as the Offmans jump up from their picnic table and rush to their frontyard to discover him and the chainsaw.

"I'll be damned!" says Honus.

"*I'll* be damned!" says Winney.

Damned though they are, they scratch their heads over what to do while Leah films their damned expressions.

The chainsaw hits a knot and growls even louder, so the Whingers in their dripping swimsuits and flip-flops slap down their driveway to take a second and third look across the lane before settling on Sam.

"Lord almighty!" says Clovis.

Then the Silvertongs clomp to their front lawn in their hunt for the cause of the botched baseball broadcast—and now there's a drove of eyeballs ranged along Orchard Lane, popping in astonishment at Sam and his chainsaw.

-2-

THE NEIGHBORS COVER THEIR EARS and make their way across the lane as Honus takes the lead to brave the gate at the split-rail fence and tap Sam on the shoulder, who puts down the chainsaw and flips up his ear protectors.

"Howdy, Honus!"

"Whacha doin, Sam?"

"Sawing this willow. And by the way, we really enjoyed the hominy squares on Monday!"

He lowers the ear protectors and goes on sawing.

Honus recoils in surprise and retreats to the safety of the crowd, and after a moment Sol gets up the nerve to struggle though the sonic force-field to Sam, who puts down the chainsaw and lifts his ear protectors.

"That's an awful big tree!" says Sol.

"You're darn tooting it is! But once I start a project it's hard to stop. Just like you, I bet, when you're mowing your lawn!"

Sol's lost for words and Winney comes to his aid. "I b'lieve he's jis thinkin it's awful *late* for this kinda chore!"

Sol nods. "I was jis thinkin it's awful *late* for this kinda chore!"

"Is it?" says Sam, checking his watch. "I make it eight minutes after six, but maybe I'm slow."

The time is flashing in the corner of Leah's monitor. "Eight minutes after six, Grandpa. Right on the bean!"

Only then do the neighbors see that they're being *filmed.* They start to protest, then remember that they're on the Ashlars' property, and that Leah's documentary work has been lauded by no less than Thaïs at her barbecue and Duffy Nicklebob in the *Wildrose Voyeur* interview.

"But it's *Friday night*," says Silt, who with Wanda and Henna paused their B&B prepping and hurried down the lane.

"That's right!" says Sam. "Doncha just love weekends!"

Po Plinkett is sucking on a Pepto-Bismol tablet to calm his stomach from another grueling set-up day at the Turquoise Tower's Lily Pad Lotions & Notions.

"We love *relaxing* on weekends," he says. "Getting some down-time!"

"So do we!" says Jenny. "And chain-sawing is kick-ass downtime!"

Sam goes on sawing, and the neighbors scurry to the split-rail fence to confer while Leah captures their every movement and sound. Even a top-grade shotgun mic has limits, and much of what she gets is garbled swear words.

Silt slips away from the group and calls Thaïs on his cell, who's herded the bankers into her library for a round of Makers Mark.

"Yes, Silt. You're calling about the Ashlars, I suspect?"

"Then you hear them!" he shouts.

"I hear *you* well enough!" She doesn't bother explaining that when you hire an architect to design a home in the Billionaire Rustic style you get walls stout enough to dampen the boom of an A-bomb. "And there seems to be a disturbance in the background."

Silt blinks. "Disturbance? It's first degree earslaughter!" He points his cell at Sam, happy as can be in a whirlwind of sawdust. "You have to do something!"

"*Have* to do something?"

"I mean, well, darn it, isn't there somethin you could suggest, or—"

"I *suggest* you look at the Village website, where an alert appeared on this very issue *three days* ago."

"Ah!"

"And your lady wife—Councilwoman Middlemarsh—should already have received Duffy's Splat, directing her to send me some ideas ahead of the August meeting!"

Thaïs returns to the moneylenders in her library, and the neighbors end their confab, having contrived a nuance that's sure to stop Sam's foolishness.

Clovis is their emissary and he treks over as Sam once again puts down the chainsaw.

"Sam. We talked it over and agreed that what we meant is that it's rather late on Friday night to be using such a terribly loud chainsaw to cut up a tree as big as a strip mall while hardworking folks are trying to recharge after an exhausting week. It could take forever!"

"Hardly. I'll be done by Halloween, or I'm Jack Sprat!"

Clovis is lost for a retort, so his wife Madge takes a shot. "Our tree-trimming service could do this in no time, Sam. It'd set you back only a couple thousand bucks!"

Sam hops back. "*Pay* someone to cut up my tree? Where'd the fun be in that? Why, it would be like you paying someone to go swimming for you!"

Madge and Clovis are thoroughly fogged and Sam fogs them some more.

"You see, what we love most about Wildrose is the gung-ho spirit all of you have, like Honus and Winney. Most people who're bonkers about restoring rusted piles of junk would do it on a deserted island, but the Offmans have the gumption to do it smack up against their neighbors. Isn't that what makes America great? Blasting one's own tunnel through life?!"

The neighbors stare like cows on Dramamine and Pru Plinkett tries to sort it out. "But they don't do it after six o'clock!"

"They could if they wanted!" says Jenny.

Winney flinches. "Wut…? Do it *after* six o'clock?"

"Of course," says Sam. "In fact, there are *several* brave hearts on Orchard Lane who regularly make joyful noises after six p.m.."

Sol rakes his eye over the crowd. "O, yeah? Who'd that be?"

Sam shuts off the chainsaw to make things easier, and Leah hits her remote—pausing the loudspeakers at the field-stone fence—which are peeling the Elm's paint with a recording of Lady Gaga's toothsome musicVid, *The Dialogues of the Caramels.*

"Well," says Silt, "there's that grunge from the Elms. But that's been going on so long I've sorta gotten used to it."

"Not me!" Wanda snaps.

"Ditto that!" says Henna.

"*Listen!*" says Sam.

Clovis gestures at his swimming pool. "You mean the Wildrose Aquanauts? But that's not really noise!"

"Then what is it? Dark Matter?"

Clovis bristles. "It's swimming pool fun. Nobody minds that!"

Silt and Wanda start to protest to Clovis that they *really do* mind the diving board bombardment and lounge-singer Muszak that burst through their windows all summer long from the Whingers' pool, but are interrupted by the Dinsmores at Orchard Lane Bottoms—whose many daughters and sons start a drag race around their cornfield.

"It's only dirt-bikes," says Figgie. "Just people havin fun!"

Sam steps up to her. "You mean like your husband, having fun with his jumbo-jet riding mower? And what about *that!"*

It's Po and Pru's Chihuahuas, who'd clammed up when Sam shut off the chainsaw, then resumed their yammering at the onset of the dirt-bike derby.

Henna lets herself go, braces flashing. "They do bark an awful lot!"

"Only when something disturbs them!" says Pru.

"They bark at every flea that goes by!" says Winney. "Some days I could jis—"

The Pepto-Bismol tablet shoots from Po's mouth. "Jis what? Some days you could jis *what?"*

Honus charges at him. "Bust their noses!"

Silt holds them apart. "We're getting off the subject!"

"This *is* the subject!" says Wanda. "Neighborhood noises!"

Then Chief Truman pulls up in his cruiser and lowers his window.

"Hello, folks!" The neighbors have known and respected him for ages and greet him amiably as he waves at the Ashlars. "Hi, Sam. Jenny. And isn't that Leah, shooting her documentary?" The Ashlars wave back and Leah gets Truman in her lens as he sizes up the crowd. "Anything I can do for you folks?"

Sol catapults forward. "We're having a friendly chat about—"

"Friendly chats are good!"

"—about chain-sawing this late on Friday night!"

"Is it late?" Truman checks his watch. "I make it 6:21. But it seems to me that deciding whether or not it's *late* is subjective. It's late to some, early to others."

"But it's 6:21 on Friday *night!*"

"You got me there, Sol. It *is* Friday night—or at least, Friday *p.m.* Words can be trickier than health insurance contracts, doncha think?"

Sam is starting to see Truman in a new light, but Clovis thinks he's being deliberately obtuse.

"We're talkin about someone running a *chainsaw* on Friday night!"

"And we want it stopped!" says Winney.

The crowd joins in, all but the Middlemarshes. "Stop the chainsaw! *Stop the chainsaw!*"

Truman raises his hand and the chanting stops. "And how do you propose to do that?"

"Ain't there a law agin it?" says Winney. "A 'No-Chain-saws-on-Friday-Night' law?"

"I'm afraid not."

The neighbors' heads whip back in astonishment, except for Henna and especially Wanda. As a councilmember she knows darn well there's no such law—any more than there's a law against hippos in G-strings.

Clovis turns purple. "You mean he can go on with that monster, spoiling the Friday night of decent folks, and you won't lift a finger!?"

"*Can't* lift a finger," says Truman. "Until 10 p.m. exactly, folks can wallop their rusty mounds of iron, race their dirt-bikes down to China, churn their swimming pools like killer whales on crack, and let their dogs bark themselves inside out." The crowd boils and Truman puts the cruiser in gear. "Now, if you'll excuse me, I'm gonna see if the rest of Wildrose is as tranquil as Orchard Lane!"

And off he goes.

At Orchard Lane Bottoms the Dinsmores are still masticating their cornfield with their dirt-bikes, and the Sonic Sisters are unreeling a Peruvian goat-bell tune from the Elms. But the only sound at Mole End is gnashing teeth.

Sam tips his hardhat to his neighbors. "Thanks for stopping by!"

They stare with pinched faces as he restarts the chainsaw and pitches into the willow—screeching like the Titanic, shredding its steel plating on the iceberg. Some of them improvise a sign-language debate, while others consider cutting back on their own noises, then abandon the idea as unpatriotic. And Leah's camera reminds them that they're still being *filmed,* probably for her idiotic flick that'll thrive for a zillion years on the Big Bad Cloud, and they scatter like mice to their homes.

Silt pressures Wanda to slip a note in the Ashlars' mailbox, saying that the wiring has gone batty in their kitchen (due to some neighborhood vibrations) and they must cancel the Saturday night dinner. It pains her, but she prays that at the August meeting the Wildrose Council will unravel the tangled knot of mad dogs and English professors who make the wrong kind of noises on Friday nights.

-3-

EVENING COMES AND LEAH FLIPS ON the tripod lights, making Mole End more dazzling than Grauman's Chinese Theatre at the premiere of *Ben Hur.* The neighbors shut their blinds and hot-glue themselves to their cellphones and e-jewelry as the seconds tick by to join the quadrillions of other seconds that preceded them after the universe's bumptious debut.

Thaïs watches from her library, sitting royally in a Windsor chair beneath the family portrait while sipping apricot brandy, and Raffia is cross-legged on a Persian rug with a mug of hot cocoa and her treasured volume of *Grimms' Fairytales.* Earlier they'd drunk a toast to Thaïs's success with the bankers, who approved the $700 million loan at three percent interest, *provided* Wildrose rezones the grape-growing Pioneer Meadows to high-density commercial. Billy Umbo has sown wallet-loads of bliss among three of the five Wildrose councilmembers and reported that the rezoning is a "sure thing!"

Thaïs holds up her brandy in the light of the fireplace—a crystal ball presaging the Mont-Obistons' Golden Age—then her masculine self takes hold and switches to Knob Creek. He pats Raffia on the cheek, who lifts her eyes from

"Rapunzel' to watch the screen with her all-too-loving sister-brother.

Freed from having to prep the dining room for the Ashlars, Wanda is in her studio with cushions propped against the windows to dampen the neighborhood noises, while she reshapes the clay wine jug from a weasel to a cuckoo bird. She at last throws up her hands and wails, "I'm getting nowhere!"

But the last three hours Sam and his chainsaw—"Growler"—have gotten quite far indeed. Sam stopped a few times to refuel, and Jenny took charge of Growler and found that she enjoys his feisty companionship as much as Sam does.

Then Leah goes to the attic to see if the Sonic Sisters are hoisting a white hanky, but is sorry to find them replacing the Elms' broken windowpane with a makeshift plywood megaphone to upgrade its sonic oomph.

So Sam takes another turn. It's 9:56 p.m., and after what seems an ungodly spell it's 9:57 p.m.. It takes forever for 9:58 p.m. to come, and a dozen forevers for 9:59 p.m.. Even Zebulon is jittery with impatience, as if the moment were stretching thinner and thinner, rather than politely making way for the next moment—when suddenly it's 10:00 p.m.!

It's 10:00 p.m. on the dot and Sam is sawing with renewed determination!

"Damn! Damn! Damn!" says Po Plinkett—glaring over the Chihuahuas' heads from his bay window.

Despite the fun they're having, the Ashlars know precisely what time it is, flashing on Leah's monitor. But as the first seconds of the 23rd hour of Friday come and go, Sam guns Growler louder and louder.

"How interesting!" Zebulon confides to Raffia.

"He's happy!" she says—intrigued by this hoary-haired man who seems to be made of fairyland dust.

"He's a maniac!" Sol screeches to Figgie, and he brings up the Police Department on his eBracelet. He rests his finger on the number as 10:00:57 p.m. comes and Leah raises her hand to signal Sam. "Late enough!" Sol hisses, punching the number.

The call is routed to Truman's bedroom on Old Farm Ridge, where the bedside clock shows 10:00: p.m..

"Here we go!" Truman says to his wife.

At 10:00:59 p.m. Leah draws a finger across her throat and Sam shuts off Growler. The sudden quiet makes the ear-lobes on Orchard Lane flap like boat hatches in a squall, and seeing that he's been hornswoggled, Sol vents a string of X-rated profanities as Truman takes note of his name.

"Sol! I think you oughta see an anger management counselor!"

-4-

EARLY ON SATURDAY THE ASHLARS breakfast at the back porch on Jenny's peach jam and Sam's walnut muffins (a trifle overdone), while enjoying the mockingbird's newest release—a sendup of Growler, sung with breast-thumping brio from the chimney top.

Sam's a bit sore from chain-sawing but is delighted that all is quiet, and Leah does a rough edit of the previous six days' footage and offloads it to some friends—a guy in Van Nuys, California who makes films, and a woman in Brooklyn who runs her own web production company, Break-Balls.now. They give high-fives on the footage's viral-worthiness and promise to share it with fellow geeks.

Then a strange noise blows in, like the offspring of a blackbird and an organ grinder.

"How weird!" says Jenny.

The Sonic Sisters stayed up well past their Midnight Mantra to connive a response to the Ashlars' loudspeakers, and decided to unleash a fresh round of "healing" by imagining the vocalizations of winged dinosaurs. An all-night effort with cutting-ear software and suspect meds birthed the effect now vibrating across the burdock meadow.

And the Chihuahuas have been restored with a good night's rest and leap to Po and Pru Plinkett's bay window with a new round of barking.

"Here we go again!" says Sam.

Honus and Winney Offman also rise early, vowing to *work on Saturday!* They prop the carriage-house doors wide open, tune their Goliath boombox to a station that features around-the-clock yodeling, and start yanking the corroded bolts from the Hudson's transmission with a pneumatic wrench so jarring it would put a tyrannosaurus's teeth on edge.

All of this shakes the Dinsmores from their bunkbeds at Orchard Lane Bottoms, who begin a dirt-bike boulder-dragging contest through their woodlot—an atonal symphony that induces Clovis and Madge Whinger to start diving-board practice at their heart-shaped pool—the *boing-boing* of their flippers resounding like an *oops!* moment at a munitions factory.

Feeling that Orchard Lane still has a noise problem, the Ashlars wash their breakfast things, insert their earplugs, and resume their tussle with the giant willow.

Wanda is in her studio—which is quickly warming up because the windows are tightly shut—and having abandoned the cuckoo bird wine jug, she begins working out ideas on a sketchpad from whatever creatures chance by her window.

"Atta girl!" says Silt.

Then he and Henna start tidying up for their impending guests. A hot weekend is forecast and Silt knows they'll be caught between powering up their ravenous swamp cooler, or running their kilowatt-greedy ceiling fans. Or all of the above! It also means their guests will get grungy from rafting on Wildrose River and hiking up Condor Lookout for the stunning selfie view, and will indulge in prolonged showers. Mumbling invectives, Silt goes to the cellar to see how the solder's holding out on their Stone Age water heater.

By midmorning the Ashlars are two-thirds through the willow when a spidery object the size of a briefcase darts overhead. It disappears too quickly for Leah to film and Sam says it's probably something whipped up by the Sonic Sisters. He makes a metal note to deal with it later on and continues sawing.

* * *

By late Saturday morning the Ashlars' competitors are foundering, largely because Sam has found that the trick is to become one with Growler. A Zen thing. Just be *in the moment* and let Growler have his way!

Then Lieut. Conklin arrives in the cruiser and hitches up his well-polished gun belt. Leah pans her camera to this stumble-on character and signals Jenny to shut Growler off, which causes the Chihuahuas to stop barking from the Plinketts' bay window.

Conklin squints at Growler. "I'll hav'ta take that in. Hadda complaint that it's terrifyin the dawgs and disruptin the peace in lots and sundry ways. Ordinance 700 or thereabouts."

Sam had never before encountered such an intellect and curses his bad luck. "Who made the complaint?"

Conklin rubs his nose. "I can't dislodge that. I hav'ta impose your chainsaw into custody, and you kin file a peel with the judge."

Jenny runs over. "It's been noisier than D Day around here ever since we arrived a week ago! The dogs next door have been barking their heads off for days. And what about the dirt-bikes, and the auto savagery across the road?"

"I don't hear no dawgs or savages. 'Sides which, nobody complained about 'em." Fast on the uptake, Conklin notices Leah. "Are you makin a movie of me?"

"Hardly. I'm just getting some bloopers."

"All right," says Sam. "Handcuff our saw, if you're able, then get off our property before *I* file a complaint about trespassing!"

Conklin does as Sam suggests, including the handcuffs.

Zebulon is playing Chinese checkers with Raffia and watched this unfold on his spycams before getting an update on the Turquoise Tower's progress from Chief Engineer Cornelius Flug. He says there's a glitch in the Tower's plumbing and points to a pipefitter, ankle-deep in water in the VIP women's room.

"Fix it!" says Zebulon.

He's disturbed that Conklin's more of a gnat brain than he'd calculated, but decides to let the chips lie where they are, since they appear to be lying in his own favor. Then Zebulon mulls over a more pressing matter. He's arranged for a doctor to land at the Manor's airstrip later in the day, and told Raffia that the doctor will be doing a "wellness checkup," in view of the recent disappearance of her monthly marvel and occasional tummy aches. The doctor had attended the Mont-Obistons in their compound outside Milwaukee before they moved to Europe, and at the private clinic in Wisconsin when Thaïs's eyes closed for good—the lights that Zebulon is so desperate to rekindle via his intimacy with Raffia.

He's suddenly distracted by cheering and returns to the spycams' screen as the neighbors unleash *hurrahs* at Conklin's triumph over the Ashlars.

Wanda is strolling about with her sketchpad and lingers by the Ashlars' gate, hoping to say a word or two of support.

If they've found the note in their mailbox revoking the dinner invitation they give no sign of it. She gives a final anguished glance and goes home—while Leah suggests to Sam and Jenny that they take another lunchbreak at the Green Goose Café.

-5-

GILES MCDRAKE FINISHES GERSHWIN'S "Nice Work if You Can Get It" and Leah asks if he'll do Gershwin's "Someone to Watch Over Me."

"Gladly! And by the way, I've heard what's going on at Orchard Lane and wish you all the best of luck!"

The Café is crammed with diners and the Ashlars are relieved that it's devoid of their neighbors, from whom they've heard more than enough the last several days. Chief Truman is lunching with his wife Daisy at a nearby booth and asks how the chain-sawing is coming along.

Sam's caught in the act of unfolding his napkin. "We were about to head to your office!"

Leah holds up her ePal and shows Lieut. Conklin's antics for Truman.

"Our chainsaw's been busted!"

* * *

Conklin is still chortling over his heroic deed when Truman storms into the office and grabs the paperwork with its belabored pictographs.

"What the blazes have you done?"

"There was a complaint 'bout that chainsaw!"

"Who made it?" Conklin's Adam's apple wobbles and Truman bears down on him. "I said, who made the complaint!?"

"Figgie Silvertongs."

Truman shakes his head in disgust. "The local Madame Currie. Where'd you put it?"

"In the cruiser."

Truman rescues Growler and returns to the Ashlars' table at the Green Goose Café.

"Your chainsaw's on the bench out front, and I guess nobody will bother it before you're done eating. I apologize for the misguided enthusiasm you suffered at the hands of my department!"

The Ashlars thank him, then after shooting Giles a grateful smile for playing the Gershwin tunes, Leah offloads her new footage to her pals in Van Nuys and Brooklyn. Right away the young woman in Brooklyn says she's putting Conklin's Oscar-certain cameo onto her BreakBalls.now web blast.

"Ur clps supr hot! Bocu hits!! Sen gobs mor!!!"

Leah shows it to Sam and Jenny. "From my pal in Brooklyn!"

"Is she ill?" says Jenny.

"She's hot for the coverage and is getting loads of hits from her 46,000 fans. The doc is building a following even before it's finished!"

Jenny stares at the ePal. "*Before* it's finished?"

"Forty-six *thousand?!*" says Sam.

-6-

THE ASHLARS RETURN HOME to find three envelopes stuffed in their mailbox. One of them has Wanda's note cancelling that evening's dinner, and another one contains a water-spotted cocktail napkin with a few curt sentences from Clovis and Madge Whinger, rescinding the invitation to their poolside lunch on Sunday and closing with, "We're sure you'd have found our hospitality all wet!"

"I was expecting something like this," Jenny laments, placing the notes on the mantelpiece.

The third envelope was crafted from a brown paper bag with a note scrawled in pencil.

Dear Mr. and Ms. Ashlar & Granddaughter,

We are struck with shame to see you treated so badly because of the chainsaw and wanna let you know we're glad about your fight to make things more respectful around here for everybody! Our birds and other friends are most grateful!

God bless!

MAD & SAD

"Makes me want to work all the harder!" says Sam, but Jenny puzzles over the signatures. "MAD and SAD…?"

She puts the note on the mantelpiece, then heartened that they have some support, they hurry into their gear and gas up Growler.

Then Sam says, "Hang on! In case that spidery thing shows its face again!"

He goes to the toolshed and digs through a trunk of family keepsakes for his old slingshot. The sprucewood handle and leather pouch have weathered well, but the rubber bands crumble in his fingers. He replaces them with Hercules Brand Extra-Stout Rubber Bands, and gets some lead sinkers from the fishing-tackle box left by Jenny's uncle, then decides he needs some practice. His eyes fall on a dried gourd, hanging from a nail on a corner-post 15 or 16 feet away. It takes all his strength to draw the pouch, then he releases, and faster than the eye can follow the sinkers smash the gourd to smithereens.

* * *

Snug in their ear protectors, the Ashlars miss Orchard Lane's collective yowl as they resume sawing. Then the spidery device that buzzed Mole End that morning returns and Jenny sees the blur of propellers.

"It's a *drone!*"

It darts at the frogs, scattering them from their pondside naps—controlled by Clovis from a floating lounge-chair in his pool, who grins at the drone's screen as Sam shouts.

"Whoever's doing this, I'm warning you to stop it!"

Clovis sniggers and shoves the joystick, diving the drone at Jenny, who barely dodges clear. Leah hurls some pebbles that miss, and Clovis sniggers again.

Sam picks up a stone. "If you're such hot stuff, why don't you give *me* a crack at you? Unless you're just an airhead!"

Clovis sees red and mutters, "I'll show ya who's an air-head!"

He shoves the joystick and the drone accelerates as Sam grows large on Clovis's screen. Sam drops the stone and whips out the slingshot, drawls the pouch and releases, and the lead sinkers shred the drone, causing it to twist erratically and crash into the Ashlars' linden tree.

"Shit!" says Clovis.

Leah runs to Sam. "Grandpa! That was terrific!"

"I'm still learning things about you!" says Jenny, then she picks up the mangled drone with a gloved hand. "It might have fingerprints!"

Zebulon watched this exchange via the spycams and has a good laugh. He's lounging in the library, waiting for the doctor to land. After examining Raffia the doctor will join them for dinner, then all will be settled, Zebulon tells himself. He returns his attention to Orchard Lane—where Sam and Growler are making great strides—and tells Raffia it's time for a litmus paper test.

Her big brown eyes widen over her watercolor. "Litmus paper?"

"You'll see!" And he gives instructions on a walkie-talkie.

Angrier than ever about Growler, the neighbors improvise a protest and wave signs scribbled, NIX THE NOISY NUISANCE! and SAVE OUR WEEKENDS! Sol bawls something over a megaphone—which no one hears because of Growler, the Chihuahuas, and the echoes from Leah's loudspeakers at the fieldstone fence, hurling the *Star Wars* theme music at the Sonic Sisters.

A half hour later the chaos worsens as a pack of motorcyclists with black lightning bolts embossed on their helmets tear down Orchard Lane.

"Right on time!" says Zebulon, and Raffia puts down her paintbrush to watch.

The bikers slow down and ogle Mole End through their dark-tinted visors, then their beefy leader gives an order over his wireless headset and they vanish down the Bottoms, pelting everything in sight with exhaust pipe carbon brickbats. The neighbors gag and cough, while Leah forwards her footage of the incident to her pal in Van Nuys—a sometime biker and gadfly of all things fringish.

And Zebulon sees another test is needed.

* * *

Come midafternoon, Growler rips through the willow's final grains and its Paul Bunyan-size bole splashes into the brook, soaking Sam in its spray. Jenny brings glasses of iced tea to toast the completion of The First Big Cut and runs her hand over the willow's smooth base.

"*Salix nigra.* We oughta count the rings!"

The sudden quiet prods the neighbors to hope that their hero, Lieut. Conklin, has rustled up another ordinance to collar Growler—or that Sam's had a heart attack. But lacking the grit to form another ring around the roadside, they watch with e-cams and spotter scopes from their decks and upper-story bedrooms and see Sam (healthier than ever, damn him!) slurping iced tea with his feet resting on the porch railing.

"Maybe they're done for the day!" Silt says to Wanda, just back from another sojourn with her sketchpad that she crammed with drawings of songbirds and dragonflies. She also sketched the willow tree roots, half submerged in the Ashlars' brook. "What the hell's that?" Silt demands.

"Gesture drawing. Force of habit!"

Leah's Van Nuys friend reports that the motorcyclists are Midnight Thunder, a rogue offshoot of the Internal Combustion Engine Enthusiasts.

"They've crossed spokes with the Little Rock Police, but what's alarming is that with such few followers, either Midnight Thunder is winning new adherents from ICEE's two million members, or you've got some Midnight Thunder *founders* right in your lap!"

Refreshed with iced tea, the Ashlars return to the willow with redoubled passion. And envisioning a vast audience for their scheme, Sam says the creature they're carving will have a lot on its shoulders and oughta be at least six feet tall.

"Oh, no," says Jenny. "It's mythic. Oughta be seven feet tall!"

"Or eight!" says Leah. "It'll be shouldering the weight of villages everywhere!"

"What are they getting at?" Zebulon muses.

Sam plants his foot by the willow's base and paces it off. He gets to nine feet—regards Jenny and Leah—then takes another step and marks the bark with the hatchet.

-7-

SAM AND JENNY SAW STEADILY, and minus the intrusion of police lieutenants (and feeling very much at Zen with Growler) they finish The Second Big Cut late Saturday afternoon. Freed from the tree, the huge piece of lumber *plonks* onto the bank by the brook and Sam runs a measuring tape along it.

"*Ten feet three inches!*"

The neighbors watch with cheek-sucking anxiety as the Ashlars remove the bark. Jenny and Leah have honed very sharp edges on the hatchet and chisel and slice off the bark like icing from an Oreo.

"Where should we put her?" says Jenny. "She probably outweighs Leah's VW!"

They pick a spot close to the cabin with mixed sun and shade, and attach a rope with a block and tackle from the magic toolshed to the linden tree and winch the willow log in place.

Honus knows "som'in 'bout tools" and is impressed by their resourcefulness, while Sol—staring anxiously through his target-rifle scope from his bungee platform—is altogether stumped.

And Zebulon orders another test over his walkie-talkie. The doctor's in the bedroom with Raffia and the family's trusted housekeeper—Petra—who was midwife at the triplets' births 44 years earlier. Zebulon is making a furrow in the library's Persian carpet with his pacing, while trying to keep up with the Ashlars' maneuvers on the sonic chessboard as Leah shinnies up the linden tree to move the block and tackle high enough to winch the log upright. Then Sam goes at the massive trunk with Growler as the Offmans watch from the carriage-house.

"He's *carvin* somethin!" Winney says to Honus.

"Matchsticks!" Sol shouts to Figgie from the bungee platform. "He's gonna stand right there and saw a billion matchsticks!"

Then the earth trembles as Midnight Thunder returns. They gun their engines and Leah picks out the beefy guy at the front of the bikers with a device clipped to his collar and—figuring he's the leader—goes super-telephoto. His orange-tinted visor looms like a washing machine lid on her monitor, and she explores the wiry eyebrows and menacing expression.

"Lookit her!" says one of the bikers.

The leader thrusts his head in defiance, but Leah's unimpressed by this D film acting and explores his leather jacket, gloves, and extra wide boot.

The other cyclists look at him and then at her as the leader boasts, "How'd ya like to snag *that* on yer fishin rod!"

They laugh nervously and he goes on leering, expecting her to back down, but he doesn't know Leah. Zebulon does know something about Leah and grabs the walkie-talkie.

"Move your stupid ass!"

The biker sinks in his saddle and shoots up Orchard Lane with his Midnight Thunder cohort in his exhaust stream.

* * *

The Ashlars break for dinner—as do the Sonic Sisters—who partake of tofu steaks and lentil pie in the Elms' funereal dining room. They're debating their next step, and Calliope shoves a weary hand through her rainbow-colored hair as she rereads the leaflet given her by the Ashlars.

"Perhaps we should attend their Sunday evening Noise Ordinance chitchat after all!"

"Given the wounds they've made in the Fabric they can't possibly still be thinking of holding it!" says Pavana. "Besides, an inspiration came to me at Noon Mantra!"

Following her vision, they hit the software and saturate Orchard Lane with chainsaw-like emanations that make the neighbors think the Ashlars have cloned Growler and are attacking Orchard Lane with *two* chainsaws.

Leah knows right off what's up and switches her audio system from Dynamic Boost to Wagnerian Boost. Then she fires off a volley of Willy Nelson tribute artists over the loudspeakers, a recoding that's reimagined by the Bavarian accordion band Blähungen ("out your backside"). The accordionized Willie Nelson meets the Sisters' virtual chainsaw noise—like Achilles getting the finger from Hector on Troy's veranda—and the chase is on.

Then Leah sends the Midnight Thunder footage to her chums in Van Nuys and Brooklyn, who get the same uneasy feeling about the musclebound biker with the wide feet as do Leah and her grandparents.

"B krful!" says Breakballs.now, then posts the footage on her website.

Fed, rested, and more determined than ever, Sam has become a backwoods Michelangelo and persists until he has the bottom half of the log roughed in. But roughed in as *what* the neighbors haven't the vaguest idea, and they watch in stupefaction through their Peeping Tom devices at the willowwood gouges, whorls, and hirsute looking ridges.

"It ain't matchsticks he's sawing," says Figgie to Sol, as she joins him on the bungee tower. "It's just plain *sawdust!*"

Night comes and Leah flips on the tripod lights as Jenny takes over with Growler, generating scuttlebutt that they're carving a giant piece of art.

"Some sorta *hex* symbol!" says Winney.

"Or *sex* symbol!" says Honus—disturbed by the carving's potent size. "And won't they hav'ta pay an art tax? Or a *sex* art tax?"

The Plinketts and Whingers can't begin to fathom what Sam is carving and send photos of it to their LoveMe cliques, eDump mates, and lawyers. But the Dinsmore clan is intrigued enough to start a lottery to see who comes closest to guessing what Sam's doing.

"I think he's carvin an animal," says the matriarch, Mynah. "A *loving* animal!"

"So do I!" says Sparrow, her youngest.

Mynah and Sparrow are MAD and SAD—Mynah Annette Dinsmore and Sparrow Arlen Dinsmore—who left the handwritten note of support in the Ashlars' mailbox.

Wanda avoids the hubbub by insulating herself in her studio. She flips through her sketches and finds herself attracted to the ones of the willow log, and wonders if she's lost her mind.

Zebulon is keeping a close eye on things when the doctor knocks at the library door.

"Raffia's about nine weeks along and doing just fine!"

Zebulon does an ecstatic turn around the aquarium and pours glasses of cherry schnapps as the doctor asks where the child will be born.

"In Milwaukee. Petra's too old, bless her, so we'll need a suitable nanny."

The doctor says he'll make some inquiries and lifts his glass. "To the Mont-Obistons' future!"

Zebulon clinks glasses. "Our *glorious* future!"

* * *

Sam ascends the ladder and starts carving the top of the willow log to conform with the lower half, but at 10:00:58 p.m. exactly Leah gives the signal and he silences Growler.

Sol is still at the bungee tower with his finger poised over Chief Truman's number on his eBracelet. But he's grown cautious, and instead of jumping the gun he hurls an expletive at the top of his lungs.

"Crapolla!"

All of the Middlemarshes are in bed but Wanda, who tossed her sketchpad aside and heaped another mound of clay onto her wheel. She's improvising and has the genesis of something she can't articulate and fumes aloud.

"What a fumbling, lumbering, conundrum!"

Zebulon is reading "The Little Match Girl" to Raffia in her bed, but it's been an eventful day and her eyes close in sleep before the match girl's eyes close in death. The radiance he saw in Raffia the night of the barbecue is blossoming and he swells with pride.

He pulls the quilt snug to her Plymouth Rock chin and whispers, "Platinum-plated dreams!" to her and her stuffed giraffe.

Unhappy with the second litmus test, he drafts a letter and seals it in an envelope with a pair of $100 bills, then gets a bucket of tar and a stout brush from the Swiss chalet maintenance building that he puts into a black plastic leaf-bag. Moments later the leaf-bag is lashed to Nightshade as Zebulon glissades down Salamander Ridge to Tread On Us Retreads.

-8-

EARLY ON SUNDAY THE ASHLARS awaken to find red paint sprayed all over their 10-foot, three-inch masterwork.

Leah films it for the record, but Sam says not to worry, as he still needs to grind off another inch or so of wood. But as he goes to the toolshed he runs right back out.

"Growler's gone!"

They glance up and down the lane to see if anyone's watching with a guilty sneer, but no one's around and Sam checks for footprints when Jenny sees the bullfrog at the far side of the pond, staring back at her from the tip of Growler's blade. Sam removes his shoes and socks, rolls up his trousers, and wades out to rescue him.

"At least we're striking a nerve!" he laughs.

Sol is already at the bungee tower with his telescopic sight and eDumps the news around Orchard Lane, drawing the neighbors to the split-rail fence.

Winney takes the lead and cries out. "Looks like someone don't like modern art!"

"That's no excuse!" says Wanda.

"They had it comin!" says Pru.

"This is supposed to be a civilized village!" says Henna.

"Civilized people don't run chainsaws at all hours!" says Madge.

But Clovis sees a chance to safeguard his and Madge's vacations that begin the next day, and he pulls Sam aside.

"This red paint ain't somethin most of us agree with, and it seems you're doing this 'cause you find things kinda roughshod around here. What exactly do you want?"

"All right, Clovis. I'll tell you. Several days ago we passed around leaflets to set up a meeting with all of you about the noises on Orchard Lane. But aside from finding most of our leaflets tossed in the ditch, we didn't get a single response—other than the Middlemarshes and Offmans, who said they couldn't come. No one else stopped by or emailed or anything!" The neighbors shuffle and lower their eyes. "What we'd have said at the meeting is we think it's time Wildrose had a genuine Noise Ordinance!"

"Well," says Honus. "If it would outlaw chain-sawin twen'y hours a day *I'd* be for it!"

"So would I!" says Dewey Dinsmore, who crept up from the Orchard Lane Bottoms with a squadron of his dirt-bike-addicted progeny.

"Then let's put it on the ballot right now!" says Sol.

"Ordinances don't go on ballots," says Silt. "They're enacted by the Village Council."

Winney shakes her greasy locks. "Village console?"

All eyes fall on Wanda, who takes a deep breath.

"Well, Sam. As you know, the mayor has scheduled the Noise Ordinance issue for the next meeting."

"That's nine weeks away," he says, "which is why we tried to engage everyone ahead of time!"

"I think we've let you down."

Clovis smells an opening. "Okay. A noise ordinance. To put the skids on chainsaws and gasoline motorcycles, like the ones that keep racing up the lane! Will that do it for you?"

Sam squares up to Clovis. "Look. An ordinance wouldn't hold up if the Council cherry-picked only noises they or certain other residents disliked."

"Such as?"

"You name it!" says Sam, surveying the vexed faces. "Our chain-sawing is getting everyone's goat because most of you are beat from a long week and wanna splash about your pools or knock off some beers with your friends."

"Well, of course!" says Clovis. "It's only natural!"

"But your swimming pool is louder than our chainsaw!"

"Bullshit!"

Silt goes face to face with Clovis. "No, it isn't. Most summer nights Wanda and the kids and I feel like we're living next to Daytona Beach at Spring Break. We have to shut the windows and put on the swamp cooler—at a God-damned 43 cents a kilowatt hour!"

"Well—why didn't you say so before?"

Wanda jumps into the ring. "We have said so, and you always tell us to get our swimsuits and join you for a six-pack. But we've told you countless times we don't care for swimming and can't stand beer!"

"Well," says Madge. "You could bring soft drinks and watch *us* swim!"

Sol waggles his arms. "This is a lotta nonsense!"

"On the contrary," says Sam. "We *know* the Whingers are louder because Leah monitored their swimming parties on Tuesday and Wednesday nights on her noise-level meter and compared it to our chain-sawing, showing the Whingers as the undisputed noise champions. But other Orchard Lane noises are almost as bad!"

"Such as?" says Pru.

Madge dashes over. "Such as your dogs!"

"They *are* a damned nuisance!" says Winney. "If Honus and I are havin a picanic, their screechin darn near takes the pattern off the plates!"

The argument boils over and Silt raises his hands for order. "But even if we know how much noise somebody's making, what good will it do?"

"As I said," says Sam. "We pass an ordinance with a *maximum* noise level."

Honus straightens to his full five-foot four. "Ya mean a law tellin us how much noise we kin make, every damn night of the year?!"

Sam straightens to his five-foot eleven. "I mean a law telling us how much noise we can make every damn *second* of the year!"

Honus flails his arms. "You're a nut head!"

Jenny runs over and grabs him by the earmuffs. "Mr. Offman. If you can't speak civilly to my husband, then leave our property!"

Honus whirls around and kicks the gatepost, stubbing his toe.

"The Council won't never pass such a law!" says one of the Dinsmores—who seem to multiply by the minute.

Thaïs is enjoying this from the luxuries of her library, as more neighbors shout solidarity with Sol and the Dinsmores.

"Have it your own way!" says Sam, taking up Growler. "Now excuse us, as we're gonna continue indulging in *our* hobby!"

"We're doing no good here!" says Silt, taking Wanda and Henna by the hand and marching off.

The others stick it out, betting that Sam won't get Growler working after its skinny-dip in the pond, but after a vigorous yank Growler roars as noisily as you please. Certainly as noisily as the Ashlars please, then Sam uses the tip of Growler's blade to remove the red paint, and in no time the wood grain gleams, as paint-free as a baby's bum.

Sam mounts the ladder and resumes carving where he'd left off the night before, and the stragglers groan in despair and go home—while Sol takes out his frustration by jumping on his Brahman Bull Bronco Trainer, backed up with the soundtrack of a besotted rodeo crowd.

-9-

AS THE ASHLARS BREAK FOR LUNCH Leah says she's worried about more trouble. "What if someone drives nails into her? Or *steals* Growler?" She opens her ePal. "I'm gonna tell Chief Truman about the paint and the drone. And I have a plan of my own!"

After lunch Sam resumes carving and Leah films, while Jenny takes the VW to Home Discomfit to get some items for Leah's idea. Meanwhile, the neighbors turn up the heat of their speculations as to what the Ashlars are contriving.

"They're carving a tornader!" Winney says to Honus, who shakes his head. "Naw, it ain't. It's a great big brain. Jis lookit the furrows he's carvin, like brains are s'posed to have!"

And Raffia tells Thaïs she knows what it's going to be, and whispers in her ear.

"Do you think so?" says Thaïs. "How odd!"

Then suddenly Mole End goes quiet and the neighbors put their eye devices on the highest magnification.

"What the hell are they up to?" Sol says to Figgie, who's hoisting beer and pretzels in the bungee platform's dumb-waiter.

And Clovis says to Madge, "They're just *staring* at it!"

Silt and Wanda are watching from their kitchen window while preparing parsley puff hors d'oeuvres, and Silt guesses the Ashlars might be finished for the day.

"We can have a quiet game of charades with our guests!"

They've come at last—two middle-aged couples from Manitoba—and having slopped up the guest bathroom after their 26-hour journey are quaffing glasses of complimentary orangeade as Henna shows them around the garden.

The Orchard Lane consensus is that the willow carving is indeed *finished*, and all the neighbors engage in feverish eDumps and Goobers as to what it is. A pouting storm cloud, hurling lightning bolts? A wooly quadruped from the Amazon rainforest?

The Ashlars stand back to admire their creation and Leah says they should name her.

Sam fires up his pipe. "Why don't we call her Moleen?"

Jenny claps her hands. "Moleen! That's perfect!"

And Thaïs turns to Raffia. "My pet! You were right! He's carved a giant *mole!*"

* * *

The Middlemarshes' guests gather in the dining room to enjoy the parsley puff hors d'oeuvres and more orangeade while Henna diverts them with a piccolo concerto, backed up by a harmonica orchestra on her digital recorder that's masking the tremoring of the Manse's prehistoric swamp cooler, toiling like a galley slave.

The neighbors who come closest to identifying the Ashlars' creation are Mynah and Sparrow Dinsmore—MAD and SAD—who're spending their summer making pastel drawings of the wildlife that's been vanishing throughout Wildrose the last few years. Mynah thought Sam was carving a hedgehog, and Sparrow a giant shrew. But the word's out, and it circulates throughout Wildrose faster than a CERN particle, chasing another bozo.

"At least it's done with!" Clovis says to Madge, sunning themselves beside their pool.

Then hoping to protect their impending vacations, Clovis throws on a lounge robe and runs over in his flipflops to congratulate Sam on his masterpiece.

"Thanks, Clovis, but we've just begun. You see, this willow's big enough to provide mole carvings for every frontyard in the county. In fact, we're thinking about busing in other chainsaw enthusiasts and making it a cottage industry!"

Clovis runs home and gasps the news to Madge, and another CERN-like report circles Wildrose while Sam resumes sawing with newfound gusto.

In a panic, several neighbors race off in hopes of a quiet Sunday dinner at Burger Queen or Attila the Bun on the Sky Vue Freeway, while others retaliate with their obstreperous garage vac systems and ramjet whirlpool bathtubs. As for the Offmans, it's their monthly drag race night, and they're joined by other kindred souls who maul their scrubby backlot with a fleet of gas-gulping DIY hotrods.

At Middlemarsh Manse the swamp cooler is sweating like a mule in long johns as Henna pitches into the piccolo concerto's 7th movement for the delight of their puff-pastry-stuffed guests.

"More orangeade?" her brothers ask.

There's a sudden *pop!* as the lights and swamp cooler go out and the harmonica orchestra falls silent on Henna's recorder. She plays a few more notes on her piccolo and gives up, in a house as black and blue as a boxer in the midnight of his career.

* * *

It's 10:00:58 p.m., and after starting another Big Cut on the willow tree Sam shuts Growler off.

Sol Silvertongs no longer has his finger on Chief Truman's number, but he seeks vengeance by bringing his TendrTokus Riding Mower to bear on his lawn—where the plutonium-based fertilizer has shot the grass blades up nine inches since he mowed it on Monday.

Then he sees Figgie waving a sign in his headlights, STOP IT, YOU FOOL! IT'S AFTER TEN P.M.!!!!!

Silt and Wanda are sitting in a stupor in their drawing room. The lights have been restored with a spare fuse, but the swamp cooler is off and the wide-open windows inhale the garden's heliotrope scent. The two couples from Manitoba tore off to the Tugboat Inn on Wildrose River, screaming that what the Manse provided wasn't remotely what the website had promised. Silt returned their deposits—and because the couples had swapped mates to indulge in some adult friskery on top of, around, and under their beds, all of the sheets, rugs, and candlesticks have to be sanitized.

A nightingale solos in the garden and Wanda says it's a lovely evening. Silt turns to her with a brow as creased as a third-hand newspaper.

"Are you outta your mind? It's the worst damned evening of our lives!"

Sam and Jenny meanwhile help Leah effect the plan she'd mentioned at lunch. They unpack the items from Home Detritus—a dozen wireless security cameras that they install around the property, with three cameras aimed directly at Moleen. Leah places one of them in the crotch of their willow tree limb where an especially handsome cone is wedged, which she puts in her vest pocket as a memento of her documentary. And Sam installs a heavy-duty hasp and latch to the shed door and secures them with a padlock. They make popcorn on the fire pit—whose perky detonations are the loudest thing for miles around—then kick back in the Adirondack chairs with glasses of Green Goose Merlot.

Moleen's black-currant eyes sparkle from the yard and Sam says, "It's night, when moles are up and about!"

-10-

SAM TAKES A SECOND BOW FROM THE stage of Emerson University's new Lyceum as the audience applauds his pithy dedication speech. Jenny and their son and daughter bask in his success from their front-row seats, but as he enters the wings he's surrounded by the chancellor's henchmen.

The chancellor cuffs Sam's ear. "We're putting this place in better hands!"

They pin Sam's arms behind him as the stage is taken over by a Las Vegas phantasmagoria of oiled dancers, chained circus animals, and writhing musicians whose lurid performances crack the Lyceum's very foundations.

Sam moans under the quilt and wakens in a sweat from his recurring nightmare, then an alarm screeches and lights blaze from the frontyard as Leah runs in in her nightgown.

"I'm going out!"

Sam and Jenny follow in their PJs and Leah shuts off the sirens with the remote.

"How's our girl?" says Sam, hobbling toward Moleen on his arthritic knees.

She's unmolested, but he trips over a bucket with a brush stuck deep in its murky contents.

Then the Village cruiser pulls up and Truman gets out.

"I just got a noise complaint. Would you mind telling me what's going on?"

Sam explains, and in an instant Truman becomes a six-foot three-inch action figure.

"Don't walk around more than you have to, leastwise not by your giant mole there." He gets the bucket by the wire handle and stows it in the cruiser, then squints at the blazing lights. "Your setup certainly scared the bejesus outta whoever did this!"

He examines the mounds of sawdust, laden with dew, moving deftly like a John Wayne who attended boot camp with Mikhail Baryshnikov.

"Sam? What size shoe do you wear?"

"Nine and a half D."

Truman unreels a tape measure where a shoe has lifted some sawdust.

"Must be quadruple E. We've got Widefoot here!"

"Chief?" says Leah. "Remember the video I sent you about the Midnight Thunder biker?"

"The one with the huge boots? I sure do!"

Zebulon has tuned in from his library, while sorting through the dozens of ore samples he's collected from the defunct mine at Wildrose Forest, samples that are a foretaste of the tons of ore he intends to extract over the coming years. The state is chronically strapped for funds, with parks at the bottom of the list. Platinum LLC can provide several rangers where now there's but one, and can pull the plug on the illegal animal trapping—which Zebulon is fueling with his late-night drop-offs at Tread on Us Retreads. Once Platinum LLC is at the tiller, he knows he can extract the precious ore from the ground, with or without the state's blessing.

He returns his attention to Mole End, but the input from spycam number five in the willow tree is on the blink. He turns up the sound on the other spycams as Truman photographs the extra-wide footprint and hands a jar to Jenny.

"Could you zap this for me?"

The substance in the jar softens like jelly in Jenny's microwave, then firms up when Truman pours it over the footprint.

Leah opens her ePal. "Chief? Take a look!"

Zebulon enlarges the image of her as she replays the security camera footage for Truman, showing *two* men invading Mole End. A thin, tall man hangs back by the split-rail fence as a lookout while the other one—thick-waisted and muscular—skulks toward Moleen with the bucket of tar when the alarm sounds, causing him to drop the bucket and make fat tracks for Orchard Lane.

Leah freezes the shot. "I'm sure that's the biker who came by yesterday!"

Zebulon zooms in until Leah's eyes hover like twin planets, inhabited by highly intelligent but very mysterious beings.

-11-

NEXT MORNING LEAH OFFLOADS the securety camera footage to Truman and he asks the Ashlars to his office. He runs the footage on his desktop computer for them and pauses on Widefoot—whose face is shadowed by a baseball cap. Truman gestures at the tar bucket, locked up in a cabinet beside the drone.

"There weren't any fingerprints, and I couldn't find a store who sold this. But the drone *does* have some prints, and it came from Knokdown Drugs. Clovis Whinger—the stock manager—was pretty sheepish when I asked about it, and I could press the matter if you wish."

Sam glances at Jenny and Leah. "I think not. Not for now, at least."

"Let me know if you change your mind," says Truman, "and I'll give Clovis a thorough scolding." He unlocks the cabinet and removes a plaster-of-Paris cast, made from the mold of Widefoot's print. "This could be our ace in the hole!"

Thaïs suddenly ducks through the doorway and gazes down at the Ashlars.

"Chief Truman told me about the appalling event at Mole End last night and I think we've reached the Rubicon. I'm calling a Special Meeting of the Village Council for this coming Wednesday night, the sole agenda item being the Noise Ordinance."

"Good Lord!" says Jenny. "That's very good of you!"

Thaïs rolls her Rocky Mountain shoulders. "The meeting will raise some hackles, due to the councilmembers' stipends and overtime for Duffy and Lieut. Conklin. But spending a few hundred taxpayer dollars *now* will save us thousands later on!"

The Ashlars thank Thaïs for her wisdom, then needing a calming brunch they go to the Green Goose Café, where a Shrinking World Tours bus is hogging enough curbstone for six or seven cars.

"The Age of Driveosaurs!" says Leah.

The bus's cargo—overfed and under-exercised vacationers—are crammed in the Café and beat their dinnerware approximately on time with Giles's rendition of "Flatbush Flanagan" on the piano. Rita and two helpers are up to their server's caps slinging food and hosing coffee, so Giles curtails the tune to get menus and glasses of water for the Ashlars.

The tour bus crowd bang their own glasses to protest the cancelling of the free music—until they see who Giles is serving, then shriek like banshees.

"It's the *mole makers!*"

Chaos ensues as the diners power up their eWallets and ePurses to send images of the Ashlars to their e-friends, and a toddler next to the Ashlars with a full diaper and zero parenting shoves an eRattle with her syrupy fist at Leah's face and goo-goos, "WannalickUbemyfrien!"

Whole families disgorge from their tables like giant beefburgers, demanding gimme-fives and chain-sawing hints from the Ashlars, their devices flashing like the Gulf War's Shock and Awe over Baghdad.

"Stop it!" says Giles.

He hoists the toddler from Leah's shoulder and plunks her and her bulging diaper with a *squish* onto the lap of her 15-year-old father, who's filming the Ashlars with his vaper-cam. A podgy boy snatches Sam's fedora and others try to kidnap Leah's camera. Giles goes for his shillelagh, while Rita brandishes a mop and Mabel rushes from the kitchen with her largest frying pan.

Then a man bursts from the restroom where he's been taking a whiz while surfing the news on his eBelt.

"Hey, everybody! The Gov'nor's done it *again!"*—which is like yelling "Panty Raid!" at an Ole Miss football game.

In an instant the crowd deletes the Ashlars from their brains and return to their tables. They shove their faces to their devices, showing Arkansas Governor Willie Blott on a Let's Do Business With Botswana junket, doing business with an orangutan.

"It'll ruin him!" a diner shouts, sharing the view on his eMoneyClip with his preschool daughters.

"Naw, it won't," says his wife, holding her eCompact for her senile dad to see. "He'll campaign on the Equal Opportunists' ticket, and will be our next two-term president!"

Realizing that the mob has forgotten that they ever existed, the Ashlars throw off their jitters and straighten their disheveled tableware while Giles returns Sam's fedora from the podgy urchin.

"I'm sorry about this! It's the last time I'll accept a bleeding *tour* bus!"

Leah presses his hand. "I'm disappointed at not seeing you carry forth with your Irish warclub!"

He laughs. "Anyway, I was about to say that your mole carving is truly wondrous!"

Sam says their Orchard Lane neighbors don't think so, and relates the chainsaw dunking, drone attack, and tar bucket stunt. Then Jenny says they also have some supporters and mentions the note from MAD and SAD, and Giles assures her that they have *hordes* of supporters.

"But what's your next move?"

"That's what we came here to discuss," says Leah. "Over Mabel's boysenberry pancakes!"

Giles gives Rita their order, then Sam relates Thaïs's decision to hold a Special Council meeting.

Jenny tucks in her napkin. "Now that the Council's taking up the Noise Ordinance, should we give Growler a rest? A gesture of goodwill?"

Sam raps the table with his fist. "No! We've shown restraint *and* goodwill by obeying the Noise Ordinance, as wonky as it is."

He raps the table again, toppling a mustard jar that draws a rash of tongue clucking from some locals, breakfasting at a nearby table.

Jenny takes his hand. "Then I'm with you, all the way!"

"And me!" says Leah, placing her hand on theirs, a Three Moleateers' oath.

The locals grumble in protest and Giles springs to his feet.

"As one of Wildrose's chief noisemakers, I declare my support of your brave efforts to get an ordinance that's worthy of this grand old Village!" He puts his hand on the Ashlars', a piano-playing D'Artagnan.

His vigorous vow pierces the diners' fixation with Gov'nor Blott, and they try to recall who Giles and the Ashlars are.

Then a longtime Wildrose resident rises from his half-finished bowl of five-bean chili. "Noise ord'nance my fanny! I'll show ya some ord'nance!"

He bends over and releases a humongous fart that scatters the napkins from the tables, then puts on his cap with a snap of the wrist and leaves the Café, farting as he goes.

-12-

LEAH SENDS TRUMAN THE FILM CLIP of the beefy motorcyclist who roared by Mole End the day before, and says he definitely appears to be the same man who tried to tar Moleen.

Truman agrees and forwards the videos to the captain of the local state police station. Then Truman pins Widefoot's mug shot to his corkboard and vows, "I'm gonna track down your fat *ass!*"

He goes to Thaïs's door to update her and hears a man's voice in a fervid speech from within. This has occurred more than once in the five months since Thaïs became mayor, and Truman asks Duffy if Thaïs has a visitor.

"Not a soul, Chief. I just took her a paper to sign and she was all by her lonesome."

He returns to Thaïs's door and hears her say, "Not yet. Not nearly yet!" Then the man, "But time is running out!"

The voices go on and Truman gently knocks. It goes quiet and he puts his ear to the door—which suddenly swings open. A vein throbs on Thaïs's temple and she glares down from her seven-foot nine onto his six-foot three.

"What the blazes is it?!"

The skin prickles at the back of Truman's neck. "Mayor…?"

She blinks. "Chief…? What the hell do you want?

He updates her on Widefoot. "And about your instruction to do occasional patrols by Mole End. I thought that rather than pay overtime to Conklin or myself, we should bring in Olive Best. It'd save on our budget, and she's most reliable."

"Good idea!" And she curtly shuts the door.

Truman phones Olive and asks her to begin the next day. She's been an exemplary security guard at All Souls College and a superb part-timer of his for five years, and if he'd had his way would have Conklin's job in a flash. But Conklin is a nephew of the previous mayor, who hired him over Truman's vehement protests. Then Truman stews over Thaïs's bizarre manner when she opened her door. He wonders if she has a secret mental condition, and his pulse shoots up as he recalls that she seemed all but ready to kill him.

* * *

After the mammoth task of creating Moleen, the Ashlars decide to do some smaller ones—mol*ettes*—and they scour Jenny's mammal books for ideas.

"Let me try one!" says Leah.

She picks a juvenile mole who's looking over its shoulder with a Bruce Springsteen attitude and goes to work with Growler, then Jenny carves a mole in a tutu, and the two molettes and their flinty eyes are put at Moleen's feet.

All of a sudden the Elms' noises cease and the Ashlars go to the attic window to find the Sonic Sisters repairing their roof.

"Maybe they're coming around!" says Leah.

But the instant she stops her music from the fieldstone fence (Suzuki's *How to Become a Champion Whistler*), the Sisters fire off a recording of snoring sumo wrestlers.

The rest of Orchard Lane is even busier, with Sol at his shooting range, refreshing his automatic-rifle skills against cardboard mole cutouts; the Middlemarsh boys playing virtual toss-the-grenade; and the Dinsmores, armoring their dirt-bikes with oil-drum lids for a demolition derby. A full-metal racket.

And it's the first day of the Whingers' annual vacation, which Clovis and Madge are itching to spend by bronzing themselves with Knoka'da Sun Gel, sandwiched between frequent naps and frequenter piña coladas. They climb to their diving platform and see the Ashlars revving up Growler, and Madge groans.

"Looks like they're gonna carve millions of moles!"

Wanda, meantime, has at last finished her wine jug—and realizes it's a *mole!*

-13-

GILES ROLLS UP ORCHARD LANE on his delivery scooter, its one cylinder gurgling like a saucepan of simmering soup, and pulls up at Mole End with a basket of Mabel's freshly baked appetizers.

Leah accepts them with a hug and steers Giles and a cup of tea to an Adirondack chair while he explains the reason for his visit.

"Lars Anderson and I are thrilled about the special Council Noise Ordinance meetin and did some brainstorming. Word is you're planning to carve slews of moles, and if so we'd like to sell them for you, at the Green Goose and Lars's Woodsculptors Loft."

"*Sell* our moles?" says Sam.

"Not the mamma and her two little ones," says Giles. "They should stay right here, as guardians of your Moles Revolt."

"Moles Revolt!" says Jenny. "I like that!"

Giles rubs his hands. "You decide which moles you wanna sell and we'll display them. I can take only the smaller ones, but Lars wants to do a bang up *exhibit* at the Woodsculptors Loft! Help spread the word about your Revolt!"

"A gallery show!" says Leah, and Sam springs from his chair to shake Giles's hand. "All right!"

After another cup of tea Giles scooters off, and Leah takes in the tea things and finds her vest hanging in the hall, reminding her of the unusually attractive pinecone in its pocket she'd found the day before.

She runs to the living room to show Jenny, who says, "Good heavens! It's a *Torrey* pinecone, which only grow in California!"

Leah shrugs. "It was in our *willow* tree, 15 feet up!"

Then she notices something smaller than a dewdrop at the tip of the cone. She slips the cone under a cushion and leads Jenny to the kitchen, then turns on the faucet and lets the water splash noisily into the sink. She searches the shelves and cabinets, then whispers.

"I think we've been bugged!"

An hour later Chief Truman and state police Captain Adron Kroft are huddled in Kroft's patrol car by the Village Commons. The Ashlars are staring from the backseat at the device in Kroft's hand—no larger than a sewing needle—and the pinecone from which Kroft extracted it rests on the dashboard.

"We should assume more of these are hidden at Mole End," says Kroft, "so I'll have my technician give it a thorough sweep."

Billy Umbo is watching from an anonymous looking car across the Commons, its tinted window lowered and a 1,200 mm lens microcam and ubermic aimed at Kroft's cruiser.

Captain Kroft secures the spycam in a plastic bag and advises the Ashlars to carry on as usual.

"If you have something especially private to discuss, put on some loud music. Whoever planted this device will probably just assume it's failed."

Before Kroft arrived to meet with Truman and the Ashlars, Umbo was listening in on three of the Wildrose Village councilmembers—Save & Spend Bank Manager Tabitha Tannenbach, insurance agent Buford Whitlow, and Certified Public Accountant Cecil Flinn—all of them conferring quietly on a bench beside the Commons, while lunching on the offerings of a corndog stand. Since all three are councilmembers, Thaïs was yearning to hear what they were up to, and was overjoyed when they vowed to vote *Yes* at the Pioneer Meadows Rezoning Proposal hearing. Then as Umbo turned his peeping equipment to Kroft's cruiser Thaïs was keen to stay tuned in.

Sam weighs Captain Kroft's advice. "That pinecone had to have been planted at Mole End *before* we put up the security cameras last night, or we'd have seen it on the footage. So someone might've been spying on us since we moved here 10 days ago!"

Kroft's techie comes that afternoon and, after a scrupulous sweep with his equipment, says with near total certainty that the cabin and toolshed are clean. But things are dicier outdoors where he finds eight devices tucked in here and there about the cabin and property.

"I can't be sure I've found *all* of them, and I advise you to lock up very carefully when you're away!"

Thaïs is watching from the library via one of the spycams the techie missed and smolders. "Another point to you, wise old owl!"

-14-

THE DISCOVERY OF THE SPYCAMS stiffens the Ashlars' resolve to bring some decency to Wildrose, and they supercharge their planning for the Special Council Meeting—while the *William Tell Overture* plays on the record player to mask their conversation.

Then wanting to make some music of his own, Sam bicycles to band practice at All Souls College, where his fellow musicians greet him with affectionate slaps on the back.

"Snowy Top!" cries the teenage girl who is Sam's Co-Principal Hornist. "I love those wooly molies!"

The band members are ecstatic to learn that he'll be selling molettes at the Woodsculptors Loft, and Pierre congratulates him on the fight he's putting up on behalf of common civility. Then Pierre motions everyone to their seats.

"Our Fourth of July Concert is coming pell-mell, and we're getting loads of coverage in the *Barleycorn* and *Wildrose Voyeur,* promising to lure our biggest crowd ever!"

Minutes later the players are deep into Percy Granger's "County Gardens" when a phalanx of semis bound for the Turquoise Tower shakes the Practice Room like a dozen

OK Corral gunfights. Pierre halts the piece and runs outside to shake his fist and shout. "Blockheads!"

* * *

Tuesday afternoon and most of Wednesday the Ashlars carve molettes, turning Mole End into Mole Nursery and luring motorists to slam on their brakes and beep their horns in amazement. One of the horn-blowers is an RV that careens into the driveway, where the parents and their myriad offspring eject from its doors.

"May I help you?" says Sam.

The kids start hauling the Bruce Springsteen and ballet dancer molettes toward the RV while the father pokes his head in the toolshed.

"Any more in here?"

"This is private property," says Jenny. "You've mistaken us for the Woodsculptors Loft!"

The daddy frowns. "My kids saw 'em on BreakBalls.now! We've come over 100 miles!"

"Hold on!" says Leah, grabbing her ePal and phoning Lars for advice.

"Go ahead and sell them," he says. "It'll be a week till I can set up your exhibit, and when it opens I'm sure I won't be able to keep them in stock!"

The Ashlars confer, then Sam goes to the daddy.

"We'll sell all of the moles but the big one and the two at her feet."

"That leaves only 10!" says one the girls, who's fast on her fingers.

"We'll be carving lots more!" says Jenny.

The offspring scream madly and daddy pulls out a roll of greenbacks. "How much ya want?"

They sell the molettes for $85 each and take $35 deposits for six more in varied poses, to be collected in three weeks at the Woodsculptors Loft. Leah makes out a receipt on Sam's Thoreau notepaper and the family motors off with beaming smiles.

Sam slumps on the porch. "Now we've done it. We'll have to get a *business* license!"

Jenny tousles his hair. "Well, wasn't Thoreau a sometime businessman? A surveyor, after all, is a private contractor. And his family's pencil factory where he worked from time to time was most certainly a *woodcarving* business!"

They resume preparations for the Special Council meeting, and charmed by what they're doing, Leah's Van Nuys' friend knocks together a toonVid, which Leah tweaks for use at their Village Council presentation.

After a while Sam yawns and Leah sends him and Jenny off for a nap while she makes dinner. As the linguini sauce simmers in the kitchen (a recipe Leah has made many a day on her VW's propane stove while filming in the wilds of Philadelphia and Boston), a *bazoing* comes on her ePal. It's a video message from Goldenhawk.news—Goldenhawk being a middle-aged woman with flaxen hair in a helicopter, who's darting about the Manhattan skyline as police sirens buzz like hornets from one of its many concrete canyons.

"Hel*looo*, Leah! I'm sooo glada meetcha 'n wanna say I adore the vids of moles on BreakBalls 'n noisy neighbors 'n comin battle with th'a Village Council 'n let's stay 'n touch 'n—!"

The copter's bellycam has fixed on a purple van, bashing through the midtown traffic and lopping off side mirrors while looking no bigger than an M&M at the bottom of a well. Goldenhawk tightens her seatbelt and roars to her pilot, Charley.

"There's the bastard—heading toward the Queensboro Bridge! Okay! Let's get this sto*reeeee!*"

Having read her mind, Charley has already begun plummeting into the midtown well on the tail of the purple van—as skyscraper parapets, satellite discs, and penthouse nudists shoot upward in a dizzying streak.

Leah hits the escape key to exit the website—while her stomach clings to the kitchen ceiling.

-15-

LEAH'S AUBURN HAIR IS LUMINOUS from the shower and she slips into a blue sundress and sandals, while Jenny zips a 1920s style lawn-party dress onto her fawnish form, then straightens Sam's aqua necktie that brings out his eyes. He's in the same brown suit he wore in his standoff with the Emerson University chancellor, and Jenny tells Sam he's "quite handsome!"

They load Leah's projector and rollup screen into the VW and head to the Village Center where they find all manner of vehicles, plastic-bumper to plastic-bumper about the Commons; and people, retro fanny pack to retro fanny pack around the shops—while the ManShot Trolley makes another killing. They scrounge up a parking space in a back alley and go to the Save & Spend Bank, where Head Cashier Figgie Silvertongs stifles her umbrage at their chainsaw antics sufficiently to point them toward Bank Manager Tabitha Tannenbaum's icebox. They find her arrayed in Undine's latest creation of hemp trousers, rattan sandals, and Nehru-inspired cargo blouse, and she shows them to chairs.

"I feel that I know you already, from Duffy Nicklebob's rapturous interview on the *Wildrose Voyeur* and ... elsewhere. Wildrose is fortunate to have you among us!"

"Not everyone feels that way!" says Jenny.

"Well, as a councilmember I'm certainly aware of the noise issue. And since it's on tonight's docket I applaud you for doing the right thing, bringing it to the mayor's attention. Now what can I do for you in the banking way?"

Sam explains about the moles and Leah flashes the wad of cash they've raked in. Tabitha lifts her brow in admiration and suggests a Small Business Checking Account (at 0.0001% interest).

Their next stop is the Village Hall, and despite the crush of vehicles for 2nd Wednesday triple-coupon binging, they slip in the foyer without difficulty to see Duffy, who says a business license will cost $95. As Sam pays, Chief Truman brings in a tall and impressively fit-looking woman in her mid-20s with a ponytail and holstered handgun.

"Duffy?" says Truman. "Olive needs to update her paperwork." Then he introduces Olive Best to the Ashlars. "The finest officer I've ever had. You'll see her patrolling Orchard Lane from time to time."

Olive greets them with a warm smile and firm handshakes. "Is it okay to commission a mole? I'd love to have one playing a saxophone!"

* * *

The Ashlars climb to the Hall's second floor with their packhorse load of equipment and are stunned to find the Council Chamber as jammed as a Macy's on Black Friday—and realize that the Special Meeting is where most of the crowd had been heading! They search for a place to sit as butts shift and necks twist.

Figgie and Sol Silvertongs are seated on the near side of the aisle that divides the Chamber's Gallery in half, and she unloads in Sol's ear. "They were at the bank, scheming with that lesbiterian boss of mine!"

Honus and Winney Offman are crouched behind the Silvertongs and hiss in unison, "The mole makers!"

Farther back are Clovis and Madge Whinger, furious that the chainsaw is spoiling their annual swimming-pool vacation, and their eyes shrink in their sockets, like vultures watching a cougar steal their roadkill lunch.

Across the aisle are Po and Pru Plinkett, scowling because the Village policy forbad them from bringing their beloved Chihuahuas to comment on the Council's proceedings.

Just behind the Plinketts is Silt Middlemarsh—still smarting over the loss of the Manitoba B&B guests—and he whispers hoarsely to Henna. "Enough for a whole month's electric bill, right through our fingers!" He takes out his ePen and sets his thumbs to work on a Snippet.

The Dinsmores have claim-staked an entire row, their hands twitching with an attack of DBHWS—Dirt-Biker's Handlebar Withdrawal Syndrome. But Mynah and Sparrow Dinsmore (MAD and SAD) are free of such tremors and gaze fondly at the Ashlars.

Others throughout the Gallery have seen Internet droppings of the Mole End shenanigans on BreakBalls.now, YouBoob, or UpYers, and just today from Goldenhawk.-news in her helicopter at 1,760 feet above Manhattan, and are comparing those images with the flesh-and-blood originals. They decide to shoot their own videos and the Chamber goes stroboscopic with e-gadgets.

The Gallery's front row is reserved for the media—the editor of *The Barleycorn*; the student reporters of the Wildrose preschool, grade school, middle school, high school, and All Souls College ezines; and web journalists have flocked in from around the region. They fuss with their equipment—as if they were covering a Mars launch at Cape Canaveral—and are streaming pre-meeting commentary, which the people around them follow on their devices, a time-blurring view of what's *right before their own noses.*

The Ashlars try to deflect this e-epileptic welcome while searching for a place to sit, and Sam shakes his head.

"I guess it's SRO!"

With Truman on call at home and Olive Best cruising the Village, Lieut. Conklin is more or less at attention at the front of the Chamber. He feels it beneath his dignity to assist latecomers (although the Ashlars are 10 minutes early) and would be happier than a fly in a cowpie if they gave up and left. He heaves a weary sigh and gazes at the framed photos on the Chamber's side walls—portraits of former mayors, clerks, and police chiefs—and prays that Chief Truman's retirement-party likeness will *quite soon* join the lineup.

"Oh, look!" says Leah.

Giles is beckoning from the back row of the Gallery with his lanky legs and arms splayed over three seats next to his. The Ashlars scramble up and find Billy Umbo occupying the aisle seat.

"Be my guest!" he says, stepping gallantly aside.

They remember him as the ostentatiously fit man who emerged from Cecil Flinn's accounting office the week before, and they thank him before threading themselves and their equipment through the meat grinder of bodies to the empty seats.

"You're a peach!" Leah says to Giles, who blushes candy-apple red.

With the Ashlars wedged among them, the public return their gaze to a lofty dais of timeworn oak at the front of the Chamber, where three of the five councilmembers are already seated. Wanda Middlemarsh is by her nameplate, reading the Snippet on her eCameo just sent by Silt, urging her to "remember the water heater!" She's yet to tell him about the mole wine-jug she made (buried in her supply cabinet) and covers her guilt with a cough, as if a lump of potting clay had lodged in her throat, and turns her eyes to the agenda sheet on the oak writing-surface, whose only item is the fabled Noise Ordinance.

The Ashlars are surprised to recognize two other councilmembers, including their insurance agent—Buford Whitlow—who went all out on this landmark night by wearing a freshly laundered shirt. They're too far back for him to make eye contact and he moons at nearer faces, toting up who's late in their premium payments and wondering with terror if they've deserted him in favor of the globe-swallowing Worldwide Insurance on the Sky Vue Freeway.

The other familiar face is CPA Cecil Flinn, who the Ashlars met the previous week, next door to Buford's aluminum eye-trash office. Cecil noted the Ashlars' arrival with a nod, but now glances fondly at his chef-wife Mabel and their two teenage sons near the front of the Gallery.

A CPA, an underwriter, an art potter-homemaker, and a banker—Sam thinks—and he wonders who the final councilmember is. Just before seven Lars arrives in a Norfolk jacket with a daffodil in the lapel. Sam notices an empty seat at the very end of his row, although it might be broken. He decides to chance it so Lars can have *his* seat.

"Lars! Up here!"

Cartilage crunches as the entire Gallery snap their heads to see what the mole maniac is up to, and Lars chuckles.

"Thanks, Sam. But I think I'll sit up *there*."

He goes through a swinging door at a railing to the dais and takes the chair by his nameplate, COUNCILMAN LARS ANDERSEN. Bottled water has been put out for the councilmembers, but he replaces his with an army canteen.

Sam sinks in his seat, redder than Santa's britches.

"I shoulda told you," says Giles. "He was elected last November as an independent. Mostly to fight idiotic developments, like the expansion of that sodding Condor Estates. And a damn good thing because he's also a highly skilled lawyer."

"Lars is a *lawyer?"* says Leah.

"He keeps office in the stockroom at the back of the Woodsculptors Loft."

There are whispers as Tabitha Tannenbach appears with briefcase swaying and sandals swishing. Away from her cash-and-strongbox banking worries she's refreshed and alert. She searches the Gallery until she alights on Undine—done up in sequined basketball trunks, yarn sweatshirt, and train engineer's cap. Their eyes meet and Tabitha takes her seat.

Just as the clock in the Village Hall belfry tolls seven, Duffy Nicklebob enters in an eggplant-colored dress (kept in her cubbyhole especially for the occasion) and a garland of Virgin's Bower at her wrist.

Her piping voice rings out. "All be upstanding!"

-16-

THE PUBLIC RISES AND THAÏS—shimmering in a cream-colored velvet gown and pearl-studded choker—enters with an aplomb that crushes all chatter and strides to a tapestried armchair on the dais. She takes in the many faces, including Billy Umbo's, but gives no sign of recognizing him.

The public starts to lower their bottoms to their seats and Duffy stops them.

"Please remain standing for the Pledge of Allegiance!"

They obey, then plop their bottoms down with an ear-wash of creaking oakwood as Duffy goes on.

"This Special Session of the Wildrose Village Council will address questions pertaining to Ordinance 22: to wit, the Noise Ordinance. There being a quorum, the session is ready to be called to order; the Right Honorable Thaïs Mont-Obiston, Mayor of Wildrose, presiding."

Having expelled her last eyedropper of breath, Duffy sinks at a small desk to one side of Thaïs that holds some well-worn legal tomes beside a Stenograph writer. She takes a gavel from a yewwood case with gold-plated corner protectors and places it in Thaïs palm. Thaïs strikes a lignum vitae block with the gavel and the public flinches as if it had been a starter's pistol. Without effort, her words permeate the Chamber's every trouser crease and woodworm hole.

"Welcome one and all. This Special Session of the Wildrose Council is called to order. First, we must hear what the Noise Ordinance says."

Duffy pops up and recites the Ordinance's lone sentence and Thaïs continues.

"With the councilmembers as auditors and Village Clerk recording, the Council welcomes comments from the public. Those who wish to speak, please present yourselves at the railing."

A paralysis grips the Gallery, as thick as the mortar on the Third Little Pig's brick house. All those who were itching to comment forget what they had to say—or tell themselves that someone else will heft their bottom to the railing and say it.

Then Sam remembers Leah's remark about his being too much of a gentleman, and recalls his vision of what Wildrose should be. A few faces are raised to him in hope, and some seem to be looking to him for *leadership*. Then he feels Jenny's hand on his and smells the lavender water she's worn on her wrists ever since he first dated her. Her eyes are warm and loving, and that's all he needs.

He turns to Leah. "Shall we?"

"Let's go, Grandpa!"

All eyes pounce on them as they push their equipment past the water bottles and ill-planted feet to the aisle and descend to the railing that seems as forbidding as the torrid face of Venus. The media point their lenses as Leah and Sam set up the projector and screen with its compact but virile speakers, then Sam grasps the railing with hands that slip with perspiration.

The journalists are streaming this from their positions along the front row, so Sam and Leah are being watched *right now* by her colleagues in Brooklyn and Van Nuys, by Sam's and Jenny's two grown children, and their many friends at Emerson University.

Goldenhawk has also tuned in, and swoops down in her helicopter with her pilot Charley at the New Jersey Meadowlands to scoop the US Cheerleader Hurling Finals. One of the contestants is a pneumatic-chested cheerleader from Ohio State University, who's hurled eight feet wide of the safety net and bounces across the artificial turf. After capturing that to the squealing delight of her half million subscribers, Goldenhawk gives the Ashlars her full attention.

In his somber brown suit Sam's as nervous as a defendant, pleading for his life in the dock of London's Old Bailey in a BBC crime saga. "I'm Samuel Ashlar, and I'm a resident of Wildrose and glad to be so!"

Clovis nudges Madge. "Glad? He oughta be *humbled* to live in Wildrose!"

Those who met Sam at Thaïs's barbecue or saw the *Wildrose Voyeur* interview know he was an English professor and author, and assume his remarks will be literate, if nothing else. And Thaïs—keen to seem impartial—gazes with the warmth of a snifter of fine brandy, as if to say, "It would be gauche of me to mention it, but of course you and your family have been guests at the Manor, and it's so good to see you here tonight!"

That shot of brandy is a shot in the arm, and Sam clears his throat.

"First, I want to thank the mayor for calling this meeting, and to say I'm grateful for the chance to comment."

Duffy's fingers fly over the Stenograph keys as his words appear in pixelated black across its screen.

"To begin, it's clear that the Noise Ordinance was meant for a simpler and perhaps more innocent age, before there were cars and trucks, amplified music or chainsaws."

Some of the public suck in their breath at his mention of the weapon of his transgression, but Thaïs is as composed as a Madonna in a fresco.

"What's more, Wildrose is more crowded than it was when the Ordinance was enacted in 1865." Sam waves a brochure. "Soon after my wife and I came to Wildrose we joined the library, and found in its 'Our Yesteryears' brochure that as bucolic as the Village is, it's *five times* as populous as it was at its founding. So we have a multiplication of people and their noises." He emphasizes some words he's underlined on the brochure. "So, to keep Wildrose as a harbor of the best of American values, I say it's time to revise the Noise Ordinance to address the changes wrought by that yawing gulf of time."

"Right on!" says Giles.

"Well said!" says Tabitha.

"Good intro!" says Lars.

Sol elbows Figgie. "Yawning golf? What's that? Eighteen holes of sleepwalking?"

"The only thing to yawn about is his prattle!" Winney says to Honus—and is rewarded with a jab in the back of the neck from an umbrella, delivered by a gray-haired woman sitting behind her. Duffy Nicklebob's granny.

"Quiet, you hussy! I wanna hear what he has to say!"

For her part, Duffy duly records Sam's words on the Stenograph writer, and he feels that from the number of attentive faces he's won a morsel of regard.

Then Buford raises his hand. "Your Honor, I'd like some clarification from Mr. Ashlar."

"You may address him directly, councilman."

Mindful that he must keep the Ashlars as clients, Buford offers up his question with a cashmere glove. "Mr. Ashlar, would you please tell us what exactly you think the Ordinance should contain?"

Sam relaxes his grip on the railing. "If a Noise Ordinance is to work it must have a measurable standard, which is the *decibel.* I ask the Council to adopt a maximum decibel level throughout Wildrose, 24 hours a day, seven days a week."

"Right on!" says Giles.

"Bravo!" says Pierre and Marie Pasquin.

"About time!" says Duffy's granny, tapping the floor with her umbrella.

Shouts of approval pepper the Gallery, but are quickly salted down by protests.

"Not our farm!" Dewey Dinsmore screeches.

"Madman!" says Clovis.

"Sociologist!" says Sol.

"*Sex*ologist!" says Honus.

Some of the public enter "decibel" in their e-things and find "dress a belle," "dongs a bell," "diss dat Bill"—and videos of Big Ben and Bette Davis in *Jezebel.*

Thaïs crushes the interruptions with a raised eyebrow, then Cecil Flinn lifts his hand.

"Mr. Ashlar? Would you please tell us exactly what a decibel is, and how it might work for the Village?"

"Gladly. But to do that I'd like to enlist my granddaughter Leah, who can do it much better than I. She doesn't live in

Wildrose, but is here as an expert witness on my behalf, if that's all right."

This is a curveball for Duffy, who dives into the tome on *Bylaws Governing Special Session Public Comments* as Thaïs cloaks Leah with a smile.

"Of course it's all right. Please proceed, Ms. Ashlar!"

-17-

ALL EYES, CAMERAS, AND FROWNS fall on Leah. And Goldenhawk (having made two flybys over the Meadowlands crowd, who're applauding the Defending Champion Cheerleader Hurlers from Baylor U, scoring two female and one male missiles in the bull's-eye) asks Charley to land on the sidelines long enough to capture Leah's spiel for her viewers, now grown to three-quarters of a million.

Leah has her gear ready and skips to the railing, the hem of her dress caressing her knees.

"My name's Leah Ashlar and I'm staying at my grandparents' place, best known as Mole End."

She presses the remote and the toonVid of a bearded man stares cheerfully from the screen, and below it, DECIBEL and its abbreviation, dB.

"That's Alexander Graham Bell, inventor of the telephone, of course, for whom the decibel is named, which is the universal standard for measuring the intensity of a sound." She holds up her dB meter. "You can measure decibels on a device like this, and as those of you in the front row can see, it shows I'm speaking at 75 decibels. But those in the back row may be getting only 30 decibels, since sound energy decreases as it travels from its source."

The media's many eyes hop with the wavering needle.

"But the intensity of my voice is compounded as it bounces from the hard surfaces of the Chamber's oak paneling and plaster ceiling. Even hard *heads* can reflect sound, though I'm sure there aren't any of those here tonight!"

Laughter rocks the hall, then carping—until Thaïs grins as though *she'd* made the quip.

"I'm sure you're right, Ms. Ashlar!"

Leah touches the remote, and Mr. Bell makes way for four people and their dachshund, picnicking in a meadow.

"So the issue at hand is to measure decibels at the location of anyone who's *impacted* by the sounds in question."

The picnickers' chitchat pours from Leah's speakers as soundwaves radiate, then thin out and fade away. She points at the dachshund, snoozing by the picnic hamper.

"This fellow's getting 60 decibels, the level of normal conversation. But the honeybee at the edge of the meadow is getting only eight or nine decibels. That's not even a whisper, so he's missing some juicy tidbits!"

The honeybee buzzes and the pubic titters while Thaïs chuckles and Cecil Flinn chortles.

"This is fun!" he says to Wanda, who smiles in agreement.

"She's great!" Goldenhawk tells her fans.

"She's clever!" Tabitha thinks, and Undine thinks, "What luscious calves!"

Leah returns to the screen.

"As you can see, the picnickers' chatter is absorbed by the air molecules and the meadow's thick foliage. But unlike this Chamber, the meadow has no plastered surfaces to reflect the picnickers' talk, and other than Fido and the honeybee, the picnickers are the sole receivers of their own conversation!"

The meadow vanishes, and the same four people and their dachshund are now picnicking next to a jazz quartet by a house on a leafy street like Orchard Lane.

Leah's eyes rove the Gallery.

"These soundwaves are heavier, and boomerang from the housefronts right back at the picnickers—who're talking at 80 decibels, just to hear themselves over the jazz band and their own echo. And by the way, the decibel scale represents sound *logarithmically*, so each 10-decibel increase is *twice* as powerful as the preceding level!"

The dachshund is jolted from his nap and claps his paws over his ears, and Sam steps in.

"If New Orleans' tunes aren't your thing, it can get a little *ear*itating!"

Then a heart-shaped swimming pool materializes as the picnickers drop their sunglasses and swimsuits and dive in to splash about, frolicking and tossing a beachball to their two pet seals. Clovis and Madge steam at this parody of their beloved pool but daren't complain, as Thaïs finds it uproarious. The seals slap their flippers and bark, and Leah has dubbed in the barking of Po and Pru Plinkett's Chihuahuas.

"How dreadful!" several people protest—including the Plinketts.

The picnickers can't hear the jazz musicians and ask them to kick it up a few notches, and the soundwaves fatten even more.

"We're at 100 decibels," says Leah. "Sixteen times as loud as the picnic in the meadow, and as noisy as a rock concert at close range."

Some of the public cry out that it's *too* loud, and Billy Umbo pinches his brow and pulls out a notebook.

The soundwaves fatten all the more as honking cars and roaring RVs clog the street, their ePlayers blasting out acid fusion and twaddle from innumerable talk-show hustlers. Leah's toonVid is now a psychosis-inducing matrix of cross-radiating circles, battering the picnickers with more ear blasts than the Confederates suffered at Gettysburg.

"We've passed 120 decibels—" says Leah. "—64 times louder than the picnic in the meadow, and as harsh as a jackhammer in your dining room. But it could be worse. Just imagine a lawn crew going at it with turbocharged weed-whackers, or a neighbor trying out the kettledrums she got for her birthday, using fireplace tongs instead of drumsticks. Without a maximum decibel level, all of this is *perfectly legal until ten p.m.!*"

The public watch with white knuckles on their chair arms as these terrors stalk the screen, blackening it with intersecting soundwaves as thick as warring beetles. The glass shatters in a framed photo on one of the Chamber walls and ceiling plaster flakes off onto the public's heads.

"Glory, glory!" cry Honus and Winney.

Leah belts it out. "You're getting 130 decibels, like a jet airplane taking off from your backyard!"

Everyone—including Duffy and Thaïs—plug their ears with their fingers and Leah cuts the speakers. The dB energy drops like a cast iron kite, and everyone's ears throb with the obstinacy of Internet cookies. They cautiously remove their fingers and the media checks to see if their mics have melted.

Goldenhawk slaps Charley on the knee. "God above! These Ashlars are *my* kinda people!"

Thaïs straightens the wrinkles in her sleeves. "Have you much more to do?"

Leah and Sam remove their earplugs, and he says, "We've sketched out the problem, Your Honor, and now we'll paint a solution!"

Leah clears the screen.

"When disputes arise, the dB level should be measured from the *boundaries* of Wildrose's various public and private places." A name appears on a house on the screen—*the Smites*—and a house next to it—*the Smittens*. "Let's say the Smites have bulldozed their backyard into a replica of Bunker Hill, to give their 17 kids some educational recreation. A laudable pursuit, wouldn't you say?"

A hill sprouts up in the Smites' backyard, and a pintsize British man-o'-war with belching canons sails across their swimming pool as red-coated kids charge up the hill with cork-popping muskets. Kids atop the hill in homespun woolens respond with cap-firing flintlock muskets, while drums and fifes beef up the drama even more.

"Who'd mind some good, clean fun like this?" says Leah. "Well, the Smittens and half the county, who have to listen to it! Now, let's say the Council adopts a maximum noise level of 70 decibels, and that Ms. Smitten finds the bricks flying off her house and suspects that the Smites' Bunker Hill frolic is causing it. Instead of a complex device like mine, she goes to her fence with a 99-cent app and finds that the Bunker Hill reenactment is 100 decibels. *Eight times* the legal limit!"

In a frenzy, the public checks to see if their e-things have dB apps, and those who have them shout *Hey!* and turn them on.

Cecil flings up his hand. "Excuse me, but that wouldn't be official!"

"It doesn't have to be," says Leah, then Sam steps in.

"Under the current Ordinance, if someone's ticked off by their neighbor's racket they ask them to ease up on it. If it's between 10:00 p.m. and 6:00 a.m. they might call Chief Truman or Lieutenant Conklin, who must decide if the noisemaker is breaking the law. If both men show up they might even disagree, causing a lawsuit that could cost the taxpayers in this Chamber and the rest of Wildrose thousands of dollars!"

"Well put!" says Lars.

"Smart man!" says Goldenhawk.

"Wut?" says Conklin.

Billy Umbo scribbles "Take off the gloves!" in his notebook, but Thaïs is unperturbed and puts a hand to a platinum ringlet to silence the protests.

"Pray go on."

"The dB app is just a do-it-yourself guide," says Leah. "Since the Bunker Hill noise is *way* above our hypothetical 70-decibel limit, Ms. Smitten is on solid ground to ask the Smites to cut down on the gunpowder, or to call the police if they don't."

Tabitha's hand goes up. "Then what should Lieut. Conklin do about it, if he's the one who answers the call?"

Conklin fixes the red slits of his eyes on Leah.

"Using a dB meter issued by the Village, he'd measure the noise, and after instructing the Smites to cease the battle, he'd offload the reading onto the department's computer and back it up on the hard drive you keep in the local bank vault."

"Hard drive?" Sol mutters to Figgie, trying to picture a Trailways bus ride across the Dakota Badlands.

Cecil raises his hand. "That glitzy gadget has to cost a lot more than 99 cents!"

"An international standards dB device costs about $600," says Leah, "which includes a calibration card to ensure its accuracy, and certification to assert that its readings will stand up in court."

Buford's voice jumps an octave. "Whew! For that much money we could buy new gloves for all of the Silver Hair Softballers!"

Sam's back at the railing.

"It won't cost the Village a dime. I talked it over with my wife and we agreed to donate four devices to the Village for the full and parttime police, so it's mitts off the taxpayers and gloves on the Softballers!"

"Hurrah!" says Marie and Pierre Pasquin, and Granny Nicklebob waves her umbrella. Giles cheers and Lars slaps the bench with joy. Buford's mouth opens, but nothing emerges.

Thaïs is thrown by the Ashlars' largesse, but an electron microscope couldn't detect it, and she asks Sam if he and Leah have finished.

"We'd like to close by asking that the Ordinance include an Exclusion Clause," he says, "which would allow the police and firefighters to use their sirens when needed, and the public works crew to drag out the backhoe to fix a broken waterline. Plus the College Wind Band's outdoor concerts and Fourth of July fireworks display—as long as they're professionally supervised. Public interest things like that."

"Good idea!" says Cecil, grinning at Mabel and his sons.

"Hurray!" says Henna.

"Bra*vo!*" and "Bra*va!*" exclaim Pierre and Marie Pasquin.

Undine pants, "I wanna spank that girl!"

There's robust applause and calls of approval as Sam and Leah get their things and climb the aisle, where Billy Umbo moves aside (less graciously than before) and Giles pats them on the back.

"Brilliant!"

Thaïs's black eyes search the Chamber. "And who is next?"

Sol Silvertongs vaults to the railing and reminds everyone that he's lived on Orchard Lane *all of his long life*—just one house down from the notorious Mole End—and was one of the very first of first responders when the Ashlars' chainsaw clobbered everyone's Friday night. He gets a stranglehold on the railing and ratchets onto his toes.

"There's a whappin big flaw in the Ashtons' little cartoon. It's the room inside the elephant and another example of the Big Brothers tightening the nails on all of us. If their scheme gets its heel in the door, in no time someone will cook up a law forcin all of us to eat at food banks and God knows what else! All of us already have our backyards and ridin mowers filmed by Gobbleups' satellites, but now we'll have our party talk broadcasted as well!"

An elderly man near the back of the Chamber adjusts his tortoiseshell glasses to get a better look at Sol.

"Heck! I'd guess from the number of devices aimed at you *right now* that everything you're sayin is already being live-streamed on Blockhead dot Duh!"

The public goes berserk with laughter and Thaïs lowers her eyelids.

"Please keep your remarks civil."

The Gallery goes quiet and Sol snorts at his detractors.

"Joke on if you want! But I'll fight any such law as the Ashfords are proposing with every nerve of my fingertips. Let's not forget our American legacy of dependency, forged at Valley Forge by Abraham Washington!" The public murmurs with astonishment, and encouraged by this show of support, Sol forges ahead. "And the legacy of Thomas Jefferson, Benedict Arnold, and Abraham… Abraham…" He knows something's amiss but can't quite pin it down, and his fingernails scrape at the railing as the seconds rush jeeringly by.

"Lincoln!" Figgie prompts from her seat.

"Lincoln!" says Sol. "The legacy of Abraham Washington Lincoln!"

-18-

CLOVIS WHINGER AND DEWY DINSMORE hustle to the railing to fling comments, a rehash of the succotash ladled up by Sol, and are countered by Mynah Dinsmore and her son Sparrow, who hold up their pastel sketches of the chipmunks, turtledoves, and other wildlife that are being wiped out by the Wildrose noise epidemic.

"A birdsong's worth 100 vitamins!" says Mynah.

Pierre Pasquin is hard on Mynah's heels to lay out statistics of the damage done to All Souls College.

"Because we champion a liberal arts education, cancelling our Fresh Air Practice Series due to the increasingly loud traffic on Chipmunk Run has resulted not only in losing students who're concentrating in music, but also Band members who focus on physics and math, languages and literature, climate and agricultural sciences, and psychology! Everyone loses out!"

The Chamber's as still as an old sock, and no one else comes forward.

Thaïs commends everyone for having attended the meeting. "The councilmembers and I will now retire *in camera* to the Conference Room to review the issue in Executive Session!"

She ends the meeting with a 93-decibel blow of her gavel, and Duffy asks everyone to "be upstanding!" The public rises and Thaïs sails out with the councilmembers astern of her. Billy Umbo torpedoes down the public stairway, pocketing the notebook as if sheaving a dagger, and a high school reporter makes a beeline for Sam and Leah with her eClipboard.

"Any final words?"

"We're trusting in the Council's level-headedness!" says Sam.

Soon afterward the Ashlars and their newfound supporters are hobnobbing in a streetlamp's glow in front of the Village Hall, where Granny Nicklebob pledges to join the Moles Revolt, and Mynah and Sparrow reveal themselves as MAD and SAD.

"Your note really cheered us up!" says Jenny, hugging Mynah as Sam praises Sparrow for his soulful pastels.

"Pierre and I are also trusting in the Council's level-headedness," says Marie. "And we want to commission two cellist moles for the College's Music Hall!"

Shouting and table-pounding cause the Ashlars and their new friends to crane their necks, and they see Thaïs silhouetted at the Hall's third-floor Conference Room window as she lifts her hand to stop the councilmembers' voices mid-sentence—except for Lars's…

* * *

"…and if we have the least bit of conscience we must revise the Ordinance, as outlined by the Ashlars!"

Lars's plea reverberates from the walls above a curly maple table, dominated by Thaïs in an armchair by the window that bears her silhouette—with Duffy and her

Stenograph writer at Thaïs's elbow and the councilmembers in side chairs.

"It's clear that we *are* moving toward adopting some of the Ashlars' ideas," says Thaïs, "but first let's be certain of our footing!"

"Then let's find the best decibel level by bringing in some acoustical experts!" Lars insists.

"If we can get them at reasonable *cost!*" says Cecil.

"*Safety*-minded experts!" says Buford, dead certain it would require coverage from his agency.

Wanda feels Thaïs's glance, who's been uncommonly generous with the pottery commission, and for appointing Silt as School Superintendent after his predecessor dropped dead of a seizure some weeks ago during a private chat with Thaïs in this very room.

"I move that we form a committee—chaired by our Mayor and guided by acoustical experts—to decide a decibel level and other provisions for a Revised Noise Ordinance."

Buford starts to second, but Thaïs stalls him. "I ask the councilwoman if she'll amend her motion for one of *you* to serve as chair."

"I so amend!" says Wanda.

Lars's hand goes up. "And I ask that she amend to allow the *general public* on the committee. Any Wildroseian, 12 years old and up!"

Buford flops back in his chair. "Good lord! What if a lotta nosey noggins like Sol Silvertongs sign up?!"

Cecil rubs his jaw. "Are we gonna provide snacks and bottled water for all these people? Or stipends?"

"No meals or stipends but the experts," says Lars. He thrusts up his canteen like a torch. "And no bottled water!"

"I'll provide the water," says Thaïs, fixing her eyes on Lars, who meets them unblinking.

Tabitha crosses a hemp-trousered leg. "Inviting the public is a smart idea. If they invest in the process, we can bank on their support!"

"I couldn't have said it much better myself!" says Thaïs, and Wanda amends her motion to include their fellow Wildroseians, 12 years old and up. Buford falls in line to second the motion and it's carried unanimously.

"All that remains is to appoint a chair," says Thaïs.

Tabitha knows that her banking skills would make her the ideal chair, and she's eager to retain Thaïs's favor by seeing that her wishes are obeyed. Thaïs has shored up Tabitha's bottom line by keeping the Village accounts at Spend & Loan (despite higher interest rates everywhere else on the planet), and swathed Undine in prestige with the commission to design the Turquoise Tower employees' uniforms.

And Cecil—a CPA who's mastered deductions, depletions, and highly lucrative but perfectly legal *de jure* tax loopholes—is confident that Thaïs will continue to use *him* to audit the Village books, and lifts his eyes to receive the royal nod.

But Thaïs looks past these two supplicants to the daffodil-twirler at the end of the table.

"I appoint Councilman Andersen as chair."

The councilmembers gape.

"Me?" says Lars.

"You!" says Thaïs.

-19-

AS THE COUNCIL ADJOURNS, Olive Best is patrolling Persimmon Lane on Wildrose's outskirts, climbing and ascending a hill behind a trailered cabin cruiser, hauled by a pickup truck that pokes along the lonely tarmac. The trailer has an out-of-state plate and one of its rear lights winks as the trailer hits a pothole. It hits another pothole and the light winks again and stays off for good.

Olive turns on her bodycam and rack lights, and after a moment the pickup pulls over. She relays the boat trailer's out-of-state license number to the police department voicemail and gets out with her hefty flashlight. The boat's portholes are curtained and she moves to the rear of the pickup, bearing an out-of-state plate that isn't current.

Okay! she thinks.

The driver is watching through his rearview mirror as Olive flicks the beam of her flashlight over the truck bed—sealed with a metal cover—then she goes to his window. He's 40-ish and grins at the nametag on her uniform.

"Well! Officer *Best.* You must be numero uno around here!"

"Sir, your trailer's got a bad rear light and your truck plate's outta date. Please shut off the engine, step outta the cab, and hand me your driver's license, insurance card, and registration."

"Well . . . sure!"

He turns off the engine—leaving the key in the ignition—and pulls a couple of papers from the glove compartment before opening the door and stepping out. He hands her the two slips of paper and slaps his pockets.

"Now where'd I put my wallet? Just had it when I gassed up at that station on the Freeway!" He digs around as the ignition buzzes.

Olive hears something in the gravel at the edge of the road beyond the boat. A raccoon or groundhog, she thinks.

"Please take out the key."

The man is still searching his pockets. "Sure! Doncha just hate gadgets that are always bitchin attcha?"

He turns to remove the key, then takes a swing at her. She swerves and smashes the flashlight against his jaw, throwing his head against the doorframe. In an instant her handgun is leveled at him—as more crunching comes from the gravel beyond the boat.

"Hit the ground with your hands on your head!" she orders.

The man is holding his jaw and moaning, but she'll never forget that her uncle—Wildrose's Police Chief when Truman was a rooky—was shot dead by a burglar he had felled with a roundhouse punch, who he thought was too woozy to do any harm.

She's in no mood to repeat her order and sweep-kicks the guy in the ankle, felling him to the tarmac, then takes cover at the front of the pickup and aims the flashlight toward the stern of the boat as a man lurches out with a monster of a rifle.

"Police! Drop the weapon and put up your hands!"

A brutal burst of gunfire shreds the door as Olive crouches by the hood. Her heart pounds, and her training says when firing at an attacker beyond 15 or 20 feet to aim at the *torso*—especially as she's using her uncle's .38 revolver with only a five-inch barrel. But she grips it with both hands, and with the sureness of Annie Oakley aims *higher up* and *to one side* and squeezes off a single round.

-20-

EARLY NEXT DAY LARS SHOWS UP AT Mole End on his soft-spoken motorcycle and joins the Ashlars on the porch, accepting Jenny's offer of coffee and a cinnamon bun.

"Have you heard the news?"

"We trust it's good!" she says.

"There are two pieces. Late last night our parttime Police Officer Olive Best collared a couple of bootleggers on Persimmon Lane. But it wasn't booze they were legging."

"Drugs?" says Leah.

"Fireworks."

"Fireworks?" says Sam.

"Olive dropped one of them with a single round to the shoulder when he opened fire with an AKA-47, and broke the other guy's jaw when he tried to punch her."

'Holy shit!" says Leah.

Lars laughs. "Indeed! The wounded one is under guard at the Clinic, and the other nut case is cooling it in our very own log-cabin clink. Olive made it without a scratch!"

"I'm very glad!" says Jenny.

"For sure! And the other news is the Council formed a committee to research and decide an appropriate dB level for a Revised Noise Ordinance—based on *your* recommendations."

Leah rushes over to hug Sam and Jenny. "Well done!"

"Well done, Leah!" they say.

Leah is especially cheerful this morning, which Sam and Jenny attributed to her having spent the night with Giles at his Colonial saltbox, a few blocks from the Green Goose Café. She'd mentioned his invitation when dropping them off after the Council meeting, and returned this morning in time to roll the dough for the cinnamon buns. She reported that Giles's vinyl collection didn't quite rival Sam's, but said they'd had a lovely time listening to recordings of Edith Piaf and Chris Botti, while sharing a bottle of Green Goose Burgundy.

Lars compliments Jenny and Leah on the cinnamon buns and says, "What's surprising is the mayor picked *me* as chair!" They wait for the punchline and he obliges. "She wanted me in the hotseat in case things blow up in our faces. But I won't let them! In fact—"

Leah takes his arm. "It might be pleasanter indoors."

They move to the living room where she puts Tchaikovsky's *1812 Overture* on the record player and explains about the hidden cameras.

"Lord!" says Lars. "You've clearly been trodding on some powerful feet! Please take care!"

"We will. Now you were saying…?"

"That anyone at least 10 years old and above who lives in Wildrose can be on the Decibel Committee, and I thought the three of you would certainly be interested."

"Sign me up!" says Sam.

"I'd love to," says Leah, "but I don't really live here."

"Your show-stopping dB tutorial last night impressed even the nematodes that you know your stuff. And we need some experts who *aren't* Wildrose residents, to minimize conflict of interest."

"Won't people think Leah's biased?" says Jenny.

"Everyone is, one way or another, but our job is to poke around and listen to *all* sides. We'll have to base our report on hard evidence, and Leah needn't fear that she'll be in the hotseat, as we'll have two other experts who're real heavy-hitters."

Leah offers him another cinnamon bun. "What if I serve as an advisor?"

***

Lars sends out a call for volunteers, and when he convenes the Decibel Committee the following Monday it's comprised of nearly 50 Wildroseians—the most bloated ad hoc committee ever to enter the ledger book in Duffy's cubbyhole. It meets in front of the Village Hall with Duffy taking Thaïs's photo for the *Wildrose Voyeur.*

"My blessings on you all!" Her Honor coos.

She bends down to pat a few cheeks and shake a few hands, then goes inside to scrub off the microbes and make online appearances concerning Olive's capture of the two dirtbags—now gone pandemic—since Olive has no interest in making the appearances herself. Thaïs had already done Internugget blurbs praising Olive's quick-witted bravery, and said that while Olive is on a few days' mandatory leave she'll receive a fulltime lieutenant's pay (at Truman's insistence). Thaïs revealed that the 2,800 pounds of highly lethal but totally legal fireworks were locked up in the log cabin jail, and that the state attorney general had ruled that if they weren't claimed in 12 days they could be auctioned off.

Lars explains the Committee's goals to the volunteers and presents the three special members, starting with Leah.

Sol Silvertongs was the very first, first responder to join up and spits on the sidewalk. "I mighta known!"

And Dewey Dinsmore kicks a pebble. "It's downright favoritism!"

Lars goes nose-to-nose with them. "It *is* favoritism—for Leah's considerable expertise! She's a graduate of UCLA, where she was voted Filmmaker of the Year. She directed five feature films around the country the last six years and won the Best Sound Design Award for her *Our Vanishing Farms* documentary at the Berlin Film Festival. And she's not taking a stipend, which saves *all* of us some tax dollars!"

Leah turns red, but is flattered that Lars did his homework.

"We couldn't of done better!" says Mynah Dinsmore.

"I agree!" says Wanda, the only other councilmember aside from Lars on the committee.

Then Lars introduces Drs. Reynolds Vey and Clara Duzzle. Reynolds is Dean of the Physics Department at the state university, and Clara is head of Marybridge Acoustics, the region's premier audio firm. She and Reynolds have satchels of state-of-the-ear equipment, and Duffy films their remarks about how thrilled they are to assist Wildrose in its quest for a more responsible scoundscape.

Lars guides the committee onto a school bus, with Leah and Sam but not Jenny—who insisted that *two* Ashlars were enough to represent Mole End. Their first stop is Orchard Lane—the cradle and launch pad of the Moles' Revolt—where the bus pulls up at the feet of Moleen and her two molettes.

"They're darling!" says the girl reporter from the high school, who joined up as a summer school civics project.

Then Lars leads the committee to the split-rail fence, directly opposite the Offmans' carriage-house, where Honus and Winney are oblivious to the rest of the universe in their possum skin earmuffs and their boombox tuned to the Bottom 40 Rock station.

"Aggh!" cries a committee member, who scrambles back to the bus. Two or three others follow and they shut the windows to wait it out.

The Offmans are reaming out the Hudson's cylinders with a giant augur that might've come from a tank factory, and Reynolds, Clara, and Leah zero in with their devices.

"I make it 88 dB," says Leah a few moments later.

"I have 87.99," says Reynolds.

"I also have 87.99," says Clara.

Thaïs is watching via the spycams from her office and tells Billy Umbo and Geoffrey Murgwynd—observing from their Condor Estates offices—that Lars seems to know what he's doing.

"I suppose they'll be sniffing around the Turquoise Tower," says Murgwynd.

"Of course," says Thaïs. "We must have a thorough-seeming process!"

Something of a recording expert himself, Umbo's bowled over by the sophistication of Reynolds's and Clara's devices. Aside from the dB level, they measure the temperature and sound frequency variances; wind direction, velocity, and fluctuation curve; relative humidity and barometric pressure; particulate analysis and distribution; distance to primary, secondary, and tertiary sound sources (plus or minus two millimeters); angle of deflection and sunspot attenuation; photon perturbation and quantum-fudge coefficient.

"Amazing!" says Umbo.

The devices also create digital files, tagged with the time, date and GPS location, and capture stray soundwaves that enter their hyper-directional mics as barely detectable trace elements—a trembling leaf or fragment of undigested bird-song.

A minute later Reynolds, Clara, and Leah press their STOP & SAVE buttons.

"How impressive!" says Wanda. She'd downloaded a dB app on her e-Cameo and is tickled that it's not many decibels astray of the experts' equipment.

"Bosh!" says Dewey Dinsmore, compressing his lips into a thin line of ill will.

"Hurray!" says his son Sparrow, doing pastel sketches of the experts.

Lars gives Sparrow a thumbs-up, then calls for everyone's attention. "For the sake of balanced fact-finding, I urge all of you to share your observations on the notepads I gave you. Or Splat me."

Sol plows forward. "I'll Splat ya right now. It's just as I warned at the Council meetin—the Big Brothers and Sisters, sneakin about and spying!"

Lars explodes. "Sneaking about…!?"

Before he can tackle Sol, Wanda does.

"This is a duly authorized Village committee, doing its work in broad daylight on the *Ashlars'* property—with their full consent!"

Sol stomps his foot. "But the sound's comin from the Offmans!"

"Indeed," says Reynolds, in soft-spoken, professorial tones. "The Offmans are making the sounds, but Councilwoman Middlemarsh is correct. The soundwaves are measured as they *enter* the Ashlars' property. One might even say that the Offmans' soundwaves are trespassing!"

Clara pitches in. "We have no microphones on the Offmans' place, Mr. Silvertongs, nor are we amplifying the sound." She holds up her device for him. "This is getting precisely the same soundwaves as your eardrums. Are your eardrums 'sneaking about and spying'?"

The elderly man with the tortoiseshell specs who'd attended the Council meeting plants himself before Sol.

"If the Offmans want their goings-on to be private they oughta shut those durn carriage-house doors! If *I* lived on Orchard Lane I'd turn the garden hose on 'em!"

Then Lars has everyone about-face toward Mole End, where by prior arrangement Sam cranks up Growler and starts a new cut on the giant willow as Reynolds, Clara, and Leah reorient their devices.

A woman frowns beneath her parasol at Clara's readout. "That can't be right! Only 78 decibels for all that hurly-burly!?"

"I assure you it *is* right," says Clara. "It may seem louder, due to the chainsaw's percussiveness and your personal response to sounds—neurologically *and* psychologically. But our equipment is state of the industry!"

The man with the tortoiseshell specs—who lives across the hall from the woman in the same boarding house—peers at her beneath the parasol.

"I betcha wouldn't complain if it was that Ozarks cookin show your TV blasts out every blessed day! What's it called…? *Eat My Zits?*"

The woman presses a hand to her throat. "You know very well it's *Heat My Grits!*"

Sam and Leah realize that the Chihuahuas must be off their feed, as they've yet to make an appearance at the Plinketts' bay window. But their matron Pru Plinkett took off work from $2 Duz It and just returned her darlings from their bimonthly checkups, where the vet treated their overtaxed vocal folds with cortisone biscuits. They hear

Growler and cut loose with all their lungpower as Leah and company swivel their devices on them.

The dogs have occasionally gotten on Wanda's nerves, but Middlemarsh Manse is farther north from the Plinketts by the span of a baseball field, and the Chihuahuas' bay window is on the *south* side of the house, broadside to Mole End. From what Wanda learned from Leah's toonVid about the logarithmic increase of a noise the closer one gets to it, she's sobered by how far more maddening the dogs are for the Ashlars.

She looks again to make sure she wasn't imagining it, and is shocked to see her cameo registering the Chihuahuas at *92 decibels!*

-21-

LARS'S WOODSCULPTORS LOFT *Moles Revolt* show opens, and Sam sets the record player's needle on trumpeter Harry James's 1942 hit recording of 'The Mole'—as the public pours in for a gander while accepting glasses of Green Goose wine and beer, accompanied by Mabel's highly prized appetizers.

Olive Best slips in to pay for Leah's sprightly wrought saxophonist molette, while Sam and Jenny let on how glad they are that she'd turned the Persimmon Lane assault to victory.

Olive hugs her molette. "She's wonderful, Leah. Very saxy!"

She heads out the door as Thaïs arrives in her Duesenberg.

"Not running off, are we?"

"My break's nearly done, Your Honor."

"Oh, posh! Surely your taskmaster Vivian Truman will allow you an extra minute or two for a sip of wine!"

"But I'm on duty!"

"Then let's have a quickie!"

Thaïs clasps Olive to her massive bosom as the media snap rapid-fire photos of them, then Olive frees herself and resumes her tour. The councilmembers show up with their families, and Thaïs makes her own show by ostentatiously purchasing a set of three ballet dancer molettes that Jenny carved. She praises Jenny for her artistry, who promises to help pick an appropriate spot for them in the Manor's arboretum.

Then Thaïs lowers her polar bear size hand on Wanda's shoulder. "Aren't these molies luscious?!"

"They're very soulful!"

Wanda has crafted several more moles of her own in the secrecy of her studio, and apologizes for her tardiness on Thaïs's glazed-mammal commission. She offers to return the deposit she and Silt already spent.

"Nonsense, my dear. Virtuosity won't be rushed!"

Silt boycotted the opening "on principle" and is sulking at home with their boys, while Henna tagged along with her mom. She's mad for a molette with a penny whistle, but the Middlemarsh financial straits rule out any such purchase.

Leah is filming the event and, noticing Henna's longing gaze, draws her aside. "What if you and I team up to carve a molette just for you? Very much like this one, but with a *piccolo!*"

"Oh yes, please!"

Lars introduces the Ashlars to ripping applause from the crowd that squeezed itself through the doors, and in no time all 62 molettes are sold and dozens of orders taken to the many Wildroseians present, including Sam's Wildrose College Wind Band mates, and the growing influx of out-of-town Moles Revolt allies.

-22-

FOR TWO WEEKS LARS RUNS Decibel Committee outings, as the volunteers and experts Reynolds Vey, Clara Duzzle, and Leah ride jauntily about in the school bus to measure every sound such a modest hamlet can beget, including the noises begat by the school bus and its tongue-wagging cargo, while they imbibe vats of Lars's cider—as he always forgets to bring the bottled water donated by Thaïs.

Reynolds, Clara, and Leah generate files on the Boutique Gas & Lube when the mechanic is using his ear-bending tire wrench; the various school playgrounds during pigtail-pulling recesses and ball-whacking athletic practices; the Burlap Factory at the cantankerous shift changes; the Gravel Works at barge-loading hours; the gas-ravenous powerboats on Wildrose River, rehearsing for the Turquoise Tower Grande Opening Gala; and the diesel trains at Wildrose's south end, dieseling so loud they wake the sleepers.

"Lars ain't missin much!" Dewey Dinsmore admits.

"He ain't missin *nothin!*" says Mynah.

During their perambulations the Committee members are amazed to see increasing numbers of handcrafted moles of every ilk appearing on porches, frontyards, and balconies, purchased from the Woodsculptors Loft or carved by the residents themselves from fallen trees or castoff wood furniture. Leah films and offloads all of this to her colleagues and Goldenhawk—who squeals from her wide-ranging news chopper, "You're making mighty mountains outta moles!"

* * *

The June equinox comes, cloudless and pure, and just before noon the Decibel Committee members unload at Wildrose's picnic area below Moonlight Knob's jagged cliff face to enjoy box lunches. Zebulon, meantime, is feasting his eyes on the Turquoise Tower from the Manor's turret, five miles away. The Tower's immensity makes it easily visible without binoculars and he contacts Chief Engineer Cornelius Flug, standing by in the Tower's command center.

"Is everything on track?"

Flug has been sweating for days to oversee the system checklist for the QuadBoard's 90 billion LEDs.

"Yes, Sir!"

"Then let her rip!"

Flug says a hasty prayer and throws a toggle that patches the QuadBoard into the Tower's chronograph. In a millisecond, untold trillions of electrons zip though miles of gold-print circuitry and the QuadBoard's 90 billion LEDs glow like molten steel. Despite the bright sunlight, laser beams form a phantom image of Thaïs above the Tower and lose themselves in space to strike a distant planet, eons hence.

"Not bad," says Zebulon. "Now start the blitz!"

Perspiration pours from Flug's face as he says another prayer and throws another toggle, and the LEDs create Olympian-size words that march around the QuadBoard.

51 DAYS TO OUR WORLD-SHAKING GALA!
RESERVE YOUR STATEROOM
ABOARD THE TUGBOAT INN!

"Good Lord!" says Sam, sharing a picnic table with Leah and Lars. "It outdoes Las Vegas!"

The man at the next table removes his tortoiseshell glasses. "Time I got a welder's mask!"

Flug heaves the sigh of his life as images of restaurants, spas, weight-loss parlors and e-gamer shops fill the QuadBoard in a mind-jarring gallop. The QuadBoard's mega effulgence distracts the golfers on Condor Links into driving their balls into Wildrose River and speedboaters to run aground, while hydrofoilers bellyflop into the water and hikers stumble on the trails below Condor Lookout.

Back at Mont-Obiston Manor, Raffia skips up to the turret with the ever-patient Petra to hug Zebulon and exclaims, "How magical!"

He pecks her on the cheek. "My dearest pet! Just wait till you see the Queen of Platinum Moment on our birthday!"

* * *

Thaïs and the councilmembers sift through the jungle of Decibel Committee data while Duffy catalogs and backs it up on the new hard drive donated by Thaïs, stored in the Council's safety deposit box at the Spend & Save Bank.

Meanwhile, to reinforce their position on the noise issue, ICEE and its compeers swarm Wildrose with placards proclaiming that ICEE is COOL! and I'M A HARLEY GRANNY!, while shouting "Moles eat dirt!" and "Moles *undermine* democracy!" at everyone in earshot. They monopolize reservations at all of the B&Bs (including Middlemarsh Manse B&B) and promise many return visits, "*provided* Wildrose stays ICEE friendly!"

"Thank God," Silt says, waving a check at a dubious Wanda on his way to the bank. "We can almost afford a new water heater!"

To further strengthen its hand, ICEE allies itself with the Truckers Conjunction, Unicyclists Limited, Sodality of Lawn Workers, Mopeds for Jesus, and Cyclists-Over-90 (on three-wheelers)—all of them governed by the Supreme Saddle and its Washington lobbyists. They book the Wildrose chapter of the Grand Order of the Boombox for dinners, and lavish donations on the local Democrats, Republicans, Independents, Neocreationists, Give-a-Damns, and Who-Gives-a-Damns; and donate swimsuits to the Wildrose Aquanauts, embossed with the Supreme Saddle logo. Their *In Horse Power We Thrust* motto appears on T-shirts, tote bags, tampon packets, and other items that monopolize the $2 Duz It aisles, and buy up all of the Maalox, beef jerky and Corn Husker's Lotion to soothe their sore backsides at Knokdown Drugs—whose shelves are resupplied by a 24/7 conveyor belt of semi-trucks from the Sky Vue Freeway.

This giant anaconda of vehicles begins to tighten Wildrose in its fumy grip, prompting the Supreme Saddle to issue an edict instructing the membership *not to worry*, as the issue is "fussy noise restrictions, not lung-rotting particulates!"

-23-

EARLY IN JULY THE THREE BALLERINA molettes arrive at Mont-Obiston Manor and Jenny accepts Thaïs's pressing invitation to help choose the most alluring site for them. She bicycles over in her workaday slacks, canvas shoes, and straw hat, and is ushered by the ever-meticulous Gallifent to Thaïs's presence in a Regency sitting room on the Manor's ground floor. With a gloved hand Gallifent offers Jenny a glass of Chardonnay and slice of almond cake, served on an 18th-century Spode dessert plate, encrusted with 22 carat gold florets.

Gallifent slips away, leaving Jenny to fumble with a damask napkin, which she fears is worth more than she once earned in an entire week as a tenured university professor.

"I'm afraid I'm dressed for the out-of-doors!"

"Exactly how you *should* be dressed," Thaïs purrs, studying Jenny over her wineglass. "This is just an informal girls' klatch, and you're doing me a favor by sacrificing some of your precious time to help me situate the ballerinas. If ever I might do a good turn for you—or Sam—you'll let me know, won't you? Anything at all?"

Jenny flushes. "Coming here is hardly a sacrifice. But if there were something, of course I would!"

She takes another bite of cake, so moist her tongue welcomes it like dewdrops on the Mohave Desert.

Twenty-five minutes later Thaïs leads Jenny down a marble pathway to the arboretum.

"I had this in mind for your adorable molies the instant I saw them!"

Jenny's breath is swept away by the sylvan vision before her, as if she's been transported to a Tuscan estate—hoarded by the same caring hands since the time of Dante. The arboretum graces a dozen terraced acres, interlaced with brick pathways and a necklace of waterlily ponds, anchored by a hothouse—and Jenny marvels at the maturity of the trees for so young a setting.

"They're *transplants*," says Thaïs. "Like me! Many of them came from properties that were being cannibalized into suburban plots or public housing, if you can imagine!"

Imagine, indeed! Jenny thinks, imagining the small farms and wineries north of Wildrose River, doomed to an equally dire fate if Condor Estates expands as projected! But she congratulates Thaïs for hosting a world-class nature preserve, and draws her attention to a copse of pine trees where the ballerina molettes might do well.

Thaïs presses a hand to her cheek. "I hadn't thought of that!"

Then Jenny stops short at the sight of a pine tree with singular, grey-green needles. "Pinus torreyana!"

"Yes! How discerning you are!"

Jenny can't take her eyes from it. "Trees were my first interest, ever since I visited my aunt and uncle here in Wildrose when I was four."

Thaïs expands. "From San Diego, the only Torrey pine I have!"

She plucks a cone from the topmost branch and leans down with it to Jenny, who rotates it in the mottled sunlight.

"I wish you luck with them!" But she's thinking that this pinecone is *identical* to the one that concealed the spycam at Mole End!

* * *

"Well," says Sam, "Mont-Obiston could very well be of French derivation!"

He's in Mole End's living-room with Jenny, Leah, and her ePal. Their uneasiness that Captain Kroft's technician might've failed to detect any spycams inside the cabin just blew a hole through their self-assurance, due to the similarity between the pinecone Leah found at Mole End and the Torrey pinecone from Thaïs's arboretum—and Beethoven's *Ode to Joy* spins on the record player to mask their conversation.

Leah hits a key and her ePal brings to life the Ville Obiston town-square in Quebec.

"How picturesque!" says Jenny.

They'd already gleaned some tidbits about Thaïs's stellar days at the University of Wisconsin and the Sorbonne, and her 16 years at Epic Builders & Repossessors in Brussels, before retiring in her early 40s with an estimated wealth of 14 billion dollars. Her origins require more keying, and Leah ferrets out that the triplets' father was French Canadian and the mother an American from Milwaukee, where the family settled when the triplets were nine. Growing up bilingual, Thaïs shrewdly chose a career in France and Belgium.

"Let's move on to Zebulon," Leah suggests.

The goods on him are scarcer. He was a bone-shattering football tackle at the University of Wisconsin, leaving a Big

Ten Conference record for sacking that's still out of reach. One entry notes that he'd also won a science fair award for creating an electric battery from heating certain ores in high-pressure chambers. He'd bragged to a reporter that when not demolishing opposing footballers, his passions were fixing up exotic cars and tinkering with computers.

"Certainly explains the Duesenberg!" says Sam.

Then Leah brings up a news item from a vacation the triplets had in Greece, where Zebulon duked it out in a taverna with four ouzo-fueled rowdies, injuring three of them and killing the fourth one with his bare hands. An Athens attorney got him acquitted by reason of justifiable homicide, and the lack of news on him since then suggests that the incident caused his near-total withdrawal from the public eye.

"What a temper!" says Jenny, noting that the Greek roughneck died of a broken back when Zebulon hurled him like a football at the taverna's stone wall.

"But that's no reason for bugging Mole End," says Sam.

"Let's keep digging!" says Leah.

She types in "Wildrose Village mayor" and her ePal disgorges clips of the Special Council meeting with Leah's toonVid presentation, the Decibel Committee's launch in front of the Wildrose Village Hall, and Thaïs's arrival at the Moles' gallery opening. Then comes the groundbreaking ceremony two years earlier for the first Condor Estates townvillas, where Thaïs mugs for the cameras while wielding a platinum shovel.

Sam does a double take. "What's she doing there? She wasn't mayor back then!"

Over the next hour they dig deeper still and find that Thaïs founded Platinum LLC just after retiring from Epic Builders in Brussels, and just before her swearing in as

Wildrose mayor she bequeathed it to her Milwaukee cousins—freeing her from election-law restraints.

-24-

WILDROSEIANS COME IN WAVES for the Fourth of July Concert, with Duffy and her granny first in line to snag a pair of good seats.

Then Duffy snags a better pair of seats for Thaïs, who rolls in behind the wheel of the Duesenberg with Raffia, mere seconds before Pierre Pasquin gives the downbeat for 'The Star Spangled Banner.' Thaïs hypnotizes her humble constituents with an ivory-colored gown and a purple, broad-brim summer hat with matching leather pumps. But for once Raffia outshines her in Undine's custom tailored, scarlet cape-and-skirt ensemble that brings to mind Big Red Riding Hood.

Truman and his wife Daisy find good seats, as does Olive Best and her parents, while Lieut. Conklin—having snorted that he has no use for musical "trifles!" —patrols the Village, protecting the citizens with his well-polished Colt.

Giles and his head server Rita shuttered the Green Goose Café to join Jenny, Mynah, and Sparrow Dinsmore, while Leah engages via her camera from her VW's roof. As the National Anthem ends she roams about filming the attendees, which Thaïs acknowledges with a stately nod, while Raffia gazes as if the lens were Alice's looking glass.

"No Zebulon," Leah notes, thinking he certainly *is* a recluse, passing up such a concert!

But he chipped in by commanding Condor Estates' General Manager Geoffrey Murgwynd to respect the day, and for once Chipmunk Run has fewer construction vehicles than *The New York Times* has Republicans.

The crowd applauds, and the All Souls College Symphony Wind Band swings into 'Country Gardens', which Goldenhawk streams for her 2.7 million fans, flying high up so her aerodynamically tipped blade-caps don't break the spell with contraband noises.

Sam is very much at home among the Wind Band members in black slacks, black tie, and white dress shirt, thrilling in the musicmaking with his Co-Principal hornist, as Henna delivers phrases on her piccolo with the agility of purple martin aerial displays. With Leah's help she carved a piccolo-playing molette—now at her bedroom window—which Silt pretends not to see when he's working in the yard. But at the moment he, Wanda, and their two boys are among the audience, drinking in Henna's honeyed notes.

Evening brings hotdogs and firecrackers at the Village Commons. The Ashlars bought the 2,800 pounds of bootleg fireworks at the auction and donated them to All Souls College to support this very event—its annual July Fourth Fête. The Village Commons sizzles with music and pyrotechnics, and Jenny snuggles against Sam on one of the benches.

"It's just the kind of event your Exemption Clause proposed!"

A Flying Spinner Rocket shoots above the treetops, drawing *Wows!* and *Ahs!* from the crowd while turning night to day—and giving Sam a BRAND NEW IDEA.

-25-

GRATIFIED WITH THE dB COMMITTEE'S progress, the Ashlars ease up on the chain-sawing. They continue carving moles—for the thrill of it and to feed their Woodsculptors Loft exhibit—but they use a Vietnamese-made electric model from Home Dislocation. It makes but a fraction of the noise of Growler and is guaranteed for 60 days. And they've rearranged the corrugated tin sheets at the willow tree from sound amplifiers to sound buffers—so the neighbors can barely hear anything.

Sam's pleased about this, as the lightweight Vietnamese chainsaw (recycled from toothpaste tubes) eases things for his back. And when he's not carving moles or practicing on his horn, he's groping forward with his book on Thoreau, mostly indoors with the ceiling fan blowing and windows shut, as the neighbors are still besieging Mole End with their own noises.

Be *patient,* he reminds himself!

It's another Monday and Sam is starting another chapter on Thoreau while enjoying his pipe in the Adirondack chair. Overnight winds felled a limb from an aging buckeye tree by the mountain laurels at the back of Mole End, but it's a cleanup that must wait because a steady rain is freshening Jenney's sweetcorn that's more than knee high.

Leah's tucked under a parka by the cattails, filming Sam's reflection in the pond's rippled surface when she gets an alert on her ePal and darts from her hideaway.

"They've done it, Grandpa!"

Jenny's doing her dancer's barre in the living room and runs out to join the excitement. It's a post from Duffy, announcing that the Wildrose Council finished reviewing the dB Committee recommendations and agreed on a Revised Noise Ordinance with a maximum noise level of 70 decibels.

The pipe bails from Sam's mouth. "Seventy decibels! That's great!"

"Have they really done it?" says Jenny, throwing her towel around her neck.

Lead reads on. "This says it'll have two readings before becoming the law, at the August and September meetings."

Then Lars comes so catlike on his motorcycle that they don't hear him until he reaches the porch. He shakes the rain from his helmet and accepts some coffee from Leah. They settle in the living room with Stravinsky's *Firebird* on the record player and Lars asks if they've seen Duffy's post.

"It couldn't have happened without your leadership!" says Jenny.

He groans. "I meant the *six a.m.* post!"

Leah finds it just arriving on her ePal.

"It mentions an 'Exemption,' which I assume is the one Grandpa suggested. For fire-engine sirens and such."

"At our meeting last night the vote was four to one in favor of the Ordinance."

"Who opposed it?" says Leah.

"I did."

They stare in shock, then he explains that the Exemption referred to on her ePal *isn't* the one Sam had proposed, but a new one cooked up by the Council.

"A Byways Exemption"—to exclude all public roads, waterways, and recreational spaces from the Ordinance. Which means that motorized vehicles, vessels, and pedestrians with boomboxes on these many places are allowed to make as much of a clamor as they want, around the clock, around the year!"

"That's total idiocy!" says Jenny.

"I tried compromising with a 75 decibel level, but only Wanda backed me. Buford argued that if we didn't exempt the roads we'd lose deliveries from UPS, FedEx, and the Post Office, and would have to exempt most of the river barges."

"But we measured those kinds of vehicles," says Leah, "and they were surprisingly quiet! As I said in my report, the drivers don't as a rule let their trucks idle while they're leaving packages, and they can't afford to beat them up with jackrabbit starts and brake-screeching stops!"

Lars dumps cream into his coffee.

"Buford ranted on about poorly maintained trucks creating an enforcement nightmare. And the diesel-engine semis that supply the restaurants and schools, the Boutique Gas 'n Lube, and that bring heating oil to the houses. A lot of it is scare tactics, but it has plenty of Wildroseians on edge."

Sam chews on his pipe. "The dollar is Augustus Decibelis!"

A Shrinking World Tours bus muscles its way up Orchard Lane, drawing Lars to the window.

"Tourists are flooding the local B&Bs—which is practically one in five houses around town! The Retailers Association loves them and snowed us under with eDumps and Snippets in favor of the Byways Exemption!"

The bus airbrakes sassily as the tour guide unloads his amplified patter through the bus's open windows.

"To your right is Mole End, ground zero of the dB crusade. And that's the mighty mamma mole and her two chips-off-the-old block!"

Moleen stares with troubled eyes as the driver gives an airhorn blast as the passengers holler.

"Hey, babe! What's happenin!?"

The airbrakes release an ear-piercing *shissh,* and the bus grinds up the lane with an undertow of cars and trucks whose sound systems rake the cabin so violently that the mantelpiece clock is shaken from its nook and smashes onto the floor. It was Jenny's great-grandmother's, and for the first time in a century and a half its voice is stilled.

Lars is speechless, and Leah holds her breath in shock. After a moment Jenney kneels to collect the pieces and returns them to the mantelpiece.

Sam trembles with rage. "Damn it!"

Jenny bushes a tear from her eye. "It's all right."

He hugs her. "It's not all right!"

After a moment Lars pulls out some papers. "I may have a solution. I'm drafting a lawsuit, arguing that the Byways Exemption is nothing but a sop to the Condor Estates' builder and owner, Platinum LLC. I've filed similar suits and will wager that some Thoreauvian, botanical, and cinematic ammunition from the three of *you* would multiply our odds of success!"

Leah clenches her fists. "Let us at 'em!"

They go to work and generate enough suggestions to turn his slender draft into a fatted calf, then Sam asks Lars how long the appeal will take.

"I'm afraid it could be a few weeks or even longer, depending on the judge's schedule and predilections."

Sam surveys the broken bits of clock. "We can't just sit idly by! While we're awaiting the judge's decision, let's open a second front!"

Then a thought strikes him—a *prelude* to the BRAND NEW IDEA he'd gotten at the 4th of July Fireworks Fête.

Leah goes to work on her ePal as he sketches it out with a conference call to Giles at the Green Goose Café, Marie and Pierre Pasquin at All Souls College, Leah's friends in Brooklyn and Van Nuys, and Goldenhawk—the empress of highflying journalists in her copter—somewhere in the skies above.

-26-

AN HOUR LATER THE ASHLARS beat a path over the sodden roads to the Village Center where Jenny hits up $2 Duz It for white plastic tablecloths and—to the amazement of Sales Rep Pru Plinkett—every last packet of balloons they have.

Pru is boiling mad that when the Revised Noise Ordinance gets its two readings and becomes the law—as seems likely—she and Po will have to wriggle their precious Chihuahuas beneath the 70 dB limit by *shutting their bay window!*

But she's relieved that the Ashlars are still willing to shop at $2 Duz It (instead of sneaking off to the giant Win-Win outlet on the Sky Vue Freeway) and floats a friendly face as she stuffs the purchases into Jenny's carryall.

"Enjoy your balloons!"

"Everyone will!"

Leah meanwhile snaps up all of the balloons at Knokdown Drugs, and after a fruitless search for the next item on her list she pigeonholes Clovis. "Where are your rubbers?"

"Ah! Ain't this just the weather for 'em!"

And he leads her to a bin overflowing with lace-on, slip-on, and zip-on rainy-day footwear.

Internally he's steaming over the new Ordinance, which will require him and Madge to muzzle their beloved pool with some sort of soundproof enclosure—at God knows what expense! But he's relieved that they'll be protected from the Middlemarsh boys' e-bongo drums, and noting that Leah seems boggled by the rainwear bin's multitudinous choices, he feels it's a good chance to mend fences and keep the Ashlars as customers. Having donated four costly dB devices to the Village and a yacht-load of fireworks to All Souls College, they clearly have very big purses with very loose strings.

"I know, Leah! So many rubbers, so few feet! But how about this?"

He takes a HuriBoot STORE SAMPLE canister from a shelf and sprays his shoe with a gooey substance that in five seconds hardens like chewing gum that's been on a sidewalk since the Hoover Administration.

"Keeps your foot drier than a martini and is guaranteed to stick to itself, but nothin else! Perfect for a rainy day!"

Leah steps back. "I shoulda been clearer. I'm looking for *condoms*."

Seconds go by before he can respond. "Condoms...?"

"As many as you've got!"

"Well... we're chock full of 'em!"

Clovis leads her through the store (leaving his shoe behind, cemented firmly to the floor with HuriBoot) and points to a counter where a sign warns, YOU MUST BE AT LEAST 12 YEARS OLD, above a rack of 87% guaranteed NoKnokUp Kondoms.

"Will that do ya?"

"Quite nicely!"

Sam, meanwhile, is trying to exchange a $100 bill for quarters at the only Save & Spend Bank window that's open. It's Figgie Silvertongs's pied-à-terror, who's still smarting from her husband Sol's "Abraham Washington Lincoln" harikari act at the Council meeting and pretends not to see Sam. Tabitha Tannenbach does see him and leaves her cubicle to show him a device that might've come from an Atlantic City casino.

"You put in coins and get out bills. Or put in bills and get out coins!" She takes his Benjamin Franklin and feeds it in the slot. "Are you pleased with the Revised Noise Ordinance? Your efforts were so crucial to it!"

A digital voice asks what coins Sam wants and he punches in a choice. "I think the Byways Exemption makes it untenable."

"Isn't it worth trying?"

Ten rolls of quarters shoot into Sam's hands. "It *will* be tried!"

His next stop is the Boutique Gas & Lube men's room, where the vending machine offers RediEddie RubHers condoms in sizes from Jiminy Cricket to King Kong. He shoves in the quarters and the packets toboggan down the chute into his waiting palms. It's Sam's lucky day, as the RediEddie rep came just that morning, and Sam's pockets sag with enough recreational latex to satisfy any sports celebrity or gov'nor you'd care to name.

"Planning a little party?" the gas-pump attendant asks with a wink as Sam leaves the men's room.

Sam winks back. "You betcha!"

Back at Mole End, the Ashlars use permanent markers to turn the white plastic tablecloths into JOIN THE MOLES REVOLT! banners that they duct-tape to the VW, then flex their lungs by inflating the balloons, RediEddi RubHers, and No-KnokUp Kondoms.

Leah glances at her ePal and sees it's nearly six p.m.

"Hey! It's party time!"

As was true of Orchard Lane, it's the hour when Wildroseians throughout the Village return from their jolly labors, thirsting for a guzzle of recreational alcohol or a puff of medical marijuana to accompany their digital distractions, so Sam and Jenny roll out their bicycles with the balloons and condoms clothes-pinned to their wheel forks, *flop-flopping* against the spokes with the effect of tommy-gun practice in one's shower stall.

They head down Orchard Lane Bottoms—boxing the ears of the Dinsmore dirt-bikers, and round the U to give the Sonic Sisters a musical shout—then enter a series of more populous byways. They miss out on some of the fun because of their earplugs, but Leah generously heightens their listeners' pleasure by cannonballing carnival music from her VW's rooftop speakers, while her camera streams the Villagers' jolly reactions for the entire world to enjoy.

The tablecloth banners invite the bystanders to

CELEBRATE the WILDROSE VILLAGE
COUNCIL'S **BYWAYS EXEMPTION!**

Olive cruises a few blocks behind to keep the peace, and Thaïs tunes in with mounting chagrin and orders Billy Umbo to head out in his spymobile.

Goldenhawk flies in from monitoring illegal crop dusters in the next county and shares the Ashlars' video with her followers, now swollen to 3.4 million—due to the feverish coverage generated the last few weeks by the Moles Revolt.

She *boings* Leah, "Supr hotsht!!!"

Whole families gape as the Ashlars come *flopping* into Hathaway Hollow, giving its residents their first up-close-and-personal Moles experience.

"Damn that Village Council!" they cry from their vibrating lounge chairs and garage-top saunas.

Hathaway Hollow is also Wildrose Ward Number Two, where councilmember and insurance magnate Buford Whitlow reigns with his wife and teenage son and daughter. It's an hour when the two teens are on the losing side of a brain-wrestling contest with their homework for the costly tutoring they're getting (subsidized by Buford's two employees' gasping pension fund), and they raise their dormer windows—hoping that a traveling circus has wandered by, with which they might run off.

Buford shuffles out the front door with a glass of Milk of Magnesia—still in suit and tie, but shoeless with a toe peeping from a hole in one of his socks—freshly returned from the jolly insurance agency where he grows senile before his time.

"Huh?" he mumbles.

His wife does better. "It's those noisy Ashlands!"

Sam, Jenny, and Leah guess from the Whitlows' expressions that they're thrilled to be served such a lively summer-night's repast, and Sam signals that they should swing their condom cavalcade past Buford's door again.

And again.

As they ping-pong up and down the street a window opens in the corner of Leah's monitor. It's a Snippet from the Bronx, where scores of families are circling the borough president's brownstone with plastic water bottles pummeling the wheel spokes of their laundry carts and baby strollers to protest the street repair work that's been dragging on for 18 years. They wave signs declaring, THANK YOU, MOLEEN!, and similar videos come from Tijuana, Rio de Janeiro, and New Orleans.

After the fifth flop-by Ms. Whitlow screeches at Buford.

"Why doncha do somethin?! Ain'cha a Village Counselor? If our kids don't learn the particles of speech they'll never get into Vassalage and Yale!"

Buford sighs, knowing that his seed will be hard-pressed to get in the local beauty school and auto-detailing institute. But he missed part of his wife's insights and cups a hand to his ear.

"Come again?"

She grabs him by that ear. "Why doncha call the CIA, or whatever it takes to shut these people up!"

"It's only 6:30 p.m.. The CIA can't do anything!"

"Well!" she screams, causing compression fractures in his ear bones. "I'm not gonna wait for that stupid Revisited Noise Orneriness to take effect! I mean, two more stupid months of this stupid noise!"

Buford staggers with pain and doesn't bother pointing out to his ever-loving backpack that the two readings won't make any difference. Since Hathaway Hollow's a public road, the Byways Exemption approved by him and his three like-minded councilmembers will make it eternally hostage to anyone who wants to create as much of a din as they like, *24 hours a day!*

The Ashlars begin their seventh flop-by, and to ease the smarting in his ear Buford pours another round of Milk of Magnesia and stiffens it with three fingers of Old Granddad. The whisky gives such a liftoff that Buford wonders what Granddad had been up to with those three fingers.

Then he feels a *ribit-ribit* from his eTieTack and finds a Dribble from Billy Umbo—parked at the end of the block in his spy-mobile—thanking Buford for "soldering on" and reminding him of the "jolly premium payments" awaiting him at the end of his travails.

Buford Dribbles back, "Thnx v'ry mch!!"

Most of the neighbors have skittered indoors like termites from a brushfire, but one of the holdouts—a Little League coach right next door to Buford—bellows from his porch.

"Hey, Whitlow! Why doncha shake a leg and get these balloon terrorists off our street?! Didn't all us coaches vote for you? I'm cookin up some pine tar and can't concentrate for shit!"

Before Buford can reply another neighbor shrieks, her voice tunneling through the drainpipe to his one ear that's still functioning.

"For Chrissake, Buford! I'm tryin to watch the Okra Channel!"

-27-

SAM NOTES THE WHITLOWS' JOLLY expressions and gives Leah and Jenny a V for Volume sign, then they replace the balloons and condoms that sacrificed themselves for the cause, while Leah's ePal reels out feedback:

"Bang on!" says Goldenhawk.

"Ball-breaking!" says BreakBalls.now.

"Monstrously musical!" says her Van Nuys friend.

"It's totally thumbs-up!" Leah tells her grandparents.

Sam says their next stop is Ward Number Three on Loon Lake Road.

"Our banker, Councilwoman Tannenbach. She was a big help at the change machine and deserves an early Christmas!"

Once underway he realizes that Tabitha might be Jewish and may not be hankering for an early Christmas, though he reckons she just might hanker for an early Hanukkah. But when they reach Loon Lake Road they find they've been beaten to the shofar. It's Lars on his motorcycle, leading his pals on their classic Moto Guzzi, Ducati, Triumph, BSA, and Royal Enfield motorcycles, and Sam recalls that at their morning ePal strategy talk Lars had promised to dish up some dBs of his own, aided by his freebooting friends.

"Good man!" Sam shouts.

Lars's other contribution is his backup strategy to rely on State Statute 83, nick-named the "mistress law," because back in the day so many lawyers funded their fleshpot recreations by arguing its loosey-goosey verbiage. Enacted in 1829, Statute 83 decrees:

THE STATE SHALL NOT MAKE OR SUFFER TO BE MADE ANY LAWS, ORDINANCES, COVENANTS OR OTHER LEGISLATION PROHIBITING, REGULATING, OR CIRCUMSCRIBING THE PEOPLE'S ACCESS TO OR USE OF THE VARIOUS PUBLIC ROADS, PATHS, OR WATERWAYS, MANUFACTURED OR NATURAL, IN THE PURSUIT OF THEIR LEGITIMATE EMPLOYMENTS, CELEBRATIONS, OR RECREATIONS.

Loose though its verbiage may be, Lars is counting on the all-but-forgotten Statute to cover the Moles from 10:00 p.m. to six a.m.—since Wildrose's 1865 Noise Ordinance *prohibiting* loud noises during those hours is still in effect.

Loon Lake Road is a cul-de-sac with a broad terminus that makes it a cinch for Lars and his pals to about-face for ongoing drivebys, and Goldenhawk adds to the fun by droning low overhead and drawing in new subscribers by the thousands.

Tabitha winces from the front door of the house she shares with her mother, two sisters, three sets of aunts and uncles, and wife Undine. A few of the aunts and uncles are deaf as warranty departments and glad of it, while the other Tannenbachs press oven mittens to their ears, a half-baked solution.

It's just as prophesized by Leah's Bunker Hill toonVid, as echoes multiply until all of the housefronts on Loon Lake

Road heave like an opera about Mike Tyson, composed by Homer Simpson.

"O God!" says Tabitha, suddenly realizing what Sam meant when he said the Byways Exemption would "be tried out!"

Thrilled that Lars and Co. have Loon Lake Road in sound shape, the Ashlars hurry to Crabtree Draw—Ward Number Four and home of Councilman Cecil Flinn. But as they coast down the hill they find they've been beaten to the Draw by the 134-piece All Souls College Wind Band, rehearsing Sibelius' *Finlandia* for the approaching Founder's Day Concert.

Jenny reminds Sam that Pierre and Marie Pasquin—who took part in that morning's conference call—pledged to give the Moles Revolt a big band boost.

"I put your horn in the VW!" says Jenny.

In an eye-blink Sam gets it and joins the band where his Co-Principal hornist squeals, "Snowy top! We thought you'd abandoned us!"

"Never!"

The Band gets stuck on *Finlandia's* stormy one-minute-and-19-second ending and Pierre has them try it again. They're in classic Roman legion formation—point blank in front of Cecil's house—because as the Band Boosters' treasurer he's entitled to a frontyard foretaste of the concert, along with his wife Mabel and their two sons. But his sons are members of the band—trombone and bass drum. Trombones have been played better but not louder, and the base drum is being walloped so hard it's getting a headache.

Cecil and Mabel are sitting uncomfortably on the folding chairs set out by the other Boosters and endure the second go at *Finlandia's* final 79 seconds, while the neighbors watch from indoors while Splatting Cecil, which he can't hear.

Others Dribble Chief Truman, who Dribbles back that he can't intervene, since it's well before 10:00 p.m. Other Crabtree Draw residents phone Thaïs, whose message system overloads with complaints, and she's engaged in a call of her own with the GlobBank VP who greenlighted her $700 million Condor Estates loan.

"What you're hearing is a minor correction, as the vector of our support will advance exactly as forecast. And tomorrow I'll introduce a tactic that'll make the world forget this sorry spectacle!"

Then Thaïs lets Billy Umbo loose, camouflaged and waiting in his spymobile on the U bend at Orchard Lane Bottoms.

He slips from his car and circles the burdock meadow to the Ashlars' fieldstone fence. Knowing that Leah's security system allows for small animals that frequent Mole End, he reasons that if wild turkeys can navigate the yard without setting off the security system, so can he. A moment later he's crawling on his stomach around the pond to the toolshed, like the glory days in Afghanistan. The shed is padlocked, but he easily wrenches loose some boards from the back wall and squeezes inside.

Meantime, two figures are hiking up the east side of Orchard Lane's U with an old suitcase and heave the Elms' door knocker. Calliope and Pavana are jarred from Evening Manta and patter through the shadowy hall with guttering candles, then pick out the two faces beneath the portico.

Calliope brushes the variegated bangs from her eyes. "Heavens!"

"We're yer neighbors. Mynah Dinsmore and my youngest, Sparrow." They plop down the suitcase. "We've come to join yer commune!"

* * *

At Crabtree Draw, Pierre asks the Band to try *Finlandia's* ending again, so the musicians lick their chops and create a blockbuster attempt that windshears an airplane, causing the passengers to slam into each other and spill their overpriced drinks.

Pierre massages his arm. "Not bad. Not bad at all. But we could use even more *punch* from the brass and heaps more *oomph* from the percussion!"

Cecil's son has broken his drumstick and grabs another one, and Mabel responds by digging her fingernails into Cecil's knee. "Maybe you and the rest of the Council oughta reconsider that wretched Byways Exemption!"

"From the top!" says Pierre, giving a mighty downstroke.

Olive beats out the time on the cruiser's dashboard, Truman fingers an imaginary bassoon, and Jenny taps her foot. Leah captures her best footage ever, whose live streaming has Wildroseians cursing the Byways Exemption and its Village Council supporters—and winning new Moles adherents from around the planet.

The Symphonic Wind Band creates *Finlandia* anew, making certain that just the lucky sods in the Village Cemetery will sleep this night.

PART THREE

-1-

IT'S 2:00 A.M. AND BILLY UMBO—still in camouflage—is shown to Mont-Obiston Manor's library by the ever-discreet Gallifent and hands Zebulon a pea-size object.

"Your Holy Grail, Your Honor!"

It's a pinDrv, which Zebulon studies like a rare coin. "Then let's have a look!"

Umbo inserts it and the computer screen shows black-and-white footage of a boy on a tractor, cutting hay under a midday sun.

"Kodak single-eight millimeter film, found in a trunk at Mole End. There was an old projector, which I used to screen this on some white cardboard to make this copy. There were other films, labeled 'Barn-building' and 'Our Smokey Mountains Camping Trip.' This one is 'Sam and the Bully.' "

Some kids in T-shirts and patched jeans are now bailing hay and storing it in a barn, then playing softball in the newly shorn field, joined by a man in overalls and straw hat.

"That must be Sam's father," says Zebulon. "And those are the Ashlar kids?"

"And no doubt some kids from neighboring farms. Sam is yet to appear."

The kids and Sam's dad hear something and dash off, and the camera pans to a clapboard house where a woman's striking a baking pan with a serving spoon. They race inside and the camera pans back to the hayfield, where a boy at second base trips on his shoelace.

"Probably one of Sam's friends," says Umbo. "Keep your eye on that tree to the right."

The boy ties his shoe, then the image jerks—as if the camera had been bumped—and another boy enters the frame. Zebulon knows at once it's Sam when he was 12 or 13—a stripling with a short, summertime haircut.

Sam approaches the other boy as a figure jumps from the tree. It's a large teen, with a neck so thick it seems to be a continuation of his shoulders and arms like cinderblocks. He waits by the tree as Sam takes his friend's arm and gestures toward the house.

"Almost there," says Umbo.

Sam starts back for the camera and the teen rushes and throws the friend to the ground, pinning him down and slapping him in the face.

Sam turns around and is paralyzed.

The teen slaps the boy again and Sam shakes off his stupor and runs over with clenched fists. The teen looks up with distain, then slaps the boy once more. Sam sees the fieldstone that serves as second base, and picks it up and says something to the teen with calm deliberation.

Umbo pauses the film.

"I showed this to my linguistics contact at Quantico and we agreed that Sam said something like, 'If you don't let him go, I'm gonna smash you to a pulp!'"

Zebulon is sobered. "I believe it!"

Umbo restarts the clip.

The teen stares warily, then springs up as Sam slams the stone against his shoulder. The teen cries out and his shirt is torn. He's riven with fury and punches Sam in the eye, who stays on his feet and circles, taking advantage of the teen's wounded shoulder. Then he shouts at the top of his lungs—startling the teen—and ducks to deliver a body blow that buckles the teen to the ground.

Umbo tightens the shot until Sam with his swelling eye dominates the screen, pummeling the bully for all he's worth.

-2-

WILDROSEIANS CRAWL FROM THEIR beds like slugs from an equatorial highway—all but the Ashlars and their growing cadre of moles.

After gifting Cecil and Mabel Flinn and their neighbors with five more *Finlandia* run-throughs, the band members refreshed themselves with Green Goose Café hoagies, napped in the College dorms, and at 3:00 a.m. boarded Leah's VW and several Band Boosters' cars, and over the next few hours "previewed" the Founders Day Concert for the other Wildrose neighborhoods. Despite some heckling and calls of complaint, Truman and the state police refused to intervene. State Statute 83—taking precedent over Wildrose Ordinance's 10:00 p.m. -6:00 a.m. noise ban—had won the night.

"Look at this!" says Leah, holding up her ePal for Sam and Jenny on the cabin's back porch. "It's a post from Duffy, declaring that to relieve Wildrose of a 'contentious seven-weeks' wait,' Thaïs has ordered the Noise Ordinance readings for a pair of special Council meetings. *Tomorrow and the week after!*"

At the First Reading the Elms' Sisters show up—accompanied by Mynah and Sparrow—and Calliope gives the

Ashlars three windchimes as peace offerings, made from old hubcaps, cola cans, and discarded Kindles.

"After much meditation—and with the insights of our novitiates Mynah and Sparrow—we've incarnated from sonics to *organics* and want to join your Revolt!"

"Well!" says Jenny. "You're very welcome!"

Calliope claps her hands. "All right, Sisters!"

They post themselves around the Chamber and shake their windchimes, agitating the air with an otherworldly tingling that loosens more plaster from the ceiling, while other Sisters roam the Commons, pressing windchimes on everyone not fleet enough to escape.

Giles and Rita sweeten up the fence-sitters by handing out Mabel's gingerbread moles, and Lars's buddies park their Royal Enfields and other classic bikes in a circle around the Village Center and hang about the Chamber like so many Will Rogerses. They have no membership cards or insignia, yet exude an air of individualistic and rugged support. Other moleites tunnel in from the surrounding counties, flaunting HOLY MOLEY buttons.

The opposition reacts swiftly as the Jackhammer League members crowd every curb and ATM machine, and the Retailers Association acolytes thrust out leaflets touting Wildrose's ever "rosier" future as a tourists' upscale pool-and-patio lodestone. They infest the Commons and chant "Chill out with ICEE" and "Moles are *revolting!*"

Olive Best patrols on foot while dodging autograph hounds, and Conklin guards the Chamber dais, alert as a hat stand.

Every seat is taken, with toddlers on their parents' laps and infants on the toddlers' laps, and the media is pinched into the front row with the spillover bunched on the floor.

The Village Hall clock gongs 7:00 p.m. and the Chamber falls silent as Thaïs takes her armchair. Duffy leads the Pledge of Allegiance and Her Honor pounds the session to order with the Sacred Gavel and gets right down to business by inviting public comment.

Sam hustles to the railing.

"Your Honor and Councilmembers. I'd like to dispel some of the confusion sown by those who support the Byways Exemption by stressing that the Moles revolt is *not* anti-truck, anti-RV, or anti-motorcycle. We are, quite simply, opposed to damaging noises and have a growing number of bikers, truckers, target shooters, and retro-rockers among us. In brief, we're *in favor* of peace, good manners, and social harmony!"

The molephiles cheer and the opponents stomp their feet and boo.

Thaïs waves a finger and the Chamber falls quiet. "Please continue, Mr. Ashlar."

Sam says he read every jot of the dB experts' findings and is baffled that the Council ignored great slabs of it.

"Noise experts Dr. Clara Duzzle and Dr. Reynolds Vey made it clear as Waterford Crystal that without a blanket maximum of 70 decibels, real physical and psychological harm will continue to be done to *all* of our citizens, domestic animals, and wildlife. So mark my words. By foisting this Byways Exemption upon us, the Council will set the get-rich interests at war with Wildrose's body and soul. We know that intense pressure has been piled onto you."

He glances at the B&B Guild director and Supreme Saddle rep.

"But all of us face pressures, and must reap the whirlwind if we yield to those which wreck the common good. If you persist with this Exemption you'll be ensconced for all time in the Internet Hall of Lunacy!"

"Darn right!" says Giles.

"Indeed!" says Pierre and Marie Pasquin.

"Listen to that man!" says Granny Nicklebob, flogging the arm of her chair with her umbrella.

Sam returns to his seat as Lars gets up and applauds, as do Jenny and Leah, the Pasquins, and the Elms' Sisters—while the ICEE members show defiance by drumming the floor with their boots and wallet chains.

"Order!" says Thaïs, and after a tense moment the Chamber goes still. "And who is next?"

Sol Silvertongs takes the railing and rails against the "good-for-nothing" moles, inspired by that "lazy bum Henry Throughout," who was "bribed by that Nazi, Fido Castro!"

A score of others speak pro and con, then Thaïs brings down the gavel.

"This concludes the Revised Noise Ordinance's First Reading!"

* * *

The instant the meeting ends the College Wind Band strikes up a jam session on the Village Commons that rattles the Conference Room windows, and calm though she seems to be at the curly maple table, Thaïs is annoyed to find Cecil Flinn shifting ground.

"I'm getting lots of guff from Mabel and my boys, who fear that the Founders Day Concert will be destroyed by people tearing up and down Wildrose River in their flyboats and turbo flippers! We've already lost the Fresh Air Practice Series!"

"I'm with you!" says Lars.

"We're *all* with him!" says Thaïs. "The College events are among the gems that drew me to Wildrose."

Tabitha is showcasing Undine's burlap jacket and culottes ensemble—revealing a growing schizophrenia over the Byways Exemption.

"My aunts fear that their lawn teas and possum-sighting meets in Wildrose Forest will be jeopardized by growing numbers of roboJeeps. Traditions that have been going on since I was a girl!"

Thaïs twists her bracelet, whose platinum facets shape the ceiling-light beams into stilettos. "Surely we can deal with those concerns without destroying the freedom of our byways!"

The Chamber is heating up, but Buford keeps his suit jacket pulled tight to conceal that a shirt button has gone walkabout. Haunted by the prospect of his two teens' careers as pedicurist and sofa slipcover salesman, he'd slipped out just before the Council meeting and drained three shots of Old Tailgate whiskey at the ManShot Trolley.

Thaïs nudges him. "Any suggestions, Councilman?"

He turns his good ear to her. "Sorry, Your Honor. I didn't sleep very well last night!"

"Most unfortunate!" Thaïs turns to Wanda, knowing that her daughter's piccolo is comforting the enemy with the impromptu concert on the Commons. "You look fatigued, my dear!"

Wanda's affection for the Moles has been growing by the day, conflicted with the $2,500 in B&B deposits Silt accepted from the JetSkaters' Club.

"I'm fine, Your Honor."

"And your precious children?" Thaïs asks.

A spittoon squats in the corner of the room, a brass-and-verdigris relic of long-gone debates and reeking social habits, into which Lars feels he might have to vent his nausea at Thaïs's cloying question.

"My kids napped a few hours," says Wanda.

Buford rubs his temples. "Well *I* couldn't nap. I had clients to deal with!" (One, actually.) "And my kids' tutoring was disrupted by all the chaos, so it was a waste of time and money!"

"I tried napping during my lunch break," says Tabitha, "as did my mom and aunts and uncles. But it was useless, given the invasion of tourists and journalists. Especially that Goldenhawk!"

"*Noisy* invaders!" says Buford.

Thaïs glances at Duffy, pecking away at her Stenograph writer. "Invaders?"

"Invaders!" says Buford, and Duffy pecks the word again.

Thaïs says Wildrose was a Shangri-La when she moved there. "How did it sour so quickly?"

"It's when the Ashlars came!" says Tabitha.

Lars smacks the table with his fist. "Nonsense! The lawn-care crews and dragracers have been grinding out mayhem for decades!"

"*I* didn't notice much noise before the Ashlars came!" says Buford.

"Let's pursue this line of thought!" says Thaïs.

Buford props himself on an elbow. "If it was a *little* noisy before, all of us dealt with it pretty well, like we do most things. We're law-abiding and civicminded!"

Lars scoffs. "The Offmans aren't very civicminded, leaving their carriage-house wide open to their medieval equipment. Our dB experts made that perfectly clear!"

"But that's exactly what the Ordinance will prevent!" says Thaïs, shaking her bracelet in triumph.

"Not on the streets. As the Dinsmores did few years ago when they went rallying on their dirt-bikes!"

"That's right!" says Cecil. "It was worse than a squadron of F-four fighter jets!"

"That was before my time," says Thaïs. "And Chief Truman should have cited the Dinsmores for taking their bikes on the roads."

"Wildrose doesn't require dirt-bikes to be licensed," says Cecil. "They were just plain *annoying*, and the Chief couldn't do diddlysquat about it!"

"The Byways Exemption will allow that sort of thing at all hours of the day or night!" Lars adds. He goes over and flings up a window, allowing the College Wind Band music to rush boldly in from the Commons. "They're doing this as a warning!"

Tabitha raises her voice above the din. "But we seem to have a consensus that it's been noisier and more dangerous *since* the Ashlars began carving those moles!"

Lars fastens his eyes on her. "It's like a doctor, cauterizing a wound with some short-term pain to prevent gangrene that would *kill* the patient!"

"I'm not certain it's short-term!" says Thaïs, unfolding her arm to shut the window, then turning to the other councilmembers. "Now. As mayor, is there any particular action you'd like me to take in this time of crisis? For we *are* in a crisis, and I'm sworn to protect our citizens!"

Buford bites the carrot. "I think you should advise Chief Truman to be on special alert for anything that might set off this mountain of TNT. Make sure things don't get too dangerous in terms of protests, and so forth."

"I second!" says Tabitha.

" 'And so forth'?" says Cecil. "What's that mean?"

"We have a motion and a second," says Thaïs. "Any discussion?"

Cecil straitens in his chair. "I *am* discussing it. And I wanna know what pit of vipers 'and so forth' might conceal!"

"It's not even a proper motion," says Lars, looking back and forth between Buford and Tabitha. "And Chief Truman is already doing what you're implying!"

Thaïs checks to see that Duffy entered it correctly. "Buford added 'special alert,' 'dangerous,' and 'TNT.' Those are new features!"

"I move we put it to a vote!" says Tabitha.

"I second!" says Buford.

"What?!" says Cecil.

Thaïs glances at Wanda and says, "All in favor?" Buford, Tabitha—then Wanda—vote yes. "The motion to vote on Buford's motion is carried. All in favor, raise your hands."

Wanda has grave doubts, but it sounds near enough the right thing to do, and she knows they've got to do *something.* She joins Buford and Tabitha in voting yes, while Lars and Cecil stare as if Thaïs had suddenly morphed into a giant platypus.

-3-

LARS UNLOADS THE BAD NEWS at the Green Goose Café as the Wind Band members pour in from the Commons for cherry pie, on the house. He's too steamed up for pie, and cools off with a tankard of Green Goose Lager as Sam asks about the exact wording of the new provision. Lars quotes it and says it's mostly procedural, but gives Thaïs more leeway to rule the roost as she sees fit.

"Cecil is wavering in his support of the Byways Exemption, but unless he and one other councilmember join me it'll stay put!"

"Then we have to turn up the heat!" says Sam. But he realizes that his BRAND NEW IDEA is too embryonic to spring on the others.

"Why don't we do an entire *week* of outdoor band practices!" says the man with the tortoiseshell glasses. "I'll get out my bagpipes!"

Calliope whoops. "That's tooo perfect! The Ashlars scored bigtime because their chain-sawing and condom parades knocked Wildrose on its ear. A week of concerts is just the medicine we need!"

"Why not focus on the waterways?" says Sam's Co-Principal hornist. "They won't be expecting that!"

"That's it!" says Giles, striking a mighty chord on his piano. "Let's drown 'em in *Water Music!*"

* * *

Early next morning Sam and four other Wildrose College Wind Band members are grinding their way through stacks of church hymnals on the *Jasmine*—a colorfully rigged Thai-food junk that's sailing north from Folkston Landing, 12 miles downriver from Wildrose.

The *Jasmine's* owner jumped at this chance to expand his clientele. And it's a surefire strategy, as the breeze that sends the junk skipping up the river while blaring 'Bringing in the Sheaves' also broadcasts the tantalizing aromas of pine-apple fried rice and tilapia rad prik to the inhabitants along both riverbanks. Although few of the hymns are especially challenging, the players are sightreading lickety-split, and the occasional muffed note or shaky intonation gives their performance a special piquancy.

Leah films the *Jasmine's* progress from the river's many inlets, as dockside families clamber aboard the junk for sit-down meals and takeouts, and Goldenhawk buzzes overhead to the delight of her 5.2 million subscribers.

"Wada hoot!" she squeals.

Billy Umbo is watching from the Tugboat Inn and Dribbles Thaïs for instructions, who Dribbles back. "Hold your position. We're going to win this game because we manufactured the playing cards!"

An hour later Sam and his fellow musicians are relieved by other Wind Band members, and the hymnal enfilade quickens with fresh embouchures as growing numbers of meals are sold. The *Jasmine's* lunch specials give way to afternoon hors d'oeuvres, then dinner specials and pitchers of Thai cocktails as other rotations of Band members arrive—raising the dander of increasing numbers of homeowners along both riverbanks.

As the hours drag by, the police and Thaïs are besieged with complaints—as is Captain Jonas Norton of the Coast Guard cutter *Maysville*, making a routine tour of Wildrose River. Norton checks his log and finds that the *Jasmine's* registration and inspections are up to date, and says that as it's cruising on a public waterway it can serve up *as much music as it wants!*

The Wind Band members carry the Water Music through to the following Tuesday—infuriating the anti-Mole factions—and when the Revised Noise Ordinance's Second Reading comes on Wednesday, those factions are infuriated all the more when dB experts Dr. Reynolds Vey and Dr. Clara Duzzle appear and rush to the railing the instant Thaïs welcomes comments from the public.

After a subtle glance from Thaïs, Buford pops up and gushes thank-yous for the experts' dedicated work on the Decibel Committee Report, but is pained to point out that as nonresidents they aren't permitted to comment at a Reading.

In the blink of an eye Granny Nicklebob hoists her umbrella. "Your Honor! Dr. Duzzle and Dr. Vey are *guests* at my farm!"

The Gallery's in an uproar, as everyone recalls that Her Honor most warmly welcomed Leah Ashlar's guest appearance at the Special Council Meeting three weeks earlier—setting a clear precedent!—beyond which Clara and Reynolds hold special status as the very dB experts hired by the Village to examine its noise problems.

Thaïs covers her chagrin with a welcoming nod. "By all means, proceed!"

Clara and Reynolds hurry to the railing with a rolled-up poster and Clara goes first.

"Wildrose citizens and respected media. We who devote our careers to studying sounds and their impact define loud noises as *sounds that are unwanted and/or harmful.* Leah Ashlar gave powerful examples of that in her toonVid presentation in this very Chamber, and in the 249-page document presented to your Noise Ordinance Committee, Dr Reynolds and I gave a comprehensive dB profile of Wildrose Village and our recommendations for improvement. Drawing on our mandate to make a few follow-up visits for additional sound checks, we want to present you with our latest findings."

Reynolds takes over.

"We'll share with you that which for many of us is the first big chapter of our lives—our school years!—as we'd spent some time at Wildrose Grade School on Holly Branch Drive, a road which most of you know was widened eight months ago to become part of the new Sky Vue Freeway. We'd already identified noise impacts from the Sky Vue Freeway at several locations around Wildrose, and highlighted them as 'very problematic,' but we returned to the Grade School on Monday to make further measurements at the midpoint of their summer session, as the teachers had contacted us about an alarming trend."

Reynolds and Clara unfurl the poster—revealing a floor plan of the typical Wildrose Grade School classroom with its desks, teacher's station and bookshelves, and capacious wall of windows.

Reynolds goes on.

"As you can see, five widows in each of four classrooms face south, *directly* at the Sky Vue Freeway—with the students' desks facing east toward the teacher's station—providing the students with some healthy sunshine over their right shoulder. But they also get a very *un*healthy dose of traffic noise, even with the windows closed—as they must always be, since all of the teachers said quite emphatically that it's otherwise impossible for them and their students to hear each other. Since the windows are always closed, Dr. Duzzle and I measured the Sky Vue Freeway noise as it's transmitted by the windowpanes from each of the five rows of desks in all four south-facing classrooms. And here are the results!"

Clara takes another turn.

"On average, the closer the students' desks are to the windows, the more their grades have dropped over the last eight months. You heard me correctly. The grades have dropped! This was consistent throughout all four classrooms, and the grades of the students seated *nearest* the windows dropped by the greatest margin—14%. Let's be clear what this means. The students who'd earned an A- before the Freeway opened are now doing C+ work, and students with a C- average are now doing F+ work. A failing grade, my friends, but what grade shall we give Wildrose for allowing this to happen?"

The Gallery roils with dismay, and Thaïs brings it to order with a raised forefinger, allowing Reynolds to carry on.

"As we said, grade school is for most of us life's first grand adventure, but our mandate's timeline prevented us from doing a similar return study of humanity's final adventure, in this case the Holly Branch Senior Care Home, a few hundred yards from the Grade School, with *dozens* of rooms directly opposite the Sky Vue Freeway. Perhaps some of you have friends or family members at the Home, and you might imagine what findings we'd have made of those souls who're traversing their final years!"

Dead silence.

After a moment, Clara and Reynolds thank everyone for their attention and return to their seats—a Chamber so hushed that Thaïs can almost be heard grinding her teeth.

Lars jumps up. "Your Honor. These findings are so grave that we must take them into account before voting on the Byways Exemption!"

In a rush, the other councilmembers call out in agreement—except for Buford—who says the problem can be solved by soundproofing the windows. But a second-grade teacher grouped with some of her peers in the Gallery points out that such a step wouldn't keep the Freeway noise from polluting the playground and ballfield, which are vital to their students' socialization and physical development, and a cohort of voices throughout the Chamber shout their support—especially the Ashlars.

Adept at decoding the writing on the wall, Thaïs announces a one-hour recess for the Council to debate the issue *in camera.*

* * *

The instant the councilmembers settle in the Conference Room Lars says Reynolds' and Clara's findings make it imperative that the Byways Exemption be scrapped.

"Not so fast," says Tabitha. "In their written report, Doctors Vey and Duzzle footnoted that highway noises can be abated by erecting concrete walls—a solution that's been used with considerable success around the country—which we could do along that stretch of the Freeway. I propose that we seek bids from experienced contractors, which of course would take some time. But if we make the outcome of this evening's vote *contingent* on obtaining a bid that meets our criteria, then surely Wildroseians would consider it a fair and democratic solution!"

Buford says he agrees, but Cecil waves his arms. "How do you propose we pay for these walls?"

Wanda ventures a thought. "Wouldn't it have to be a tax? And if so, would the voters support it?"

Cecil echoes Wanda's concern, and Thaïs rolls her shoulders. "Must it be tax? What other alternatives have we?"

Tabitha smells an opening.

"I propose that we fund the walls with *user fees*, levied on the Wildrose River Marina recreational facilities and activities. Docking slips. Fuel sales and engine repairs. Gondola rentals and keelboat cruises, plus the Tugboat Inn cabin suites and its Michelin Two Star restaurant. These fees would *only* affect our wealthier residents and well-heeled tourists!"

"Perfect!" says Thaïs. "And once the walls are paid for, the fees could be phased out. A victory for one and all!"

"Absolutely positively!" says Buford.

Cecil rubs his jaw. "We'd have to work out the details most carefully!"

Lars jumps up. "Walls along the Freeway wouldn't address the traumas that the Byways Exemption will cause on the rest of Wildrose's roads, waterways, and public areas!"

Cecil says he agrees, but Thaïs rises.

"Gentlemen. One step at a time. We must give Tabitha's idea a chance, and one way or the other we must return to the Chamber to decide the Revised Noise Ordinance's fate. Democracy at work!"

In a heartbeat Tabitha wraps her idea into a motion as the Marina User Fee Proposal and Buford seconds. Then a ribbon is tied around the motion as it passes with Yeas from Tabitha, Buford, and Wanda—over vigorous Nays from Lars and Cecil.

* * *

Thaïs reconvenes the Public Reading, and after Duffy summarizes the Marina User Fee Proposal for the Gallery, making clear that it's "contingent on getting a contractor's bid that's acceptable to the citizens of Wildrose," Thaïs takes the helm.

"All that remains is for Council to vote on the Revised Noise Ordinance, which in Wildrose tradition will be taken by public rollcall."

The public stirs, the media aim their lenses, and the Elms' Sisters shake their windchimes; yet despite the hardball run-up, the vote is over in 23 seconds.

Duffy goes to the tally board and calls the council-members by name, who say I vote yes, I vote no, or I abstain, and she shoves the slate with each name to the appropriate column. Despite Thaïs's supple maneuvering and Platinum LLC's $5,000 Wind Band Boosters' "donation," Cecil joins Lars in proclaiming, "I vote no!"

But Thaïs can live with his apostasy and smiles serenely as the Supreme Saddle members romp about in ecstasy, shaking the Chamber with the force of a bison hip hop meet.

The *Walleyed Street Journal* reporter dashes over to get the Ashlars' reaction.

"The Council's made a huge blunder!" says Sam. "Building walls along the Freeway won't be nearly enough!"

Jenny throws her arm around him. "The battle's just begun!"

-4-

WANDA IS LEAVING THE VILLAGE HALL as Thaïs peers out her office.

"Got a sec?"

She makes Wanda cozy on a Chesterfield sofa that was installed during Thaïs's swearing-in as mayor, where she entertains visiting dignitaries from other towns and villages.

"How about a glass of sherry? We must toast the Revised Noise Ordinance!"

Wanda runs her hand over the sofa's buttery leather. "I oughta get back, Your Honor."

"Surely Silt can manage without you a few more minutes!" She fills a glass to the brim and slips it in Wanda's hand, who shudders.

"Heavens! I won't be able to drive!"

"I'll drop you." Thaïs pours a glass for herself and settles in an armchair. "To our success!"

The sherry is finer than Wanda could've dreamed, and her throat receives it like Joan of Arc getting her own password to the Pearly Gates.

Thaïs twirls her glass. "From Portugal. I'll bring you and Silt a case."

A case! Wanda thinks. She takes another sip and her head goes into orbit around her shoulders.

"Now, Wanda. It seems to me that of late you've been rather blue, and I wondered if something's nagging at you? A small burden which I might lighten?"

Wanda starts. Is it possible that in addition to having been a monumentally successful corporate executive and a keenly astute politician, Thaïs is also a skilled mind reader? The sudden movement causes Wanda to spill some sherry on her skirt.

In an instant Thaïs whisks a tissue from her desk and whisks away all trace of the sherry before it can even think of staining Wanda's skirt. "See! I'm *good* at banishing troubles. Now tell me what's eating at you!"

Wanda feels Thaïs's massive hand on her thigh, but instead of acknowledging it she shifts her eyes to the computer screen, replaying Goldenhawk's coverage of the Wind Band's church hymnal antics on the *Jasmine* restaurant junk.

"Well, it's true that the Ashlars have somewhat disrupted the Village; but all the same, I can't help feeling that the Byways Exemption isn't the best we might've done."

"How right you are!"

Wanda blinks. "You agree with me?"

"Wanda. Running a village is a good deal like running a corporation. We aim for perfection, but if we're provident we settle for gradual improvement, one milestone at a time!" She withdraws her hand from Wanda's thigh. "Of course the Exemption is flawed—as is the Marina User Fee Proposal—but it's one we must live with until we find a better way."

The computer shows a closeup of Sam on the *Jasmine*, delivering a stirring high note on his horn.

"Just be patient. In time things will settle down and Wildrose will be more hospitable than ever!"

"Thank you!" says Wanda. "I feel so much better!"

And she throws back her head and polishes off the sherry.

* * *

After the Council vote Lars took the moles to the Woodsculptors Loft for cider and donuts. Everyone is shocked by the outcome, but he reminds them that the district judge has yet to rule on their lawsuit.

Jenny takes the floor. "And we've come so far! Let's turn what seems to be defeat into greater determination!"

Granny Nicklebob waves her umbrella. "That's the stuff! We've done well to keep the opposition guessing, and must pummel them harder than ever!"

"Well!" says Sam. "Since we have a Byways Exemption, why don't we pummel our opponents by exempting ourselves, and do it *to the max!*"

-5-

IT'S EARLY FRIDAY, JULY 18, and the *Luella Mae's* two-story paddlewheel thrusts her from the Folkston Landing with the blue-and-gold uniformed Wildrose College Wind Band members bedecking her like candles on the planet's biggest wedding cake—backed up by the thunderous voice of the *Luella Mae's* slightly offkey calliope.

Pierre's on this prowl of the magnificent paddle-wheeler, conducting ' The Yale Strut'—one of the hundreds of marches in the All Souls College Music Department backfile that fed generations of moths from the College's annual March & Fight Song Competition, 97% of which haven't been played since getting their thumbs-down tryout.

As the *Luella Mae* churns her way upriver, the leaden notes pry anglers from their nets, berry pickers from their patches, and vintners from their arbors. Granny Nicklebob is skimming along in her dory, with Leah aboard to film the *Luella Mae's* journey, as Goldenhawk hovers above to stream it to her 8.9 million viewers.

Thaïs has tuned in from her office and rouses Billy Umbo on her ePendant, viewing from his own office at the Tugboat Inn. "What the hell's going on?"

"There wasn't a hint of it, Your Honor! On the College's website or anywhere else!"

"Well, get your backside over there and report to me!"

"The 'Yale Strut' ends with a clash of flugelhorns, and over the next several hours the *Luella Mae* steams past sandbars and tributaries as the doltish marches smoke out families from their A-frame relaxations and woodlot meditations. The pilot gives a hearty *Toot! Toot!* and steers the *Luella Mae* to the College boat dock, where the players enjoy a lunch buffet, provided by Cecil Flinn and his fellow Band Boosters.

Billy Umbo parks his spymobile on a bluff overlooking the dock and alerts Thaïs. "I'm watching and listening!"

He reports an hour later as the *Luella Mae* slips hawsers and continues upriver while the Wind Band and calliope unload 'Getta Touchdown Now' onto Condor Estates' first avenue of townvillas. The baleful tune wrenches the stay-at-homes from their infidelities and Cloud surfing, and the nine-to-fivers returning from their jobs, where they'll be shackled the next 30 years to pay off their colossal mortgages.

* * *

Night comes and Thaïs is marking time in her office with a cup of cappuccino, her arms planted on the burgundy blotter that covers her desk like a field of ripe poppies. She takes a sip and her tastebuds oscillate as her computer exudes images of the eternal now. It's the *Luella Mae*, docked at Wildrose Marina—a closeup on Sam, happy as can be in the brass section as Goldenhawk narrates.

"It's the original mole and his agile horn, who orchestrated all of this just weeks ago with his wife Jenny and granddaughter Leah—and now he's using that horn to gore the Wildrose Village Council backsides!"

Thaïs's ePendant chimes 10:00 p.m. and she goes down the corridor as Truman asks Lieut. Conklin if he has anything to report from his traffic patrol.

"Just those mole people, makin more noises by the river." He sees Thaïs and jumps to attention.

"At ease," she says, then lowers herself over Truman's desk. "No doubt you know about the Declaration made by the Council last week…?"

"The one about special mayoral powers?"

"Based on that, I want you to act before there's a repeat of the Wind Band's all-night concert."

Conklin is listening from his desk, while pretending to count the bullets in his cartridge pouch.

"But the Band is performing on the river," says Truman, "which State Statute 83 exempts."

"The Statute pertains to 'legitimate' pursuits. It isn't the Band's legitimate purpose to shake the citizens from their well-earned rest, or Sam's to sit in with them!"

Conklin shifts all five watts of his gray matter to their discussion.

"The Wind Band has a tradition of performing in public," says Truman, "and to accept non-credit players, who pay tuition. My cousin Elmo is in the Band, and in years past *I've* sat in, playing the bassoon!"

Truman as a bassoonist gives Thaïs pause, but she sloughs it off.

"I'm not going to mince words with you. I instruct you to arrest Sam if he refuses to stop playing, and to tell Pierre Pasquin to cease the music at once."

"I acknowledge your instruction but decline to act on it." He gets his hat to begin his final rounds.

"Then I order you."

"And I refuse to obey." He sees that Conklin is still at his desk. "If you're thinking about putting in for overtime there's nothing doing. Your shift ended five minutes ago and out you go!" He points at the door.

Conklin jumps to his feet. "I was just about to—"

"Stay right there!" says Thaïs, freezing him in place. "Lieutenant, you've witnessed Chief Truman's refusal to obey my order."

"Yes…?"

"I also want you to witness that I'm relieving Chief Truman of his command."

Truman is stunned, but holds his peace to see if it's a ruse to get him to relent and carry out her outlandish order.

Then she makes it clear. "You're fired, under Section 19 of the Village Code, laying out the Duties and Powers of the Mayor. Now give me your badge."

Truman sighs. "Very well."

He unpins it, but ignores her outstretched hand in favor of putting it gently on his desk, then gathers his framed photo of Daisy and some other personal items before going with dignity up the hallway and out of the Village Hall.

Conklin watches with his eyes starting from their sockets, expecting Truman to pop back in and shout, "Ha! Fooled ya!"

But Truman doesn't return, and Thaïs gets Duffy and Wanda on her ePendant and asks them to hurry over. Then she turns to Conklin, waiting with eyes atwitter.

"It'll be some minutes until they arrive. How about a cappuccino while we wait?"

He hasn't the vaguest idea what she's talking about, but reckons he's also gonna be fired. He averts his eyes from the impending blow and they land on his lieutenant's cap, on a hook beyond Thaïs's shoulder. His mind races. Cap … cap you … cap you see now…?

He gushes. "Ya wanna see my *cap?*"

-6-

DUFFY STEADIES THE BIBLE under Conklin's clammy hand as Wanda witnesses.

"Look at me," says Thaïs.

He looks up from the badge, newly pinned to his chest.

"Now—*Chief* Conklin—you realize the menace that's facing the Village?"

"Yes…?"

His ears gyrate at being called "Chief," but he fears that when midnight comes his uniform will turn to rags and the cruiser will become a giant pumpkin.

"And you recall the order I gave *former* Chief Truman, which he disobeyed?"

"Yes…."

But to be sure he's got it down she asks him to repeat it, which he nearly does.

"Not quite. I want you to *arrest* Sam Ashlar, not *harass* him—if he refuses to stop playing his horn at the Marina, and order Pierre Pasquin to return the Band to the College. Use your training!"

The only real training he's had was the *Earn Hundreds Monthly as a Law Enforcement Officer* course he'd taken when he flunked out of grade school at 18. It finally seeped into his skull that the paltry wages he was making as a substitute night security guard at the Gravel Works meant one could earn hundreds of *pennies* monthly.

"Right," he says. "Use my training!"

Soon afterward he's racing up the Sky Vue Freeway as Wildrose's 28th Chief of Police. At first he was miffed at being flung so quickly into the breach, as he was yearning to lay claim to Truman's desk—so much larger than his own!—and to earn a few hours overtime at his higher salary by arranging the paperclips to his own liking. But he guesses there'll be plenty of opportunities for that after he's nabbed Sam and locked him in the log cabin cooler. He makes sure he's strapped on his cartridge belt, and imagines himself as Poncho Vanilla, leading his gang of tacos through the cacti.

Then a once-in-a-lifetime event occurs. He has an epiphany. It comes with such force that he nearly head-ons a pack of ICEE motortrikes coming the other way. The secret to carrying out the mayor's order, he realizes, is go in *disguise!*

He pulls onto the shoulder to consider this insight without the distraction of driving, and 40 minutes later has pasted together a plan and takes the Chipmunk Run exit. He parks at All Souls College and enters the Music Hall, left open for late-arriving Wind Band members. He rummages through the cloakroom and finds an overcoat with acres of gold braid that he throws over his uniform, and replaces his cap with a plumed drum major's hat. Then feeling that he needs a finishing touch, he happens by a wire cage where band instruments are stored, also unlocked.

"Thank the Lord for the trusting All Souls College!" he squeals.

He finds a huge, brassy thing and recalls that it's a Suzie Phone, named for the plumber's wife who invented it from castoff pots and broken down boilers. He shoves it in the cruiser and speeds to the Marina, where he slips into its coils and infiltrates the crowd that's spiraling with increasing density throughout Condor Estates.

"Make way!" he barks, elbowing a path between the moms, dads, and cranky kids to the *Luella Mae* as the Wind Band ends a march that climaxes louder than the high tide at the Bay of Fundy.

"Fifteen minute break!" Pierre calls from the prowl.

The players disperse down the gangplank and Sam goes to a portable restroom marked BAND MEMBERS ONLY.

"Aha!" Conklin mutters, and he throbs in anticipation of seeing his very own photo and life story in *The Barleycorn.* But the throbbing shakes his bladder and makes him want to take a tinkle—due to the foul tasting coffee with the queer name that Thaïs foisted on him before his swearing-in.

A door opens at a restroom *not* reserved for Band members and Conklin makes for it like an incontinent guided missile. Others are waiting at the same restroom, so he shouts "*Make way!*" and shoves aside a woman at the front of the line with a babe in arms. The restroom's occupant comes out and crashes into him. Or rather, her titanium lens hood crashes into him—smack against his nose.

"Is that you, Conklin?!"

As the stars clear Conklin recognizes Leah Ashlar, granddaughter of the very man he's about to nab. A red light flashes on her camera—and knowing that red means STOP—he's relieved that for once in her life she's not filming one damn thing or another.

He clenches his teeth. "Outta my way, manx!"

They're clenched because his nose was bloodied by the lens hood, and because his bladder reached critical mess.

He shoves at Leah, but she holds her ground and indicates the woman with the baby.

"She's next in line, you oaf!"

"I'm Chief of *Po*leece!"

"And I'm Teddy *Roo*sevelt!"

The woman jabs Conklin in the ribs and shoots into the restroom, just as Sam leaves the other restroom and sees a sort of *Saturday Night Live* character inside a sousaphone with a hand to his ribcage. Then he notices Leah, lens-to-eyeball with this twit, and figures she's getting some background roughage for her film.

Through tears of pain Conklin sees Sam approach, and despite the aching in his ribs and the bursting dam at his nether regions, he recalls Thaïs's command. As half the planet watches Leah's sharply focused shot he grabs Sam's collar and shouts, "You're under arrest!"

Then to cement his place in history that'll be memorialized with a footnote in *The Oxford Book of Morons*, he clutches Leah's wrist with his other hand and bellows, "And you, too, for trying to instruct me in my duties!"

-7-

THAÏS FREES SAM AND LEAH from Conklin's pulpy grip and Jenny returns them in the VW to the *Luella Mae*, where the Wind Band kicks off its 217th march of the day—while Thaïs orders Conklin to sit at his old desk. His nose is bandaged and hurts like hell; and although he's puzzled by Thaïs's frigid reception he manages to salute.

"Mission done!"

"Mission down the toity!" she says.

He starts to protest that he no longer needs a toity, but hits the brakes on his tongue, as she's making a call on her ePendant.

"Olive? I need you at the Hall, on the double!"

Olive comes straight over and sees Conklin with his bandaged nose, then follows Thaïs to her office.

"You can probably guess from the chaos at the Marina and Truman's dismissal that you're sorely needed."

"The Chief's been fired?"

"Details later. Until further notice *you* are Acting Chief of Police!"

* * *

Sam returns to the Wind Band on the *Luella Mae*, playing 'Pass dat Ball!'—jarring the Condor Estates' residents from their overly groomed townvillas. Word has spread about Statute 83 (not to mention the pending Marina User Fees to pay for the miles of noise-reducing concrete walls), and furious that the Village Council failed to address the Statute with an appeal to the state legislature, the residents get into partisan brawls about what to do. Tourists from the Tugboat Inn join in, as the marches are wrecking the eBingo and neo-breakdancing exhibitions that comprise their exorbitant weekend packages.

'Pass dat Ball!' ends to increasing rage and Sam tells his fellow players that they "seem to be gaining traction!"

* * *

Right after Olive was sworn in as Acting Chief she hurried to Truman's home on Old Farm Ridge. His mind is in turmoil and Daisy's calming him with a cup of chamomile tea as Olive joins them in the sitting room to relate Conklin's cockup.

"The mayor demoted him to Traffic Warden and put *me* in his place!"

"Thank goodness!" says Truman. "You'll do a wonderful job!"

"My only interest is to get you reinstated!"

"I'm not sure I want to be reinstated. Wildrose is changing beyond all reason!"

Daisy takes his hand. "You put in for your pension and have nothing more to do with that mayor!"

"Just hear me out," says Olive, moving her eyes from Daisy to Truman. "I'll never forget that you gave me my first job, deputizing me to help at the county fair. That's why I went into police work. My models are my late uncle and *you!*"

"Six thirty-five an hour, as I recall. Not much of a job!"

"I gained a lotta confidence, watching you calm down the crowd when that Black Angus bull broke loose at the cattle show. And the bunch of rowdies you faced down at the football game last year! Anyway, I want to ask you a couple'a big favors."

"Of course, Olive. Anything at all!"

"The first is that you don't do anything final about your pension, till you've had time to think it over."

Truman presses Daisy's hand. "I suppose there's no hurry. We won't be destitute."

"Thanks, Chief. The other favor is I'm gonna need some hands-on help."

"Whatever you want!"

"What I mean is, until we get past the craziness of the Turquoise Tower Grande Opening—and if you don't think it's an insult—I'd like to make you *my* deputy!"

-8-

EARLY ON SATURDAY THE MOLES deal the opposition another haymaker as its Wind Band Music Armada sails forth on an All Waterways Blowout.

To be exact, few of the participating vessels have actual *sails*, which are 10', 14', or 18' skiffs or runabouts, shoving off from family docks with Wind Band members aboard, kicking up a ballyhoo of duets, trios, quartets, and quintets—fed by the 700 years of classical, folk, religious, pop, and show biz tunes, from Gregorian Chant to neuronmelt, that form the Planet Earth Music Book. Other Band members perform on kayaks, catamarans, rafts, and shanty boats with banners waving:

SICK OF ROAD & WATERWAY NOISE?
TELL WILDROSE COUNCIL TO SHOVE
THE BYWAYS EXEMPTION!

Caught with its leather britches down, the Supreme Saddle scrambles the ICEE and SUV Collective, whose members swarm Wildrose like locusts. But they're unable to intimidate Pierre and the Wind Band into turning tail, given the media's high profile presence and the unflinching eyes of Acting Police Chief Olive Best and Deputy Vivian

Truman, backed up by a dozen other handpicked deputies from Lars's motorcycle buddies and rounded off with a couple of State Police Captain Adron Kroft's cruisers. Olive's and Truman's approval ratings are about 98% positive, so the protesters bite their tongues and ride with easy throttles and forced smiles.

Fuming in her office, Thaïs gets Billy Umbo on her ePendant and orders him to "Take off the Goddammed gloves!"

* * *

By early afternoon the Moles' musical armada has assailed every tributary and pond larger than a teaspoon, and disperses to prepare their next episode. The armada is the preamble to Sam's BRAND NEW IDEA, which he finally shared with the other moles. His target is August 9—the day of the Turquoise Tower Grande Opening Gala—and wanting to reconnoiter key points to launch it, Jenny suggests Condor Lookout.

They bicycle to Wildrose Forest, with Moonlight Knob louring 1,250 feet overhead. Decades earlier the poorly maintained gravel road leading up to it was shut down and blocked off with a post atop a pair of stone pillars. Sam and Jenny bike up a nearby logging road with Leah following in the VW, a road that winds its way up Condor Lookout, a tunnel of sumac, hickory, and monkey puzzle trees that form a Rip Van Winkle portal to the past.

Billy Umbo is tracking the VW on his ePalm and gives an order on his walkie-talkie.

"We oughta go berry picking here for one of your cobblers!" Sam says to Jenny.

Higher up, a stretch of gravel has been washed out by a vigorous stream where boulders sun themselves like napping armadillos, and Leah pokes her head out the VW's window.

"I'd better not risk it. I'll wait for you down here!"

She settles in the campstool to review the day's footage as her grandparents walk their bikes over the armadillo stepping stones and continue peddling up on their bikes. The road is steeper than Jenny recalls and it takes a while to reach the top, but they're in good shape and are breathing easily as they reach the one-acre patch of earth that forms Condor Lookout's peak, the highest point in the region.

"My Lord!" says Sam. "It *is* breathtaking!"

The Constable-like view of distant, bluish hilltops and All Souls College Chapel's glimmering spire four miles away takes hold of them, as a breeze brings the groaning of the Supreme Saddle's myrmidons exiting Wildrose on Chipmunk Run. Far below, the defunct trail up Moonlight Knob stares down onto Wildrose River, laden with tourists under the 90 billion-LED QuadBoard that startles eyes for miles around.

21 DAYS to the TURQUOISE TOWER GALA!
RESERVE YOUR TUGBOAT INN STATEROOM!

Sam and Jenny rub their startled eyes and return them to the College chapel.

"We better start back," Jenny says a minute or two later. "Before we doze off!"

Down at the washout, Leah hears Goldenhawk flying overhead, and is impressed that she and her pilot Charley are still on the story. Leah logs on to say hi, and downloads the copter's bellycam view of the Forest as Goldenhawk regales her 14 million fans.

"The frenzy seems to be over! And the Ashlars—who began all of this with their splashy Water Music—left some minutes ago."

Then Goldenhawk's bellycam focuses on a pair of gleaming helmets that peel off from the ICEE herd and disappear beneath a canopy of trees leading up Condor Lookout by another logging road.

That instant is enough for Leah to see the black thunderbolts, and her heart jumps with a premonition. She hops from the VW and shouts.

"Grandma! Grandpa!"

She beeps the horn, but the sound is thrown back by the stiff breeze from Condor Lookout. She alerts Goldenhawk, then grabs her camera and a tire tool, and skips over the stony stream and dashes for all she's worth up the gravel road.

Sam and Jenny are descending Condor Lookout's summit when they hear the two motorcycles, and Sam tries peering among the dense foliage on the Lookout's slopes.

"I guess somebody else wants some fresh air!"

A short way down the gravel road they come head-on to a dead tree barring their way that wasn't there when they ascended the road, and they slam on their brakes as two men emerge from the brush. One of them is tall and thin and the other one is strongly built, and they're masked with bandanas.

"Well!" says the taller one.

The two men seem to be a cliché, but the Ashlars' hearts begin to pound. The tree that's blocking the road has been dead for years and Sam snaps off a six-foot limb.

"Lookee there!" says the taller man, in an oily voice that makes him even more of a cliché.

"What do you want?" says Sam.

"Only to have some fun," the man says, who Sam thinks of as "Oily."

"Don't be foolish. You can leave right now and it's all over."

"We'll leave when we're damn well ready!" says the beefy one.

They start for the Ashlars and Jenny screams. "Help, somebody! *Help!*"

"Let us be!" Sam shouts, threatening with the jagged end of the limb.

Oily circles toward Jenny while the hefty one—"Meat," as Sam considers him—starts forward. He flicks open a knife, large enough to butcher a steer.

"Wanna play rough?"

Oily grabs Jenny, who struggles as he shoves a hand over her mouth while Sam starts over.

"Let her go!"

Meat is coming with the knife as Jenny kicks Oily's shin and gets a hand free to scratch at his eyes. He grabs her wrist, but his bandana slips down.

"Ya done it now, ya stupid bitch!"

Meat stops in his tracks. "Cain't ya handle an old woman!?"

Sam knows he's out of time, and pulls out his wallet and throws it, thumping Meat in the chest.

"It's all yours!"

Meat bends down for it and Sam lunges, piercing the bandana with the limb's jagged end. Meat yelps and drops the knife as Sam shoves with all of his might. Oily is frozen in place and clings to Jenny as Meat tumbles backward onto the ground with the limb impaling his cheek.

Sam shouts at Oily to let Jenny go, but Oily stares wildly and pulls her farther away. A searing pain shoots up Sam's spine and his back spasms as the tree limb pulls free of Meat.

Christ! Sam thinks. He tries to move, and against the crushing pain drags himself closer to Oily. "I said let her go!"

"*You'd better let her go!*"

It's Leah, dashing up the road and wielding the tire tool with her camera aimed at Oily.

Sam's in agony and sweat pours from his face as Meat thrashes about the rotting leaves in search of the knife. Things move so fast that only Leah seems aware of Goldenhawk—drawn by the video that's streaming from Leah's camera.

Meat gives up on the knife and staggers to his feet. "I'm gonna tear ya to bits!"

A siren wails in the distance and Leah turns the camera on Meat's bleeding face.

"Oh yeah? But first I think you oughta say hello to your *audience*, which numbers about 14 million. If you were around earlier you'd have seen the news chopper, which is streaming this!"

Oily and Meat crank their heads at the sky and Meat sputters. "You're a fuckin liar!"

He puts a hand to his face to stanch the flow of blood while Sam keeps him at bay with the limb.

"*Somebody's* comin!" says Oily, looking frantically through the treetops.

"Maybe it's an ambulance," says Leah, "to collect your battered hides. Or the *cops*, to batter them some more!"

Oily suddenly releases Jenny and fumbles with his bandana as Leah runs to Sam and picks up a stone the size of a baseball.

Leah laughs at Oily. "It's too late, amigo. You're getting your closeup, and I've got great footage of your pea-brain partner. And when I said you had 14 million viewers, I meant *right now!*"

She flips the monitor and Oily sees his own panicked face as Goldenhawk blares over the speaker, "That's one of the men on Condor Lookout!"

Billy Umbo is watching helplessly on his ePalm from his spymobile at the edge of the Forest because Meat's walkie-talkie was smashed in the tussle.

Thaïs is watching from her office and digs a fingernail into her beauty mark as Leah scoffs at Oily and Meat.

"It's you're lucky day! Those sirens *are* the police!"

Jenny threatens with the stone, and Sam struggles against the pain while edging closer to Oily.

"From the sound of things I'd say you've got about 90 seconds to make a try for me—if you want a sinkhole in your face like your friend has. Or you can use those 90 seconds to get the hell outta here!"

Then another vehicle joins the fray. It's Conklin's six-wheeled military DUKW—"Ducky"—obtained by his father when he mustered out of the National Guard 19 years earlier. Conklin was in Wildrose Forest when the alert came on his two-way radio, and is joining up in an effort to reclaim some of the face he'd lost in his swift fall from Police Chief to Traffic Warden. He mostly uses Ducky for illegal trapping, and a tarp over its large hold conceals his animal traps and well-thumbed collection of *Benthouse* and *Raunchy Ranch* magazines.

All of this bounces about in Ducky's hold as Conklin jounces down a deer path that follows Condor Lookout's southern slope, figuring it might be the assailants' escape route. He slaps his hip to make sure he's brought along his .45, then bucked up by the feel of cold steel in warm leather, he shouts "Charge!" as Ducky rips through the underbrush.

Leah sees that Oily and Meat need another nudge and waves the tire tool.

"I'm a strict vegetarian, but this guy just can't get enough meat! Which of you is first?"

She closes in on Oily and Meat as Sam thrusts out the limb and Jenny takes aim with the stone.

Then Goldenhawk tells her fans it's time for a "pimple-popping close-up" as Charley puts the chopper into a stomach-purging dive.

"God!" says Umbo, and Thaïs yells, "Bloody hell!"

Oily and Meat swivel their heads like gimbaled ship lanterns in a typhoon, and they suddenly realize that—judging from the sirens—the police are but a coon's fart away.

In the final moment before touching ground, the chopper blots out the sun as the beating rotors whip up a maelstrom of rotten leaves and gravel dust, blinding one and all. Oily and Meat do an about-face and feel their way into the dense underbrush behind them, then head likely-split down Condor Lookout's heavily wooded southern slope.

The Ashlars cough and cover their mouths, then Goldenhawk's engine shuts down and the rotors gradually come to a stop. Moments tick by as the police sirens grow louder, and two vehicles finally pull to a stop amid the swirling dust, with Truman and Olive in the first one, and Captain Kroft right behind them.

PART FOUR

-1-

LEAH RETRIEVES THE WALLET FOR SAM, who is consoling Jenny with a hug, then Leah fills in Truman, Olive, and Captain Kroft about the attack. She adds that her VW is at the washout on the southwestern logging road and jingles her keyring.

"If they find it, they won't get very far!"

Kroft radios this to his other cruisers and orders a helicopter and canine unit to begin searching the thousands of acres that comprise Condor Lookout's slopes.

Olive helps the Ashlars into the cruiser and drives them to the Happy Family Clinic. Then Truman and Kroft begin scouting the area just below Condor Lookout's summit and find the Ashlars' bicycles and the dead tree, then focus on the trampled shrubs where Oily and Meat ran off.

Conklin meanwhile meanders down the deer trail in Ducky, a route he can do with one eye shut from years of setting traps. Ducky mashes some baby firs by the gravel road that Sam and Jenny had bicycled up 18 minutes earlier, and farther down Conklin sees a large, blue object beyond some ferns and stops Ducky to hike down for a closer look.

It's Leah's VW, and he decides to avenge the bloody nose she gave him with her camera lens hood by letting the air from her tires. Then his heart leaps at the sound of panicked voices.

"It's the misfeasors!" he gasps.

Feeling he may need more firepower, he gets his pa's double-barrel shotgun from Ducky. He sees a muscular man slouched against the VW with a bloodied bandana tied to his face, and another man poking around below the steering wheel, who whines out loud, "This foreign wirin's got me all confused!"

Conklin lowers the shotgun. "You cheese heads! My mum's ol' rooster could do better'n that!"

The men jump as though they'd been goosed with tent-poles, then Conklin appears from behind the ferns and they recognize their illicit pelt-trade accomplice.

"Hot damn!" says Oily.

"Fwank Gwad!" says Meat, pressing a hand to his blood-soaked bandana.

Conklin knows straight off he won't arrest them—as he's hoping for a lucrative autumn's trapping season with them—and fears they'd squeal on *him,* were Olive to put the screws on them with a 2nd or 3rd degree grilling. No. What he must do is use his good luck as a bargaining chip for a larger share of the fur-trading profits.

"I suppose ya put yer grimy mitts all over this thang! Well, there ain't much time, so pay attention!"

They follow his lead and use their shirttails to wipe off every inch of the VW they might've touched, then break off some ferns to sweep away their footprints.

"Now. I wan'cha to wade downstream a couple hunert yards to that boulder that's shaped like a huge buckeye."

"Then wut?" says Oily, the official spokesman for Oily Meat Ltd.

"Jis wait *in the crick* till I git there!"

They do as his says, sloshing thigh deep in the current that rushes down from Condor Lookout. They slip and slide on algae as slick as cellphone contracts and soak themselves to the waist, and are shivering among the tadpoles by the buckeye-shaped boulder when Conklin arrives in Ducky and backs her up to the stream.

"This water's colt as hell!" says Oily, and Meat croaks something that neither Oily nor Conklin can make out.

Conklin scowls. "Hell ain't colt, ya gizzard head. It's hotter'n hell, and that's where you'll be if ya don't do as I say!"

He removes Ducky's tarp and hastens about the hold to rearrange the spotlights and girly magazines.

"Now git in!"

"Ya want us in *there!?"* says Oily.

Meat starts to protest and spits out a broken tooth. Then a black-and-white copter soars overhead and Conklin hisses.

"It's the state *po*leece!"

Oily and Meat scramble into the hold and Conklin ties off the tarp above them, then climbs behind the wheel and shouts over his shoulder.

"I might run into Olive Best, so stay quieter 'n slabs of ice. *Frozen* slabs of ice. And keep yer muddy guppies off my magazines!"

-2-

OLIVE LEAVES THE ASHLARS in the care of the Happy Family Clinic staff and returns to Condor Lookout to assist Truman.

A nurse attends to Jenny's bruised wrists, and Sam gets a CT scan, which shows his inflamed sacral vertebrae. He's injected with painkiller and anti-inflammatory juice, then Giles drives the Ashlars to Mole End. They settle in the Adirondack chairs where Jenny soothes her rattled nerves with iced tea and rum. Leah dives into a cold root beer, and Sam—denied the solace of alcohol at doctor's orders—joins her. His and Jenny's son and daughter are among Golden-hawk's 23 million fans and phone to say they're flying out, but are dissuaded by Sam, who assures them that he and Jenny will be okay.

When Olive arrives at Condor Lookout, Truman says the canine unit has traced the assailants' trail as far as the VW at the washout, where their scent ends.

"They apparently tried clearing their footprints with some ferns, and the dogs are still trying to locate where and if they got *out* of the stream."

"Any fingerprints?"

Captain Kroft shakes his head. "Not yet, but there's no end of tire tracks throughout the Forest, where quads and pickup trucks run amuck thicker than wood ticks. And Lieut. Conklin apparently left some tracks with that army DUKW."

Truman says Conklin's in the doghouse at the moment, and he himself is a deputy under Olive's authority. It hadn't passed by Kroft that Truman was wearing civvies and a different badge.

Truman turns to Olive. "Conklin radioed that he just searched some of the stream and didn't find anything. He sees himself as Daniel Boone as much as Sylvester Stallone, and he knows these woods pretty well."

Olive finds the switchblade, and Truman comes across some footprints and beckons to Kroft. "Would your team mind making a cast of these? I especially want *this* one."

He indicates a particularly wide footprint, then the three of them look over the assailants' motorcycles, one of which is a dead ringer for the chrome model that weeks earlier harassed Orchard Lane with its herd of Midnight Thunder bikers. They pull on latex gloves and open the panniers, finding beef jerky, beer cans, and Twinkies. The broken walkie-talkie is lying nearby, where Sam felled Meat with a thrust of the tree limb.

"You don't see these much anymore!" says Kroft.

"Construction crews and surveyors use them," says Truman. "And pennyante crooks!"

* * *

Goldenhawk's streaming of the attack has inquisitive motorists thronging Orchard Lane for a rubberneck at Mole End, and Lars threads his way through this gruel on his motorcycle with a gallon of hard cider.

"To heck with doctor's orders!" says Sam, accepting a mug full.

Then Thaïs comes in the Duesenberg with a vase of her yellow hothouse gladiolas. It's her first visit to Mole End since Moleen's advent and she's stopped pointblank by her Delphic gaze. Few creatures are so tall that Thaïs must look up at them, and it puts her on edge.

"What am I gonna do with you?" Thaïs murmurs.

Then realizing that the Ashlars and their guests are watching, she tears herself from Moleen's spell and goes to the back porch to present Jenny with the gladiolas.

"Let me say how shocked I am by this outrage against the three of you!"

Sam starts to offer his chair and gets a karate chop in the spine. "We appreciate your stopping by."

"Thank you, Sam. I promise to use the full powers of my office to track down these vermin!"

"I don't think they acted alone," says Lars.

"Nor I," says Giles. "As stupid as it was, someone with actual brains must've put them up to it. It smells of something worse than just a mugging gone haywire!"

"Regardless," says Thaïs. "I've instructed Olive and her deputies to make certain there are no further excesses by partisans on either side of the noise issue—if indeed these men are partisans. They might be just madmen!"

And with that she departs.

-3-

CAPTAIN KROFT DRIVES OFF TO ASSIST his officers on Condor Lookout's lower slopes while Truman and Olive continue down the deer trail.

The police copter is still maneuvering here and there above the tree line, but the woods are silent, and a few hundred yards farther down the slope Olive makes out fresh wheel tracks—most likely from Conklin's DUKW, she says to Truman. Some baby firs have been mauled where the trail's wide enough for Conklin to have avoided them, and Olive's aghast at his disregard for wildlife.

Then Truman sees something glistening on a cloverleaf, which smells of oil.

"Conklin radioed that he'd left his DUKW to look around, and this must be where he stopped."

They check the area, and sure enough they find more mashed ferns. Olive snaps them with her cellphone, and Truman marks the spot with a pyramid of stones from the stream.

Then they follow Conklin's footprints down to the washout. It's roped off by yellow tape and Kroft's forensics team is still processing the VW. They have nothing new to add, and Truman asks if he can get the VW back to Leah later that day.

One of the officers wipes his brow. "Absolutely. As soon as the captain signs off on it." He motions at the washout, frothing with whirlpools. "Our canine unit found some boulders *below* here with the moss scraped off, so we know those two jerks must have gone quite a ways downstream!"

Truman and Olive return to the stone pyramid and follow the DUKW's tire tracks farther down the deer trail and make a curious discovery. The tracks continue downhill from there, but a similar set of tracks veer off and come *up*hill—like the left arm of a Y—ending beside the stream by a large, nut-shaped boulder.

"The canine team would've come by here," says Truman. "And since they didn't find the two men's scent, they must have left the stream *below* here."

Olive finds a dark stain on a twig.

"It's oil!"

They examine the Y's arms and trunk, and it's evident that all of the tracks were almost certainly made by Conklin's DUKW.

"It looks like the diverging tracks are because he stopped his DUKW a *second* time on the way down the hill," she says, "then backed up to the stream by the boulder."

"Do you suppose he saw something on the way down and came back for a closer look?"

"But once he reversed the DUKW up to here, why *back* into the stream, instead of pulling *forward* to it? That would've been easier and safer!"

-4-

CONKLIN TAKES DUCKY TO ORVIS ALLEY, Wildrose's tarpaper enclave, and stops at a two-acre scab of land where the alley dead-ends.

It's the Conklin estate, and he opens a rickety wooden gate that drags like a drunken man in the chalky soil. He gets Ducky through, scrapes the gate back to its hitching post, and drives past a hardscrabble shanty to a browbeaten henhouse. It's hugged by a chicken-wire pen, where some Road Island Reds and their henpecked rooster are pecking at the corn that was scattered there when Conklin's mum fed them earlier on.

Conklin hops down from Ducky and surveys the premises. Smoke escapes a stovepipe above the shanty's kitchen, assuring him that his mum is cooking his supper of cornpone-fried chicken, broiled chicken, chicken wings, chicken cacciatore, chicken stew, chicken noodle soup, chicken 'n dumplings, chicken potpie, chicken 'n gravy on biscuits, chicken fingers, or his favorite, chicken croquet.

It's also a signal that Mum's made her final henhouse visit of the day and whacked the head from the chicken who was too lazy to escape—freeing Conklin to carry out the scheme he's been hatching on the way home with his Ducky load of devilment.

The homestead is hedged on all sides with thorny locust trees that make trespassing an act of self-immolation, assuring Conklin of privacy. And the kitchen window where his mum is alchemizing his supper is sooted over, as it hasn't been washed since she went into mourning 16 years ago, when Conklin's pa failed to return from a spelunking trip down their cistern. So his mum can't see him either.

Conklin unties Ducky's tarp. Oily and Meat are crouching in the hold and blink in the sunlight, and he's relieved to see that his girlie magazines are untouched by their grimy paws—especially the treasured ones with foldout body parts.

"Took ya long enough!" says Oily, scowling at the grim surroundings.

"Damwite!" says Meat, wincing from his cheek that's swollen like a cherry muffin.

"Would ya ruther I'd left ya to the bloodhounds?!" says Conklin.

They drop their eyes and follow him into the henhouse, covering their mouths from the odor of chicken piddle.

"I know it's dampish in here, but you're already soaked to the gills and will git used to it. Till I can fig'er out how to git ya outta the county."

They stare uncomfortably and Conklin pokes his toe at the ground.

"You kin stretch out on the straw—and there *is* straw down there, som'ers—as the hens have their places above."

Some hens are already roosting and cluck craftily under their flopping combs, fixing their beady eyes on Oily and Meat as though they were sacks of cornmeal.

Conklin opens the door. "I'll bring ya some grub before I leave for my policing shift."

He goes to the shanty's kitchen and finds mum, a portly woman in a feed sack dress and gumboots, hardly taller than the coal stove where she's stirring a mess of something in a skillet. She's ghostly white with flour, as though as a last resort she might throw *herself* in the skillet. She sucks on a cigar, rolled from the tobacco plants she nurtures in the chicken-pen soil.

"Supper's well-nigh done. A spankin new recipe!"

Conklin gropes his way through the gritty atmosphere. "Wut is it, Mum? Ya have me on tender forks!"

She exhales a stormfront of cigar smoke. "You jis wait, Reevas F. Conklin!"

His nostrils quiver at the odor of fried fat, singed bread, cremated chicken, and homegrown tobacco that fog the kitchen like a Los Angeles intersection. A four-slotted toaster *zumps* and a quartet of crusty things that began life as slices of bread leap to their freedom.

"Medium well!" says Mum, snaring the slices with a floury paw and tossing them onto a tin plate. "Jis the way ya like 'em!"

She ladles on chicken gravy—submerging them like a shipwreck—pours on Tabasco sauce, and folds this enticing dish in a brown-paper bag that bears the creases and stains of long service.

"It's chicken gravy on *toast*, instead'a biscuits! A double servin for a hardworkin lewdtenant of the law!"

Conklin rubs his hands. "That's choice! As choice as choice can be! And Mum, would ya mind whippin up another servin? I want the Chief to enjoy som'a yer fine cookin!"

"That so-called boss of yurn? Chief Trudeman?!"

"The mayor fired 'im, though I reckon he'll worm hisself back in. So if I treat 'im nice he might look closer at my abilities!"

She gives a hazy cigar blast. "Alrighty!"

In no time she vulcanizes two more slices of toast, shipwrecks them in chicken gravy and slathers on Tabasco sauce. He starts out the door with the two bags of victuals and hears the hens cackling.

"Oh, Mum. Yer always workin so hard to cook for me 'n sponge off my uniform and all, it's time *I* took over collectin the aggs and bringin our daily hen to the choppin block. The next few days you're gonna have a *va*cation, and won't hav'ta go anywheres *near* that ol' henhouse!"

-5-

AS OLIVE AND TRUMAN LEAVE THE forest, Captain Kroft radios that several Goldenhawk fans have recognized the assailants as Jimbo Tavener and Brick Hakker—owner-operators of Tread On Us Retreads on the Sky Vue Freeway.

"I'm heading there now, and just phoned their part-timer, who said they left this morning on their motorcycles and haven't returned."

Truman agrees to join Kroft and arrives as an officer brings a search warrant. They peer into the concrete-block garage, where the part-timer is fitting an UpChuks truck with tires, then look into the office with its decades-old calendar that features a gaudily-colored Miss Retreads and her 49-inch Goodriches. A desk is blackened from unwashed hands and burdened with a dump-truck load of unfiled paperwork.

They find nothing of interest, then enter the dusky Quonset hut and brave its rows of reconstituted roadwear to Hakker's and Tavener's private den. A wall switch awakens a florescent bulb at the domed ceiling, disclosing a makeshift kitchen, bathroom, and party-guy bedroom. Soiled clothes and empty Chinese food takeout cartons form a range of foothills, whose valleys are cluttered with discarded ice cream cartons. Then they find some papers above a wardrobe—the unsigned, computer-printed letters that were dropped overnight through the mail slot the last few months. There are also instructions for the walkie-talkie found at Condor Lookout.

"Well!" says Truman. "Maybe we can trace who they've been talking to!"

* * *

As Olive finishes her paperwork on the assault, Conklin arrives for his Traffic Warden shift and she asks him to cover the office a few minutes before his starts his rounds.

"If anyone asks about the attack, tell them the investigation's ongoing."

"Righty ho," he says, belching Tabasco sauce.

Knowing she must work with him until she can get Truman back as Chief, she extends an olive branch by thanking him for having brought his DUKW to bear on the incident in Wildrose Forest.

Then she strolls around the Village Commons to ease a charley horse she's gotten from sitting too long. She's furious that the men haven't been caught, but the law's slogging on and she's confident of success. For one thing, the cast made by the state police lab matches *exactly* the one Truman made of Widefoot's boot print that was found in the Mole End frontyard a few weeks earlier, when the two men tried to coat Moleen with tar. Better still is the Condor Lookout videos shot by Leah and Goldenhawk, and the evidence of the switchblade, walkie-talkie, and the two motorcycles with their gobs of fingerprints and DNA. The videos were shared with law enforcement networks, and the Arkansas State Police confirmed the men as Brick Hakker and Jimbo Tavener, good old Arkansas boys with petty crime rap sheets who vanished a few years ago.

Olive thinks of them as the Ashlars did—Oily and Meat—and takes a turn past the stable behind the Village Hall. It lost its doors in the misty past, when it was requisitioned to provide parking for the Village Hall employees, and Olive notices the DUKW, parked by the adjacent shrubbery. Although she knows the two men might still be in Wildrose Forest, she doubts it, as the police dogs sniffed every walnut hull and woolly worm without finding their unwholesome scent, and found no further footprints, Widefoot or otherwise.

She notices some fresh algae on the DUKW's stern and takes a photo of it. The DUKW is on Village property and she sees no harm in scraping off some algae with her pocketknife. Then she sees a drop of oil fall from the towing winch.

-6-

DURING CONKLIN'S DINNER BREAK HE wolfs down the chicken 'n gravy on toast, then phones a medical associate of his with ties to the fashion industry, and when his shift ends Conklin says "Good nighty!" to Olive and slinks out.

He guides Ducky over a backroad to Wildrose's trailer district and through a log archway with a floodlighted sign, TRADE WIND COURT. He pulls up to a double-wide trailer marked with silver reflective-tape letters, FURRIER FASHIONS WORLDWIDE.

He flashes his lights and a figure emerges from the trailer and climbs aboard. Although it's a warm evening, the figure—Frederick Libretti—wears sunglasses and a squirrel-skin duster with signature split tail, a groundhog fur cowboy hat, deerskin slacks, and beaver-hide boots with two-inch Elkhorn heels. He coddles a pigskin bag in his lap.

"Thanks for comin on such short notice," says Conklin. "This'll make us even-steven!"

Libretti owes Conklin on a muskrat-pelt deal and says he's glad to hear it, then Conklin takes a screwball route to Orvis Alley to shake off anyone who might be on his tail (a trick he learned from TV detective show reruns), and after the ritual opening and closing of the laggard gate to reach the family turf, he pulls up by the henhouse, crouching in the gloom.

"Oops! I shoulda give 'em a *lantern!*"

He gets a couple of flashlights from Ducky and they enter the henhouse as the chickens squawk and fill the air with pin feathers, their rheumy eyes glowing like embers suddenly woken by a bellows that can't tell time. The odor is as gag-me-with-a-pitchfork as ever, but Libretti was a defrocked veterinarian after he was a defrocked podiatrist—his footstool to the MD trade—and is used to fetid smells.

He sees two gunnysacks on the ground—supplied by Conklin when he brought the chicken 'n gravy on toast, and curled beneath them are Oily and Meat, well known to Libretti as Jimbo Tavener and Brick Hakker.

Conklin nudges the gunnysacks with his boot. "Hey! I brung the doctor!"

Oily jerks awake and Meat cranks himself to his feet with a groan as Libretti shines the flashlight.

"Open your mouth." Meat complies. "Wider!"

Meat opens up with his cheek on fire as Libretti explores with his flashlight, then looks for a clean spot to set down his bag.

"Apart from the wound in your cheek, you've got a gaping hole from a recent absentee molar and a busted incisor. And your tongue's punctuated. If it gets infected I'll hav'ta amputate."

Meat recoils in fright, banging his head against the slanting tin roof.

"Should I boil some water?" says Conklin. "Or git clean towels?"

Libretti furrows his brow. "What for?"

"Well, that's wut they always do on the TV, when someone's havin a baby or been shot up. They git hot water and clean towels. Or they tear up a petticoat."

Libretti hangs his hat on a nail. "If you wanna boil some water, I could do with a cup of coffee. And I guess you can bring the petticoat, just for the hell of it."

Mum's gone to the shanty's front room to enjoy a few hours of *Beat Yer Clits* on the TV, so Conklin has the run of the kitchen to make coffee, which he more or less does, then returns to the henhouse with the pot, three mugs, and one of Mum's old undergarments he found among the dish-rags.

Libretti spreads this wonderment on the straw and sets the pigskin bag on it, while Conklin pours the sorta coffee for Libretti, Oily, and himself. They raise their mugs to Meat.

"To the patient!"

They down the coffee, then Libretti opens his bag and selects an instrument.

"Stiff upper lip!" he says to Meat, more observation than encouragement.

The instrument is the offspring of a scalpel and a machete, and he scrapes off the encrustation of blood while Meat whimpers. Then Libretti selects a needle used in his current profession as custom leatherwear-maker-taxidermist and threads it with 18 inches of size XXXX catgut, donated by the subject of a recent commission.

Meat is shaking like a three-legged washing machine on spin, and Libretti tells Conklin and Oily to hold him still.

"If he moves, I might accidentally sew his cheek to his tongue. Or to his tonsils."

They take a hold of Meat, who shrieks something Libretti can't make out, and Oily makes a stab at translating.

"Somethin 'bout pain."

Conklin shakes his head. "Somethin 'bout swabbin off the needle."

Meat squeals another incoherent demand and Oily says, "*Anti* somethin or ruther."

"Anti*freeze!*" says Conklin. "He wants some antifreeze!"

"It ain't colt in here," says Oily. "Maybe he means anti-*perspirant!*"

"Nonsense," says Libretti. "He smells worse'n the Village dump, and it'd take a shipload of antiperspirant to—"

Meat makes a final effort, firing off some grotesquely wrought syllables directly into Oily's ear—who slaps his thigh.

"I got it! He wants ya to use an *antibiological*, so he don't catch no violent disease!"

"Likker!" says Conklin. "That's wut they always use!"

He runs to the shanty for a pint of 197 proof *Fourteen Acres* bourbon left by his absentee pa, which according to the label was distilled "somewheres in northeastern Kentucky."

Libretti breaks the seal and pulls the cork, getting a sharp report as an outgushing essence assails his nostrils. His irises shrink to singularities far smaller than anything theorized by Stephen Hawking, and he hears singing, probably the Mormon Tabernacle Choir.

"This'll do!" he croaks.

Finding that he can move without using his legs, he floats across the henhouse to his mug and fills it with *Fourteen Acres.* Unleashed in quantity, it rids the henhouse of chicken poo odor and replaces it with what might be the musky aroma of a grand vizier's seraglio after a decade of foreplay with his harem. Libretti ascends to the topmost barracks of

Rhode Island Reds, and amid their cackling he throws back his head and swallows the magical draft.

"Beatrice!" he cries.

He's wrapped in a transcendent womb, and from his perch watches himself grasp the needle and stitch up the wound in Meat's throbbing cheek.

-7-

THE DAY AFTER THE CONDOR LOOKOUT assault the Ashlars meet Pierre and Marie Pasquin at the All Souls College and follow them to a concrete-block room where science lab supplies are stored. The Pasquins have rounded up some students, and over the next few hours they and the Ashlars inventory the hundreds of fireworks—the Aerial Reverberaters, Flying Pythons, Sky Bombs, Mammoth Mandrakes, and Triple Goblin Terrors.

Olive meantime joins Truman on his back porch swing at Old Farm Ridge, and he says he doubts they have enough evidence to search Conklin's homestead.

"But the lab showed that the oil we found in the Forest and Conklin's DUKW are i*den*tical," she says. "As was the algae on the DUKW!"

The porch swing creaks as they follow the pranks of a covey of bobwhites in the meadow beyond them, then comes to a standstill as Truman sets his grey eyes on Olive.

"I guess it can't hurt to poke around a little. But your hands are full, Olive. Leave it to me!"

That night he pulls up in the service lane behind Orvis Alley and explores the briars and thorn trees barricading it from Conklin's homestead, and finds a gap a foot or so overhead. He has two of Daisy's hand mirrors that serve as a periscope and he sees Conklin's mum, her floury shape a phantom in the starlight as she pushes a wheelbarrow to the henhouse. She kicks the door with her gumboot and is answered by a burst of cackling. Lantern light etches her shadow on the ground as she enters with the wheelbarrow and shuts the door—and her shadow emerges soon afterward, the wheelbarrow heaped with something beneath a gunnysack that sinks its tire deep into the soil.

-8-

THE JUDGE IN FOLKSTON LANDING responds to Lars's Revised Noise Ordinance lawsuit by tossing out the Wildrose Council's Byways Exemption—leaving the rest of the Ordinance intact.

Thaïs counterattacks by ordering another Special Council Meeting for the following evening, Tuesday, July 22. Snippets race among the councilmembers like carrier pigeons on caffeine over what stance they should take. The pressure is fierce as ICEE, the Truckers' Guild, and Gatling Gun Reenactors storm Wildrose to make sure the locals don't forget them.

An hour before the Special Meeting the Council Chamber is as glutted as a cattle drive in a minicab, where Olive's laid on security with a forklift truck. The opposing camps are growing increasingly vociferous and deploy on opposite sides of the Gallery as the councilmembers elbow their way in to claim their seats.

Then the Hall's belfry clock heralds the hour and the crowd gasps as Duffy comes from the door atop the aisle bearing the Yewwood Ark of the Gavel, then Thaïs follows in Charlemagne purple among cries of wonder as she bestows fingertip greetings while descending the aisle.

"Welcome, my dear, dear friends! Welcome!"

Before you can say Bu!, Buford is on his feet, hurrahing like an evangelist in heat, and Tabitha is upstanding and uttering something like, "Oh, yes! Oh, yes!"

The media's eCams swing to Lars, lounging in his chair with arms folded. Then Thaïs passes by Cecil's wife Mabel, who's not applauding; nor are Cecil's sons, seated with their many Wind Band buddies who'd fought for a seat in the Gallery. They're looking with pride at Cecil, sitting anxiously in his chair.

The eCams pan to Wanda, who's on her feet and applauding, but her heart's not in it. The eCams linger on her until Olive opens the railing door for Thaïs, whose eyes bore into the councilmembers as she sits on her tapestried throne.

Duffy pipes up. "This special meeting has been called to consider the Third District Judge's stoppage of Wildrose's Revised Noise Ordinance *Byways Exemption*. There being a quorum, we're ready to proceed."

Thaïs accepts the gavel from Duffy and whacks the lignan vitae block. "We're pleased to welcome comments from the public."

The elderly woman with the parasol grasps the railing and implores the Council to appeal the judge's ruling. "The sooner the better!" and her neighbor with the tortoiseshell specs is right after her.

"What bunkum! We have a chance to reaffirm Wildrose's tradition of respect and good manners by supporting the Revised Noise Ordinance—without that wretched Byways Exemption!"

Twenty minutes later Duffy's fingers are breaking the speed limit on her Stenograph writer as Sam hobbles to the railing on a willow cane Leah carved for him.

"Your Honor. Let's not forget that the wisest laws need time to find their feet. Think of Dodge City with its 19 saloons, when its Sheriff Wyatt Earp banned six shooters. He was advised by some of the townsfolk to surrender his ideals, but as the weeks went by Dodge City became safer, more prosperous, and more civilized. We must be patient!"

The moleites cheer, and others take to the railing to harangue pro or con, but after another 45 minutes no one else comes forward, and Thaïs leans forward on her throne.

"Our esteemed councilmembers will now air their several views."

Lars says Sam is right, the Revised Noise Ordinance is good legislation and needs time to make its way. "There are no perfect laws, but there are perfect fools who expect there to be. Let us be wise in our glowing evolution!"

Hearty applause and calls of elation pelt the Chamber. "Well put!" and "Lars for mayor!"

Then Buford pulls himself up and demands that they forget all about the Noise Ordinance. "Neither the feds nor the state require us to have one!" Puzzled murmurs sweep the Chamber, but he turns up his nose at them. "I move that we strike down the Revised Noise Ordinance *altogether!*"

The Gallery convulses, until Olive steps forward to quash it, and Thaïs lowers her eyes at the councilmembers.

"There's a motion on the floor. Do I have a second?"

"I second!" says Tabitha.

"The motion is seconded and open to public comment."

Giles beats everyone to the railing and warns that without the Noise Ordinance Wildrose would sink into anarchy, and Sol says striking it from the books would be the best thing since sliced butter. Pierre and Marie Pasquin plead that abandoning the Ordinance would put the final nail in the coffin of the College Wind Band concerts, and after a dozen others have their say, Thaïs calls the comments to an end.

"The Council will now repair to the Conference Room to—"

Lars springs up. "Your Honor. I move that due to the unparalleled interest in this matter that we hold our discussion *and* our vote here in the Chamber, in full view of the press and public!"

A spark shoots from Thaïs's eyes. "A generous sentiment, councilman. But the vote will be taken by rollcall, and the comments and vote duly reported in the *Wildrose Voyeur* by our ever-reliable Duffy Nicklebob."

"That's more than fair!" says Buford.

Sam strikes the floor with his cane. "Horseshit!"

The Chamber heaves in amazement, and for once in 44 years Thaïs is speechless.

After a moment Lars laughs. "I agree, Your Honor. Horseshit! Our citizens want to observe *firsthand* the twists and turns of our deliberations. The backroom maneuvering, if you will, rather than rely on a report on the Village website." He takes his carnation to Duffy. "With no disparagement meant to our respected Clerk."

Cecil's fist resounds on the oak writing surface. "Councilman Andersen is right! These people wanna see not only our destination, but the jalopy we ride in!"

The Chamber goes wild and Thaïs jibs.

"I can of course order that the deliberations be held in this Chamber, but I prefer the more democratic route of a vote on the issue." She peers at the councilmembers. "All in favor of holding the discussion and vote *in this chamber* on the motion to revoke the Revised Noise Ordinance raise your hands." All of the councilmembers do so. "The motion's carried and the floor's open for discussion!"

None of the councilmembers can stomach further words, and Lars moves for a vote.

"I second!" says Cecil.

The vote is unanimous in favor of Lars' motion, and Thaïs eases back in her tapestried throne. "Very well. Let's have the rollcall."

Duffy goes to the tally board. "Ward Number One. Councilwoman Middlemarsh."

Wanda rises and is struck by the many eyes on her. She's suddenly lightheaded and steadies herself against the oak writing surface. She dares not look at Lars, whose moral leadership is unshakable, or at Silt, who's desperate to clinch their financial security by accepting B&B bookings from the Supreme Saddle supporters.

But Thaïs's black eyes are laser beams and Wanda struggles for air as Duffy rises from her stool. "Councilwoman?"

Wanda fumbles for her water bottle. "My throat's a little dry…"

"Please calm yourself," says Thaïs. "We'll return to you directly."

Wanda sinks in her seat and Duffy calls Ward Number Two, Councilman Whitlow.

The Gallery turns to Buford—a dwindling few of whom are his clients. But the only eyes he feels are Billy Umbo's.

"I vote yes!"

Duffy slides his slate to the Yes column. "Ward Number Three. Councilwoman Tannenbach."

Tabitha glances at Undine, who's painting her toenails. "I vote yes!"

Duffy moves her slate to the Yes column and calls Ward Number Four, Councilman Flinn.

Cecil melds eyes with Mabel and his boys. "I vote no!"

Duffy pushes his slate to the No column and the public bristles with tension. "Ward Number Five. Councilman Andersen."

Lars looks up at the American flag and says in his rich, bass-baritone timbre, "I vote *no!*"

"Lookit!" says the woman with the parasol as Duffy shoves his slate to the No column. "It's tied!"

Her boardinghouse neighbor says they aren't done voting, and Pru Plinkett screeches, "It's up to you, Wanda!"

Others call out and Olive steps forward, quelling further interruption as Thaïs turns to Wanda.

"How are you feeling, councilwoman?"

Wanda pulls herself to her feet. Her heart pounds and the Chamber starts to gyrate, then coalesces into a searing ball of light that shrinks until it could be the mouth of a tunnel—seen from the back of a train that's rushing full steam ahead into the black bowels of a mountain.

-9-

ONE HOUR LATER THE MEETING reconvenes. As everyone had run off to refresh themselves at the Green Goose Café, the corndog stand, or the ManShot Trolley, Duffy e-blasted them, and the Chamber is once again crammed more tightly than a discount airline cabin.

"I've just returned from the Happy Family Clinic," says Thaïs, "where the nature of Wanda's fit is uncertain. Meanwhile, we're obliged to finish the business on which we'd embarked when she was struck down."

Duffy touches a hanky to her eyes. "The vote on the motion to remove the Revised Noise Ordinance *in toto* is tied with two in favor and two opposed—and it's the mayor's sworn duty to decide the issue." She goes to the tally board. "Her Honor, Thaïs Mont-Obiston."

Thaïs rises like a flag on a battleship. "I vote yes!"

Duffy pushes Thaïs's slate to the Yes column.

"The motion carries, three in favor and two against. The Revised Noise Ordinance is struck from the books!"

Silence. Thick as nougat.

Then the Chamber explodes with e-flashings and shouting as Thaïs thunders. "The First and Second Readings will come at the regular meetings in August and September. This special session is adjourned!"

She slams down the gavel, smashing the lignum vitae block to bits.

* * *

The Ashlars are keeping Henna company, who's keeping an eye on her brothers in the Happy Family Clinic cafeteria, while Silt keeps an eye on Wanda in the Intensive Care Unit. An IV drip eases the effects of the stroke as she wakens from a fitful doze and blinks at her surroundings.

Silt takes her hand and explains what happened. "You're gonna be just fine!"

"Silt! I was having such a dream and—!"

"Try to rest!"

"But I've been so troubled... and did something I haven't told you about!"

"Henna found the mole jugs in your cabinet."

"Oh, Silt! I—"

He puts a hand to her cheek. "Wanda! Those jugs are beautiful!"

-10-

CONKLIN RUSHES HOME IN A GROWING panic over Oily and Meat, as Olive's nab-the-bad-guys aura is looming ever nearer.

He's been sprouting ideas all evening while scribbling parking tickets, and negotiates the gate as the tender shoot of the leading contender peeps from the thick clay of his brain. The idea is to fob off Oily and Meat onto Libretti, with oceans of room at his double-wide trailer in Trade Wind Court, among his racks of made-to-order leatherwear and stuffed-animals-in-progress.

This plantlet so dominates Conklin's skull that he's inside the henhouse before noticing that it's pitch dark, and he figures the lantern he lent Oily and Meat ran out of kerosene. He gets a flashlight from Ducky and is greeted by flapping and cackling, but nothing else, and he runs outside.

"Jimbo…? Brick…? Don't play no games, ya assholes!"

The wind snickers in the thorn trees, seeming to say that Oily and Meat have run off and are sure to get arrested and spill the beans. The whole 50-pound sack!

The wind shifts, bringing Mum's chuckle from the shanty, and Conklin realizes it's the hour of her favorite TV show, *Tweet Those Twits*. Then ribald laugher blows in—Oily's and Meat's!

He runs to the shanty and finds the kitchen door locked, and goes around and finds the front door also locked. He peers in the window and, between the flour-sack curtains, sees the glare of the TV on Mum's wrinkled grin as she slaps her stomach in hilarity in her oak-barrel armchair. Sitting on the beanbag sofa where *he* usually sprawls are Oily and Meat, rolling about with unbridled mirth.

He bangs on the door. "Mum! Open up!"

She's chuckling too hard to stir, so Oily drags himself up and lets Conklin in. It's a den of raillery with the TV showing some giant sloths on a Ferris wheel, which Conklin doesn't remotely comprehend.

"Mum! Wut the hell are ya—!"

"Hush!" she says, her eyes screwed to the TV.

Conklin appeals to Meat, who takes no notice, while trying to yuck-yuck without upsetting his thickly sutured cheek. Mum treated it with poultices of arnica distilled from her tobacco plants, and it's had a Lourdes-like recovery that brings Frankenstein's monster to mind.

Conklin unplugs the TV. "Wut are *they* doin here?"

Mum is wrenched from her spell. "Wut'da ya mean, 'Wut are *they* doin here?' I brung 'em in the wheelburl, that's wut! Imagine, leavin 'em pent up with my chickarees!"

"But the *po*leece is lookin for 'em!"

"Good Gwad, I knowed that already. If you'da ast me, I'da showed ya a much safer hidin place!"

"Ya would? Wut place?"

"You jis plug in the TV, Reevas F. Conklin, so's we kin watch the rest of the program. *Then* I'll show ya!"

He does as he's told and 50 minutes later—after *Tweet Those Twits* has calcified another 78 million brains around the planet—Mum turns off the TV, takes a blast-furnace draft on her cigar, and heaves herself to the pantry with the three men in her nicotine contrail. She pulls the string on a light bulb at the ceiling and plants her gumboots by a rug.

"Show 'im, boys!"

Oily and Meat roll up the rug and open the trapdoor below it. The light bulb sketches a deep and bulbous space—the very cistern into which Conklin senior vanished 16 years earlier. Lying on the stone floor among the crates of potatoes, apples, and rutabaga are Oily and Meat's gunny-sack bedrolls.

"Wut the hell!" says Conklin.

All those years ago the cistern had dried up, and Conklin senior found a crack near the bottom of the cylindrical stone wall where the water had seeped into the surrounding earth. He poked about with a pickaxe, and to his amazement found a tunnel, glittering like a profusion of eyes in the Amazon rainforest at midnight.

He crawled through and found that the eyes were gemstone-rich ore. He knew right off it was an offshoot of the Wildrose Mine that had played out in the 1910s, and keeping quiet until he could capitalize on it, he told Mum the solution to the leaky cistern was to connect to the Village waterline in the back alley. She wailed that the monthly bill would swallow his measly National Guard pension, but he said they'd *save* money by converting the cistern into a "fruit 'n spud cellar"!

His slick talking brought her around and he built the ladder and shelves, letting the mine's inrushing air chill the cistern. He bought a Ducky load of produce from local farmers—then vanished. Mum inherited a food supply that could've aced the *Kneejerk Time's* Best Cellar List, and Conklin Jr. was bequeathed the title to Ducky and a mind as quick as molasses.

"I s'pose it's all right," says Conklin, easing back from the opening. "Fer now!"

"Only thang is," says Oily, whose trouser cuffs are whiplashing in the frosty updraft. "Can't ya warm it up a little?"

* * *

Based on what he'd seen from the alley behind the Conklin homestead, Truman phoned Olive to say he thought they had enough evidence for a warrant.

"But I advise surveillance cameras, rather than a search."

Olive meets with the judge in Folkston Landing, who finds the evidence sufficient to approve the devices, and Captain Kroft's techie installs four cameras, disguised as crabapples. Olive puts the code on her cellphone and a crisp view comes into focus. The techie shows her how to pan, zoom, and switch cameras, and she finds it child's play to snoop about the Conklin homestead.

"Makes me feel kinda cheap!"

Truman rests a hand on her shoulder.

"Keep in mind that we made the request on the basis of compelling evidence, and the judge agreed. We're playing by the rules, Olive, and we won't be peering into bathtubs or bedrooms!"

"I suppose you're right." She glances at her cellphone as a possum toddles by the henhouse. "And if Conklin *did* play a role in the Ashlars' attack I'm gonna nail him to the wall!"

Early next day Olive stops by Mole End and is shown by Leah to the living room, where she steps back in amazement at the floor-to-ceiling books and records.

"Holy Pete! No wonder you all are so interesting!"

Sam is practicing his horn in the bedroom and hobbles out on his cane to say hello as Jenny offers coffee.

"That's very kind of you," says Olive. "But I hav'ta run, and just wanted to let you know we're following a couple of good leads in search of your assailants!"

* * *

Conklin probes the breach in the cistern with his lantern as Oily and Meat crouch behind him, shivering like a couple of mutts with a real bitch of a mom.

"Cain't we jis plug it up?" says Oily.

"We ain't gonna do no pluggin till we do some 'splun'-kin!"

They squeeze into the tunnel that Conklin's pa discovered 16 years earlier, flecked with stones lit up like fireflies on their fifth cocktail. They follow the pickaxe incisions until the pale iris of the cistern vanishes behind them, and a few hundred yards farther on Conklin stumbles upon a moldy pack of Camels.

"If these were Pa's he was in a tur'ble rush, leavin his smokes behind!"

Oily shudders at the surrounding gloom. "We musta hiked a mile by now, and oughta be som'ers under Condor Lookout!"

"*State* property," says Conklin. "Pa use'ta pay taxes, now 'n then, so Mum and me are part owners!"

They push on and some minutes later enter a subterranean chamber the size of a barn where they find a rusted pickaxe and some buckets, heaped with gem-studded rocks. They look closer and nearly slip into a crevasse that's wide enough to swallow a truck.

"Shitfire!" says Meat.

Conklin's flashlight shows the crevasse running deep and dank from eons of seeping water and, at the bottom—80 or 90 feet down—the flashlight beam reveals a human form. It's clothed in a moldering, green-and-orange checkered hunting jacket—similar to the one his pa was wearing the day he disappeared.

* * *

Sam and Leah are hoeing weeds that have shot up among Mole End's sweetcorn and green beans, and Jenny follows with a watering can as the three windchimes given them by the Elms' Sisters tintinnabulate in the breeze. Under Mynah's and Sparrow's influence, the Sisters have ceased all noisemaking, and the Ashlars removed Leah's loudspeakers from the fieldstone fence.

"It's progress!" says Sam, striking an obdurate dirt clod with his hoe.

A lawn crew is shearing the Whingers' yard, the same men and their surly boss who drowned out the Ashlars' first Monday morning in Wildrose. They're louder than ever, as if wallowing in the Council's erasure of the Noise Ordinance from the Village books.

"Augustus Decibelis," says Leah. "They're raising hell because they don't want to pay for quieter alternatives. Although hand-brooms *would* be cheaper!"

That evening the Pasquins and several Wind Band members help the Ashlars load the fireworks onto the VW and distribute them to kindred spirits throughout Wildrose, as Sam reminds one and all to "Wait for the Titan!"

Libretti meanwhile joins Conklin, Oily, and Meat in the barn-size cavern, deep in the earth below Condor Lookout. Before he became a podiatrist, veterinarian, and leatherwear couturier, he was a lapidary, and he whistles in astonishment as he inspects the sparkling surroundings with his jeweler's loupe.

"There's aquamarine, beryl, citrine, moonstones, and God knows what else! But extracting them from the ore demands expert hands!"

"Hands like yers?" Conklin asks.

Libretti pockets the loupe. "I think we oughta take a road trip in your six-wheeler. Tucson has the granddaddy of gemological shows, and I know a trusted gem cutter who'd fall down on his knees to get ahold of these!"

-11-

IT'S DAYBREAK, AUGUST 9, AND HEAVEN bestows Wildrose with clear skies and fair breezes. Stadium bleachers and a Special Persons Stand gleam in the Turquoise Tower Plaza, overstuffed with families, political factotums, and virtual-gossip columnists from around the continent, lured by the Tower's Grande Opening. Condor Estates' boulevards fatten with vehicles packed with vacationers, Shrinking World Tours busses, and pick-pockets on eSkates. Vessels of every social-economic niche cruise Wildrose River, up to their gunwales with sightseers and vying for mooring spots along the banks—gorged with revelers on folding chairs with picnic hampers and fully charged e-thingies.

Thaïs and Raffia awake to find the pristine sky a validation of their birthday and the splendor that'll flower from it. After breakfasting in the Manor's atrium, Thaïs presents Raffia with a tooled-Morocco edition of Perrault's *The Tales of Mother Goose*, and Raffia gives Thaïs the watercolors she painted that summer, framed by the multi-talented Gallifent. They've agreed to give Zebulon his gifts at 10:49 p.m.—the precise moment of their triple nativity when the Gala strikes its zenith.

"How pretty!" says Petra, helping Raffia into a pink, water-taffeta dress with a blue sash and matching sandals. Then Raffia paints on Thaïs's beauty mark with extra care, given the relentless hi-definition closeups she'll face the next several hours, and assists her into a double-breasted lamé pantsuit. It was spun from unalloyed platinum, created especially for the day by Undine.

"What a queen!" says Raffia, and Thaïs fancies that her sister is starting to show. "And what a princess!"

At Orvis Alley, Conklin is still nursing his wounds at losing the Chief of *Po*leece shield—but salves them with visions of becoming rich enough from gemstone mining to indulge in around-the-clock girl ogling.

He crawled out of bed at the rooster's croaking and hikes around to be sure no one's spying on the Conklin territory. He's irked by the humming of a *Rolling Stoned* news drone and fires a round from the double-barrel shotgun. It's a harmless warning aimed at a hickory tree, and he returns the shotgun to Ducky and backs her snug against the pantry door.

Meat is watching from the kitchen while stroking his cheek, now healed like the seam in a rawhide satchel. He turns to Mum, who's traded her feed-sack dress for a black oilcloth number to mourn her late husband—whose body Conklin promises he'll "one of these days" haul from the mineshaft for a proper burial behind the henhouse.

"Wha'd he do that fer?" says Meat.

Mum exhales a plume of cigar smoke. "Ya mean the potshot? My Reevas has 'is ways!"

Truman and Olive are still monitoring the crabapple cameras from the service lane behind the Conklin homestead, and after checking with the Food Bin and Win-Win outlets on the Sky Vue Freeway to see if Conklin's been buying extra groceries, suggesting he might be shielding Brick Hakker and Jimbo Tavener.

"They never buy much," said the Food Bin manager. "Word is old lady Conklin has the best stocked pantry in the county!"

Conklin rigs a washtub to a rope and pulley above the trapdoor, then supervises Oily and Meat as they hoist the ore-crammed gunnysacks from the mineshaft to the cistern, up to the pantry, and finally into Ducky's capacious hold.

Libretti arrives in a van he just bought on his expectations of becoming rich, and Conklin asks if he's plotted their route.

Twin miniatures of the shanty glint in Libretti's sunglasses. "We'll take Wildrose River to the Folkston Landing, and follow the road from there to Tucson. Among the Grande Opening dazzle we'll be less noticeable than a pimple in a mosh pit!"

"Did ya get aholt yer contact?"

"He'll take the entire load, and I know we can get eight- or nine-hundred thousand for it without breaking a sweat!"

At Old Farm Ridge, Truman is breakfasting with Daisy and logs on to the cameras to find the DUKW backed up to the shanty, and the van parked beside it. He phones Captain Kroft.

"Would you mind checking a license for me?"

* * *

While the masses pour in to Wildrose Marina, life is remarkably calm at Middlemarsh Manse, where Wanda is convalesceing under Silt's and Henna's care. Wanda told Silt that as soon as she's well enough to return to the Council she'll ally herself with Lars and Cecil to reinstate Truman as Chief of Police with Olive as Sergeant, and they'll bring back the Revised Noise Ordinance.

"I'll tell Thaïs about the mole jugs. If she doesn't want them, I'll let Giles sell them at the Green Goose Café and return Thaïs's down payment!"

All of Wildrose's B&Bs are overbooked, and some Wildroseians are still accepting guests in their garage lofts and treehouses. Lean-tos and mosquito-netted hammocks have sprouted up on lawns and porches, and more than one Villager has shipped off an aunt or granddaddy to a distant relative—COD—and turned over their room and its treasured knickknacks to the highest bidder.

At the Marina, Olive deploys her first shift of deputies, then gets Truman and Captain Kroft on her cellphone for a three-way chat to review their plan to keep the Gala peaceful.

-12-

THE *VICTORIOUS* BREAKS FROM the horizon and darkens the sky over Wildrose. A blimp of portentous size, it was retired from the US Meteorological Survey, then bought and refurbished by Zebulon for this most special of days. Its navigation lights flash and the earth shivers beneath its swiftly trolling shadow that consumes whole farms and neighborhoods as its propellers thrust it to a mooring mast atop the Turquoise Tower.

The crowds below watch agog as a hatch opens in the *Victorious's* gondola and three men and three women descend on haltered wires. It's the world-renowned pukeRok band Gimme-More, who with their guitars, hipboards and cheekpods strike up their diamond-plated release, "Rat Snot."

"Rat snot you and rat snot me!" they wail, gyrating around the plaza.

Gimme more!" the crowd pleads, waving their arms and bashing about like tin cans in a windstorm.

The band rips loose, "Rat snot every frigging one of us!"

Goldenhawk is hovering nearby and remarks to her 39 million fans. "The highly touted Turquoise Tower Gala has launched, and the planet's number five band is giving it a sleazy kickoff!"

GimmeMore burps out another stanza as the spectators bray and flagellate themselves, while the *Victorious* unhitches from the mooring mast and sails over the Sky Vue Freeway to entice more traffic to the festivities.

Thaïs and Raffia watch from their library and Raffia grimaces. "That band is awful!"

"They're worse than awful. But we must keep the little people in mind, who adore them!"

The crowd bumps and humps, and Thaïs and Raffia are relieved when Billy Umbo arrives, spiffy as ever in a dapper suit of gun-smoke grey and an indigo bowtie.

"Good morning, Your Honor. Ms. Raffia. Please lemme say what a stellar presence both of you make, and how happy I trust you'll be on this most glorious of birthdays!"

"You're ever the faithful adjutant!" says Thaïs.

The tall-case clock strikes 8:50 a. m. and Umbo escorts them to the Manor's airstrip to board *Mont-Obiston Ace*, its turbo-engine blades flashing like scimitars before an epic battle as Petra waves from the Manor's turret.

"Go safe, my lovelies!"

The pilot roars off on a low-altitude circuit over Wildrose as Umbo trails in the black van and motorists gawk from the bloated roads.

Geoffrey Murgwynd gets word that *The Ace* is coming and signals GimmeMore. After finishing "Rat Snot" they played their super hit "uFug'em," then conclude the audience warm-up with their hyper-cosmic, one-chord screamer, **!*!**, which reverberates from the Turquoise Tower as the crowd flings about in ecstasy, refusing to let the band leave until it plays the chord again. GimmeMore socks out **!*!** a second time and rushes off amid paroxysms of adoration.

Murgwynd dashes onto the plaza with a caressing sweep of his arms. "Wasn't that it? I mean, wasn't that totally, totally *it!?*"

"Totally *it!*" the crowd brays.

"And now for something much, much more momentous," says Murgwynd, "and the reason why all of you came to Wildrose Marina on this day of days!"

He puts a finger to his lips and the vast stadium grows stiller than a union worksite an hour before quitting time. A high-performance *vrooming* tickles the heavens and grows louder until *Mont-Obiston Ace's* chromium body blinds the crowd. It circles and descends, lowers its pontoons and skims to a stop at the Marina.

Billy Umbo had parked the black van in the underground VIP lot and leads Raffia up the gangway among stares and whispers to a private box in the Special Persons Stand.

Murgwynd sweeps his arms.

"And now, please say howdy to our Most-Special-of-All Guest. Multi-decorated European Union CEO, Philanthropist, Arts Patron, and Mayor of Wildrose. The Most Honorable Thaïs Mont-Obiston!"

Thaïs ducks out the *Ace's* doorway, unbends to her full height and parades up the gangway, tossing out smiles shinier than bitcoins. A battery of mics await but she blows them away.

"Dearest friends, treasured neighbors, respected constituents and citizens; honored business leaders, vacationers and tourists; beloved moms, dads, and kiddies! Welcome!"

The crowd whoops.

"What a lovely sight you are, and what a memorable day this is for you, for Wildrose, and for our region!"

A bigger whoop.

She introduces the governor, commerce secretary, and key legislators, whose faces beam massively from the Quad-Board's 90 billion LEDs.

"And I want to thank my good friend Geoffrey Murgwynd for including me in this ceremony—your humble mayor—and ask if you're ready to enter the Promised Land?"

The crowd roars like a tank battle.

"I'll take that as a yes!"

The crowd roars like a warship battle, then Murgwynd approaches with a pair of scissors taller than he is, but Thaïs signals him to wait. The *Victorious* returns from its flight above the Sky Vue Freeway as Thaïs's black eyes survey the crowd.

"Before you become the first-ever explorers of the sensational Turquoise Tower, what would you say to a fistful of freebees to its untold treasures?"

The *Yes* comes like Staten Island, slamming into New Jersey, and Thaïs touches her pendant.

"Admiral? Do you read me?" The *Victorious's* navigation lights twinkle. "Then give us a heavenly shower!"

The *Victorious's* hatch opens and a cloud of platinum-foil coupons descends as the crowd lurches from their seats and stretch out their hands. Thaïs takes the scissors and cuts the ribbon, whose severed ends drop from the Tower's nine sets of double doors.

A woman with a mound of coupons anchored to her bosom with both arms shrieks *Praise Thaïs!* and waddles into the Tower as uniformed greeters meet her with well-rehearsed smiles. The woman's eNasal piercing scans the coupon on the top of her stack (99 cents toward a meal in one of the Tower's 168 eateries) and she waddles along Lapis Lazuli Concourse to an escalator, obeying the directions in her earbud. The Dinsmore dirt-bikers are right behind her, clutching coupons for $1.99 discounts toward pairs of MotorPanz, and in mere seconds the nine doorways swell with dozens, scores, then hundreds of shoppers, clinging like clams to their coupons.

Thaïs joins Raffia in the Special Persons Stand. "What say we quadruple the fun?" She touches her ePendant. "Admiral? How about another flyby?"

The *Victorious* twinkles and glides over the Esplanade to drown the swelling crowds in coupons. Goldenhawk is streaming this for her 57 million fans and laughs.

"It's a dead cert that Wildrose won't have to worry about a cleanup bill!"

The Ashlars are watching on Leah's ePal, as fellow Moles throughout the region await the Titan.

-13-

THAÏS AND GEOFFREY MURGWYND RUSH from store to store, giving rapid-fire interviews amid countless vids and eSnaps as they greet shoppers and goad employees to brisker sales. From nine to two they eat on the hoof, nibbling and sipping and engaging patrons in a large sampling of the Turquoise Tower's 1,007 enterprises, making the Gala planet Earth's biggest show.

But gigantic as her energy is, even Thaïs needs a respite, which she takes with Raffia from 2:00 to 3:00 in their Tower Penthouse, while a team of masseuses restore Thaïs's calves and feet. Images of her play throughout the Tower and across the Internet, convincing the public that 50 or 60 Thaïses are still on the move.

Meanwhile, the Wildrose College Wind Band members polish their shoes and brush their uniforms.

By late afternoon the first-wave shoppers have exhausted their credit and debit cards, their eBuks and their feet, and straggle from the Tower by its quick-exit ramps—making the incoming shoppers think that *nobody's leaving!* The shoppers who began with pilfered cash return to the Tugboat Inn to reap another ID-theft stash. But for every two or three shoppers who leave the Tower, a dozen strain to replace them, a contagion of borrowed wealth that turns the roads into varicose byways. Sales figures are sky-rocketing, but as record-breaking as the morning and afternoon have been, Thaïs is focused on the all-nighter, the Gala's empyrean that'll set it above all other venues around the planet.

"We're winning hands down!" she gushes to Murgwynd.

And yet her best card is yet to play. Her Queen of Platinum Moment at 10:49 p.m.

Captain Kroft meanwhile radios Truman that the van parked by Conklin's shanty is registered to Frederick Libretti, known to the state police as Furry Freddie—a double bookkeeping, clothier-pelt purveyor with a score of behind-the-bars visits.

"Given the crowds, he's probably planning some tailgate trading," Truman says to Olive and Captain Kroft.

Hidden from the crabapple spycams, Oily and Meat drop the final gunnysack of ore into Ducky's hold, then shovel on a layer of potatoes from the cistern, as if it were potatoes all the way down. Conklin kicks at Ducky's tires, pressing into the soil like a woolly mammoth with an extra pair of feet.

* * *

Shadows thicken at Mole End as the Ashlars follow Goldenhawk's coverage. The bullfrog and crickets are hanging fire, as there's fire enough from the Turquoise Tower Quadboard's 90 billion LEDs, six miles away.

"I think it's dark enough!" says Jenny.

Sam buttons his band tunic and Leah brings out a seven-foot Titan and shoves its spike in the ground.

"The Moles Revolt!" they cry.

Moleen and her two molettes hold their breath as Leah strikes a match and the Titan shoots far above the treetops on a fiery plume and explodes in a supernova burst of colors.

Lars is watching from Condor Lookout and sets off a ring of 10 Titan Candles that shoot up and detonate in equally vibrant palettes. They're seen by Giles and Rita at the Village Commons, who set off 20 Titans.

"Look at 'em go!" says Rita.

Another Titan soars above Middlemarsh Manse B&B—launched by Henna as Wanda gives a thumbs-up from her bedroom window—and yet another Titan ascends from Granny Nicklebob at her farm.

Goldenhawk is watching with Charley from her news copter above the Marina and updates her 87 million fans. "Hey! It seems the Turquoise Tower Gala has some competition!"

Charley takes them skyward and the bellycam captures other Titans that answer the Ashlars' CALL TO NOISE from hundreds of locations around the Village and outlying farms.

The Ashlars are watching from their back porch, and Sam turns to Jenny and Leah. "Off we go!"

Orchard Lane is nearly deserted, so Leah swiftly guides the VW toward Chipmunk Run, heading for the College Wind Band, gathering at Lars's farm—smack across Wildrose River from the Turquoise Tower.

***

Olive is at the Turquoise Tower's Grande Concourse, supervising her deputies and coordinating things with Condor Estates security. Sam had briefed her a few days earlier, sharing enough details to satisfy her that the fireworks would be set off safely, without compromising her neutrality.

She's put in 13 hours and is famished, and goes to Ninja Bagels on the Tower's fifth floor for a quick bite. As she finishes she's approached by a Tower security guard who worked with Olive at All Souls College.

"Lucinda! How's it going?"

"God! I've tracked down 10 or 12 missing kids and snagged a truckload of women *and* men trying to walk outta Boobs & Bums with $1,000 bras under their armpits. How's by you?"

Olive laughs. "It's gonna be a long night. And speaking of long, there's an impossible line at the restrooms on the Esplanade, and I wondered if you could point me to the nearest indoor john." She holds up a coffee mug. "My eyes were bigger than my tank!"

"Go to the main floor security window and Sadie will let you in the VIP women's room. There won't be *any* lines and it's fit for movie stars!"

Olive phones Truman that she's taking a short break and goes to Sadie's window, who looks up from her galaxy of monitors.

"What's doing, Chief?"

"Acting Chief, actually. May I have the code to the VIP women's room?"

"Would you believe it? The Grande Opening and it's *outta service!* A plumbing problem they overlooked, so you'll have to use the men's. But there's no one about, so you're in the clear!"

Olive takes the VIP elevator to the 11th floor and enters a bamboo-paneled corridor. OUT OF ORDER is taped to the women's and she goes to the men's and enters the code. Inside, she finds a harpoon displayed above an oil painting of a majestic sloop, *Monarch of the Sea*, in a space done up like the interior of a 19th-century whaling ship. The door clicks shut behind her and she passes through an oak bulkhead to a row of pewter urinals and washbasins with coral-framed mirrors. Opposite are cypresswood stalls, their doors fitted with shiny brass hinges and doorknobs, all of them showing UNOCCUPIED.

"Gosh," she thinks. "It's everything an elegant *lady's* room should be!"

-14-

AS TITANS EXPLODE IN EVER-WIDENING arcs around Wildrose, Billy Umbo rushes to the Turquoise Tower Command Center and asks Cornelius Flug what's up.

Flug runs his hand over his brow, gleaming with sweat. "Damn if I know!"

His monitors show hundreds of would-be shoppers splitting off from the Tower's nine entrances to gape at the Titans, and countless vehicles pulling off the roads, putting a tourniquet in the transfusion tube of incoming customers.

Umbo checks his ePalm and finds Thaïs wooing a crowd at the Crispy Cruller on the Tower's eighth floor, and decides the situation is dire enough for an in-person meeting. He takes the VIP elevator and Thaïs slips with him to the head baker's office, where Umbo holds up his ePalm for her to see, showing Titans alighting like a foretaste of doomsday. The ePalm also shows crowds leaving the Tower and lines thinning out at the escalators—then a Titan streaks above River Road, causing an RV caravan pileup.

Thaïs's eyes darken. "How clever. Those bootleg fireworks the Ashlars donated to the College!" She checks her ePendant and finds the pulsing blue star of Leah's VW, moving north on Chipmunk Run. She plants a hand on Umbo's shoulder. "I want you to make a tactical intervention."

* * *

The heavenly perturbations draw Conklin and his team from the shanty, stuffed with Mum's chicken gumbo.

"Wowie!" he says. Who'd'a thunk!"

"Even less chance anybody'll notice *us!*" says Libretti.

"Ya best git goin!" says Mum.

Oily and Meat say awkward farewells for all she's done for them, then haul themselves up Ducky's stern and plop onto the potato mattress. Conklin fastens the tarp over Oily and Meat, then climbs behind the wheel with Libretti beside him and salutes Mum.

"See ya next week!"

She exhales a blotch of cigar smoke. "We'll celebrate with a nighty cap!"

Conklin pilots Ducky to the gate, its axels creaking and its six tires with their 19,000 pounds of payload grinding out dust motes that marry with the dusk.

Shortly afterward Truman checks in and sees Ducky's exodus. It's clearly loaded with *something*, and he asks Captain Kroft to alert one of his helicopters. The pilot is investigating the collision of a Shrinking World Tours bus with a news van, and Kroft orders her to follow the DUKW.

* * *

Having dispatched Billy Umbo on the search-and-thwart mission, Thaïs has another 73 stores to visit before she can join Raffia in the Penthouse at 10:49 to open Zebulon's gifts and celebrate the Queen of Platinum Moment, and seizes this opportunity to empty her bladder from the many toasts she's drunk. She's rankled that on this of all nights the VIP ladies' is out of order (which'll cost Cornelius Flug a certain appendage), but is glad there are precious few celebrities at the Gala with the status to use it. She goes to the men's room and punches in the code.

Moments before, Olive's toilet flushed and she's buckling on her holster when the outer door opens and a pair of hard heels beat across the oak-plank floor.

From the sound Olive guesses it's a large person, though it doesn't matter as her stall is showing OCCUPIED. But to avoid the awkwardness of encountering a *man*, she decides to stay put while the stranger enters one of the other stalls or uses a urinal and exits. At 5'11" Olive can't quite see over the door, but a spray of platinum hair whips by and she realizes it's Thaïs. She expects her to enter another stall, but Thaïs moves on and Olive guesses she's come to wash up from all the handshaking she's done among the shoppers.

Olive waits for the splash of water at the basin and when it comes her ears perk up. It's coming from a urinal, and instead of a splash it's a torrent!

Her head whirls and she tries to think. Of course! She'd forgotten about Thaïs's brother Zebulon, whom she'd occasionally glimpsed through the Duesenberg's tinted windshield the last several months as he gamboled around the Village. He'd certainly be on hand for such a big night—hovering in the background—and even standoffish brothers must pee from time to time.

Then Olive hears humming and her heart slams. It's *Thaïs* humming! But Olive asks herself, why is she using a urinal?

She holds her cellphone lens just above the stall door—getting a view of Thaïs's back in her lamé pantsuit at a urinal. Thaïs goes on humming and reaches in front of her to "shake off," as Olive's brother used to say in his teasing way, whenever Olive entered the bathroom when he hadn't bothered to lock the door. Stranger and stranger!

Olive hits RECORD as Thaïs finishes her business, zips up her fly and turns around to button her jacket, then goes to a basin where Olive can't see her, due to the intervening stall. Water runs and the hand-dryer whispers.

Thaïs hums another phrase and says, "You're looking like a trillion dollars!"

Olive lowers her phone and waits as the Titans boom an eerie backdrop throughout Wildrose.

"And now let's make more history!" Thaïs says to her reflection.

Her heels retreat across the floor. They pause… then pass through the bulkhead, where the outer door opens and clinks shut.

Olive lets out a breath and waits a good 30 or 40 seconds to make sure Thaïs is really gone before leaving the stall. She washes up and splashes water on her face to calm her nerves, then gets Truman on her cell. There's a busy tone and she leaves a message.

"Hey, Chief. I'm in the VIP men's room at the Turquoise Tower. That's right—the *men's room.* I need to meet you at the Tower's main doors. I'm curious to know what the law says about someone who's impersonating a public official!"

She sends him the video of Zebulon's performance at the urinal, then straightens her cap in the mirror.

"All right, Chief. We're gonna find out what's going on and get you back to your desk where you belong!"

She hurries past the stalls and through the bulkhead, right into Zebulon.

"Hello, Olive!"

It seems forever before Olive can move her tongue.

"I… I… "

"What's that, my dear?"

Olive stares at the impenetrable black eyes peering down at her, and tries to fathom who she's talking to. Zebulon? Thaïs? *Both?* Whoever it is must've seen the OCCUPIED sign when pausing beside the stalls, Olive realizes, and might've heard her message to Truman.

She's always thought of herself as very capable. Some inches taller than the average woman and especially strong. Captain of the Wildrose High School girls' track team and the best softball player in town—man or woman. And a dead shot with a handgun. But she stares up at this immense being, who might've sprung from the Serengeti at the dawn of the Neanderthals.

"I should get back, Your Honor. With the fireworks and all."

"That's right. It's the night of nights and you're on the front line. But two ladies shouldn't be seen leaving a men's room together. You know how tongues waggle in small towns. Let's just see if the coast is clear, then we can go our separate ways and no one's the wiser."

Olive nods, but as Thaïs opens the door Olive starts inching her hand up her thigh. She'd never prevail against this Goliath of a woman in a physical contest, but if she can reach her .38.

Thaïs checks the corridor. "All clear, my dear! I'll let you go first so you can return to your duties!"

"Thanks!"

Thaïs holds the door as Olive grips the .38, knowing she can have it against Thaïs's ribs in three-tenths of a second. Then Olive's head is wrenched 190° sideways with the *Monarch of the Sea* staring her in the face as she's wracked with unimaginable pain.

-15-

THE POLICE HELICOPTER CLOSES IN AS Ducky climbs the eastern logging road toward Condor Lookout, where other vehicles are jammed up to watch the growing sky battle.

"It's awful damn crowded!" says Libretti.

"That ain't a problem!" says Conklin.

He shifts down and plows over the guardrail, plunging deep among the trees and flinging Oily and Meat across the potatoes in the hold.

"Shitfire!" says Oily.

Rather than take the deer path he'd used the day of the Ashlars' assault, Conklin follows Condor Lookout's northern flank, cutting an arc among the evergreens and veering westward toward Wildrose River.

Truman meantime gets Olive's message, and plays it again to be sure he heard correctly. Impersonating a public official? Which one? There are oodles of them at the Gala. Then he finds Olive's video of Thaïs at the urinal and presses REPLY.

"I'm on my way!"

* * *

The legions of fireworks are spawning mass confusion as vehicles choke off the northern stretch of Chipmunk Run. Realizing it could take forever to get through this bottleneck to reach the Wind Band at Lars's farm, Leah guides the VW toward Condor Estates and takes an EMPLOYEE'S ONLY down-ramp to the Turquoise Tower. She updates Goldenhawk, who says, "Smart move!" then follows the ramp to the underground STAFF PARKING area.

"There's gotta be an exit to the river!" Leah says to Sam and Jenny.

Sam laughs. "Nothing searched, nothing found!"

His watch shows 42 minutes until the concert, plenty of time to get there, and they emerge in a subterranean honeycomb of parking carrels where an arrow points, WILDROSE RIVER TUNNEL →600 YARDS.

Zebulon is returning from the Tower's master electrical room, where he disabled the CCTV in the elevators, the 11th-floor corridor, and underground parking areas.

Sadie sees right away from her monitors that there's a problem and alerts Cornelius Flug, who growls that his hands are full up with "ass-loads of more urgent technical glitches, 'cause of the Turquoise Tower's dumbshit, premature opening!"

Zebulon returns to Olive's body on the VIP men's room oak-plank floor where he'd left it minutes earlier, her head wrenched toward *Monarch of the Sea.* He lifts her to his shoulder, warm but lifeless, then goes to the elevator and selects the underground service floor, knowing that the CCTV camera is blind to him and his burden. His ePendant shows 10:17, enough time to dispose of Olive and get to the Penthouse to greet Raffia at 10:49 for the Queen of Platinum Moment.

Then Truman's message comes on Olive's cellphone that he's on the way, and Zebulon mutters, "You're most welcome!"

* * *

The Moles' fireworks are creating such pandemonium that the police copter pilot isn't worried that Conklin will notice *her*, and she stays tight on Ducky's tail as it bushwhacks through the Forest's northern slopes in Conklin's mad dash for Chipmunk Run.

The northbound traffic is light because there are few departing shoppers to form it, but the two-vehicle collision north of the Forest is now an 86-vehicle collision, leaving the southbound lane momentarily empty in front of Conklin, and he shoots across the road and down the steep, wooded bank into Wildrose River's swift current. Ducky yawls in the turbulence, throwing Oily and Meat against the hold.

"Now wut…?!" says Meat.

Conklin engages the propellers, thrusting Ducky downriver past other watercraft, whose well-lubricated passengers imbibe the uncivil war that's rending the sky. The police copter relays this to Captain Kroft and Truman, who's heading to the Turquoise Tower.

"Let's pull her over!" says Kroft. Truman agrees and says he'll join in after he meets up with Olive.

Kroft gives the order and there's an all-hands alert aboard the Coast Guard Cutter *Maysville* at the Marina. The coxswain flips on the forward spotlights as the crew reels in the mooring lines, and moments later the *Maysville* is pushing upriver at a brisk 23 knots. It rounds a bend and the Captain picks out a pair of slitted headlights approaching, 3,400 yards ahead. The coxswain turns on the searchlight and aims its searing beam at Ducky's bow.

Conklin blinks. "Sheeit!"

The *Maysville's* horn sounds and the loudhailer booms from the mast platform.

"This is Captain Jonas Norton, Coast Guard Cutter *Maysville*. Please pull your craft portside, on the east bank of the river. I repeat! Pull your craft to the river's east bank and hold for inspection!"

Libretti sees the sinister form of the cutter's 55mm Bofors machine gun, and knowing it could turn Ducky into a colander in about six seconds, he yanks at Conklin's arm.

"We can't outrace that beast!"

"We don't gotta outrace it!"

He flashes the spotlight to acknowledge Norton's instruction, then shifts course for the eastern bank. The *Maysville* closes distance and cuts to 12 knots as its searchlight tracks Ducky toward the shore.

"Sumpun's gone assways!" says Oily, peering from under the tarp. "What if they're after *us!*"

Meat rubs his scar. "Wul, they ain't gonna git us!" He raises the lantern and sees a tool box, where he finds a flare gun. "Reckon I kin do som'it with this!"

Oily rummages and pulls out the shotgun. He breaks it open and finds shells in both barrels. "And I reckon I kin do som'it with *this!*"

Then Ducky's prow runs aground on the river's eastern shore, throwing them against the hold.

Captain Norton alerts Kroft and Truman. "The vessel's pulled over, about 1,600 yards above the bend." Then over the loudhailer, "Hold your position. We're coming in for boarding!"

"Hang on!" Conklin says to Libretti.

There's a *clunk* below deck as he cuts the propellers and engages the transmission, then he shoves the throttle and releases the clutch as Ducky's prow wheels touch mud below the waterline. Ducky starts forward, and an instant later the midship wheels engage the mud as Ducky edges up the bank.

Norton stares from the *Maysville's* bridge. "What the hell…?" The coxswain brings the searchlight full onto Ducky, and Norton roars over the loudhailer. "Hold your position on the bank. I repeat! Hold your position!"

Libretti squints in disbelief under the brim of his cowboy hat as Ducky's stern wheels touch mud and she gains speed up the bank.

Kroft alerts his two cruisers. "They're making a run for it!"

The cruisers respond that they're stuck in traffic. Truman is also caught in traffic and tries Olive, once again getting her voicemail.

"I'm trying to get there, Olive. Call me when you can!" He pulls over and jogs ahead on foot.

At the Turquoise Tower, Zebulon is descending in the elevator with Olive over his shoulder and, hearing Truman's call, knows she'll return it *when she can!*

Ducky jounces up the steep bank, shuffling Oily and Meat among the cascading potatoes.

Captain Norton knows he'd have to be facing hostile fire before he'd even consider using the Bofors, whose slugs could penetrate a hull much thicker than a DUKW's 1/8" steel plating; and he also knows that innocent people might be aboard. He orders the coxswain to deploy the motor surf boat.

* * *

Leah brings the VW to a stretch of the underground driveway flanked with metal rollup doors—MAINTENANCE & INCINERATOR—AUTHORIZED PERSONNEL

ONLY, beyond which a sign beckons, RIVER TUNNEL — 240 YARDS.

"Almost there!" says Sam.

She laughs. "Almost!"

When the VW is halfway to the curve, Zebulon emerges from the elevator with Olive's limp body over his shoulder and her ponytail dangling to the floor.

"My God!" says Jenny.

Zebulon drops Olive by the elevator, snags her .38, and raises his hand for Leah to stop—who tells Sam and Jenny to duck as she shoves the peddle to the floor.

The VW roars and Zebulon raises the .38.

"What's happening?" says Goldenhawk over Leah's ePal.

The VW closes on Zebulon and whines as if it's about to throw a rod. One hundred feet. Seventy feet. Zebulon points at the driver's side of the windshield, then at the last instant aims higher. The VW engine screams and Leah scrunches against the wheel as Zebulon fires two rounds.

They ricochet from the concrete ceiling and rip through the windshield's metal trim, spraying Leah with hot bits of lead and glass.

-16-

DUCKY IS GAINING SPEED UP THE riverbank when the motor surf boat darts from the *Maysville* and Captain Norton calls over the loudhailer.

"This is your final warning. Stop your vessel and come out with your hands above your heads!"

Libretti clings to Conklin. "This is nuttier 'n squirrel shit!"

The motor surf boat reaches the bank and the crew scrambles ashore. A boatswains mate says she's got a clear view of one of DUKW's tires, peeping beneath the steel skirting—80 or 90 yards up the bank from them. The coxswain agrees and the mate fires her M16, puncturing a tire.

"Goddamn!" says Libretti.

The mate is about to fire another round when a tree blocks her aim.

A gage shows the sudden loss of pressure and Conklin throws a lever that reinflates the tire. "We're gonna make it!"

Ducky climbs another 50 or 60 feet, then trembles as the starboard wheels happen onto the mouth of a defunct mine-ventilation shaft. The men cry out as Ducky flips sideways and slams into a huge boulder, spilling her five tons of ore, seasoned with 60 bushels of potatoes. A mate crawls under Ducky and shuts her off as the coxswain shines his light on Conklin and Libretti—moaning among the tree trunks.

* * *

Leah grips the wheel as the VW follows the tunnel beneath the river, then reaches the surface below the booming fireworks and crosses Chipmunk Run to the picnic area at the western edge of Wildrose Forest.

"Oh God!" says Sam.

"Leah...?" shouts Goldenhawk from the ePal.

Leah hits the brakes as blood soaks her shoulder and the pain sets in. Sam presses his handkerchief to her as Jenny settles her in the passenger seat and fastens the seatbelt

Sam takes the wheel when a shadow falls over him. A man's at the window with a shotgun, his eyes red with desperation. Then the rear side-door is yanked open by an ugly hunk of a man with a scarred cheek and a flare gun.

Leah starts up and he climbs in and shoves her down. It's her wounded shoulder and she winces in agony.

"Leave her be!" says Jenny. Then she recognizes them as the two pieces of filth who attacked them five weeks earlier at Condor Lookout.

"But how?" Sam wonders. He turns to Oily at his window, hoping to reason with him, but his eyes are like flames and Sam twists around to Meat. "Someone's been killed and my granddaughter is wounded. We've gotta get her to the Clinic!"

Meat sees the darkening area of Leah's shoulder and the gaping holes in the windshield. "Git back here next yer wife!"

Sam gets out and limps around to Jenny, then Oily takes the wheel and hands the shotgun to Meat. Oily finds Sam's cane and tosses it in the woods, and Meat—reeking of soiled clothes and sweat—settles in the campstool behind Sam and Jenny with the shotgun trained on them.

Oily sees the gas gage and grins at Leah. "How nice'a ya to fill 'er up! But where's your tire tool, Ms. *Vag*itarian?"

"Why? Don't you have one of your own?"

He grabs her by the jaw. "Ya wanna find out?!"

Sam pulls Oily's arm away. "Let her be!"

Then he feels the shotgun at the back of his neck.

"*We're* givin the orders," says Meat. "Un'erstand? Now gimme yer cellphones!"

"My wife and I don't have one."

Meat jabs with the shotgun. "Don't fuck wid me!"

"It's true!" says Leah. "Haven't you been following the news? Everybody on the planet knows it!"

"They're too hoity-toity for cellphones!" says Oily, and Leah gives him her own cellphone.

"Give hit 'ere!" says Meat, and Oily tosses it to him.

Leah's ePal dropped to the floor when Meat shoved her, and with Oily turned away, she shuts off its speaker, leaving the mic on and nudging the ePal under her seat with her heel.

Meat stares at the icons on her cellphone and smashes it against the propane stove.

Far overhead, Goldenhawk grabs Charley's arm. "There are some men with the Ashlars!"

Meat tells Oily to get moving. "And keep yer mind on yer drivin!"

Oily glares at Leah, then puts the VW in gear and follows a trail to the foot of Moonlight Knob. He gets out and removes the log from the stone pillars and takes the VW through.

Leah sees her chance and catches Meat's eye in the rear-view mirror. "If you're hoping to drive up Moonlight Knob, I don't think the VW can make it!"

"Ya better pray hit can!" A minute later Oily is guiding the VW up the base of Moonlight Knob in first gear and Meat scoffs. "Seems all wite to me!"

Goldenhawk passes this on to Truman and Captain Kroft, and begs them to keep the sirens off until things are clearer. Then she claps Charley on the knee.

"Moonlight Knob!"

* * *

After firing at Leah's VW, Zebulon pocketed the .38 and put Olive's body in his black van—parked around the corner from the elevator in his private bay, where Umbo had left it that morning. Zebulon's ePendant shows the VW starting up the sinuous gravel road that climbs Moonlight Knob. He takes Nightshade from the van, flips on the infrared lamp, and charges up Moonlight Knob, threading its way through the trees by a far steeper but much shorter hiking trail to the top.

* * *

Leah presses the handkerchief to her shoulder. It stings like hell, but she doubts it's seriously damaged—knowing from injuries on a war documentary she did that skin lacerations can yield fearful amounts of blood. She rests her other arm on the back of the seat and forms an OK with her thumb and forefinger. Jenny sees it and squeezes Sam's hand, who squeezes back.

From his seat behind them, Meat watches the tree silhouettes judder by, their topmost limbs lit by brilliant spears of fireworks which, combined with the blaring of

Tchaikovsky from the College Wind Band at Lars's farm, are deflecting more shoppers from the Turquoise Tower. Meat reckons that all of this confusion increases the odds of him and Oily getting away.

Goldenhawk and Charley soar overhead and detect a pair of lights like glowworms, crawling a quarter of the way up Moonlight Knob. She radios Truman and Captain Kroft. Kroft is driving on the shoulder of Chipmunk Run with his flashers on, mere inches from the sluggish chain of traffic as he goes to collect Conklin and Libretti from Captain Norton's crew.

A minute or so later Truman reaches the Turquoise Tower VIP men's room, but Olive is nowhere in sight and he phones Kroft that he'll try to find her.

Nightshade climbs swiftly up the steep hillside—a panther on a scent—and the ePendant shows the VW's blinking star 570 yards below Moonlight Knob's summit. The .38 is heavy in Zebulon's pocket, with four bullets left. Enough to do the job, he thinks, and there's plenty of ways to dispose of it. The Turquoise Tower's incinerator, with Olive Best! But it's 10:23 and he hurries upward…

From the VW's back seat, Sam hears the Wind Band and wonders what Pierre thinks of his absence. Leah is intent on the trees skipping by her window, and Jenny's eyes are large with worry. Sam doubts that the men intend them serious harm. Their capture was just bad luck, and the two men must know they've a better chance of escaping if they avoid bloodshed. But he knows he must keep his wits about him.

They're three-quarters of the way up Moonlight Knob where the trail begins to level off, and Oily shifts to second gear as the VW chugs along.

Leah stares in awe at the colorful maelstrom, visible for miles around. Despite her warning to Meat so Goldenhawk would know where they were headed, she knew her camper would make the grade. But she has no idea if Goldenhawk is listening to her ePal.

-17-

NIGHTSHADE SPRINTS UP THE FINAL yards and breaks from the trees to the crest of Moonlight Knob. Zebulon dismounts and goes to a log railing at the far side of the road. It's 1,250 feet above Wildrose River, whose surface mimics the fury in the sky. Here and there a boulder broods in its swift current, and a mile upstream the *Maysville* is anchored, with Ducky topsy-turvy on the bank.

Zebulon's chest expands in joy at his sparkling empire, then he hears the VW approach. He takes out the .38 and checks the cylinder. Four bullets. Then he gets a better idea and shoves it back in his pocket. He takes Nightshade to the far side of the trail, in full view of the straightaway.

* * *

Oily leers at Leah. "These wheels ain't so bad!"

"Keep yer eyes on the trail!" says Meat.

"They're nearing the crest," Goldenhawk tells Kroft and Truman.

The VW gains speed and bounces over the rutted gravel, and ahead of them Nightshade could be a black boulder beside the trail. Zebulon waits until the VW is a few hundred feet away, then locks in the laser and delivers a quarter-second burst.

Oily screams and the VW reels with confusion.

"Christ!" says Goldenhawk.

The VW lurches toward the Knob's sheer cliff face as Leah grabs the wheel with her good arm and tries to pull it back on course while Oily wails in agony. Sam reaches over the seat for the key and the engine stalls. The VW jerks and smashes through the railing as he pulls the emergency brake and the VW jolts to a stop.

Oily is flung into the windshield; Leah is caught by her seatbelt, with Sam and Jenny thrown against the back of her seat and Meat piled behind them as the VW teeters at the edge of the cliff.

Blood spurts from Oily's face and Jenny reaches for Leah. Meat is dazed and staggers up with the shotgun as Sam grabs its barrel.

Charley goes for the spotlight and Goldenhawk asks him to wait.

Zebulon hears Sam and Meat struggling and sees the VW's front wheels, suspended over the cliff. He goes behind the VW and lifts it by the bumper.

"Turn it on!" says Goldenhawk.

The spotlight zaps the VW in a blinding oval and Zebulon lets go, throwing Sam and Meat against the propane stove. Zebulon gets the .38 and shields his eyes from the copter's spotlight. He fires and the gun blast reverberates as a starburst appears in Goldenhawk's lexan bubble.

Charley kills the spotlight and jets the copter forward as Zebulon empties the cylinder.

Ping! Ping! Ping!

Sam and Meat thrash about the VW, knocking Jenny aside as Leah struggles to get the fire extinguisher from its mount.

Goldenhawk's lexan is fractured with two more bullet holes and the gage shows that the fuel tank's been punctured, spewing petrel onto the treetops. In an instant Charley engages the auxiliary tank.

Zebulon swears, drops the .38 and returns to the VW.

"Take us down!" says Goldenhawk. They descend and she turns on the spotlight, engorging the VW in brilliant white light as Zebulon lifts it by the rear bumper.

"Let go!" Sam yells at Meat. "Or we'll be killed!"

Meat shoves him against the rear window. "*You* leggo!"

Charley settles the chopper on the gravel as Meat forces the muzzle toward Sam's head. Leah is struggling with the fire extinguisher as Sam ducks. She frees the extinguisher from the mount and directs a foamy stream at Meat's face. The shotgun goes off, blowing out the rear window and swamping the VW in gun smoke.

Zebulon jerks and his shoulder gushes blood.

The VW slams down, flinging its occupants about like dolls. Meat gets to his feet and wipes the fire-retardant foam from his face, then pushes out the door and raises the shotgun at Zebulon.

"Git outta my way!"

Zebulon is silent and Meat pulls the trigger. The hammer snaps but nothing happens. He pulls the other trigger. Nothing. He remembers the potshot Conklin took that morning at the hickory tree and turns ashen. He throws the shotgun at Zebulon and starts for Nightshade.

Zebulon grabs him by the throat and whisks him from the ground as he squirms helplessly.

"I ain't done nothin to you!"

"Totally my fault. Casting swine before pearls!" He smashes Meat against the VW and lets him drop lifeless to the gravel.

The Ashlars spill from the VW and see Zebulon's mangled arm, and Sam gestures at Goldenhawk.

"Listen. I'm sure she can get you to the Clinic!"

Zebulon laughs dryly. "And I thought *you* were the fool!"

He summons the last of his almost godlike strength and mounts Nightshade, guiding it though the broken railing to the edge of the cliff with his arm hanging helpless at his side. The QuadBoard's 90 billion LEDs are soaking the sky with ecstasies of color, and the Wind Band is playing the *1812 Overture* as the Turquoise Tower shimmers like a dream.

Zebulon sighs from deep within his being and twists the throttle…

* * *

Leah is strapped in beside Charley with Goldenhawk behind her. She has slit open Leah's blouse and is holding a compress to her injured shoulder from the chopper's first-aid kit.

"We'll be there in no time!"

As they ascend, Leah sees Sam reverse the VW from the cliff and start down Moonlight Knob with Jenny beside him—the river a dark mirror far below them.

Truman reaches the riverbank and finds Zebulon with a broken back. The current threw him ashore and Nightshade sank to the bottom of the channel, its infrared beam haloing a school of catfish. Truman makes a tourniquet from his shirt for Zebulon's mangled arm and calls for an ambulance.

Zebulon's chest heaves. "You shouldn't have bothered."

"Try to stay quiet."

"What happened to the Ashlars?"

Truman says he hears Goldenhawk heading off for the Happy Family Clinic.

"I'm glad!" says Zebulon. He sees another Titan firework redden the sky and licks his lips. "What time is it?"

"Nearly 10:50."

At the Turquoise Tower Penthouse, Raffia is waiting to give her brother his birthday hug. She watches a shaft of platinum streak heavenward, carving Thaïs's portrait, 10 miles high and brighter than the noonday sun. The Queen of Platinum!

FINAL THINGS

IT'S SATURDAY, SEPTEMBER 27, and Mole End is the noisiest place in Wildrose. But it's a modest 68 dB, the laughter of friends and families and the pleasurable lilt of music. It's Wildrose Founders Day and the Ashlars are treating the Village to a cookout. An earthen-pit, willowwood fire crackles at the foot of the driveway, where Cecil and Mabel Flinn preside with good humor and ready spatulas.

Eat up!" Mabel commands.

Hotdogs, hamburgers, piccalilli, and potato salad spice the air. Goldenhawk settled her news chopper in the burdock meadow and Charley helps her serve sweetcorn from Jenny's garden, roasting in their husks. Her news is on pause, and her 1.3 billion fans will have to gnaw their fingernails in suspense until the cookout is over to begin their next adventure.

Folding tables under Rita's eye tantalize with Green Goose Café quiche, brown-sugar baked beans, meat or veggie casseroles, and Jenny's apple-crumb cookies.

"There's plenty more, yous guys!" says Rita.

Sam is by the Virginia bluebells, cranking an ice cream maker. Sparrow Dinsmore and the Middlemarsh boys watch hopefully and Sparrow says, "I'd like to try that!" and Sam laughs, "It's yours!"

He hopes to finish his book on Thoreau in three months, and the publisher is planning a print run of 200,000 copies—earning more money than he and Jenny could've dreamed. They realize they'll be able to enjoy a lengthy European trip and increase their giving to some favorite causes—including The Thoreau Society—but they also know that such a lot of money will complicate their lives.

Sam gives the ice cream maker a final turn and surrenders it to Sparrow, then gets the new willow cane Leah carved for him and joins Jenny and a few of their many guests at one of the folding tables, scattered about the pond. Earlier that week Jenny began teaching a weekly hydroponics workshop at the library, and has agreed to choreograph the ballet sequence for the All Souls College production of *Carousel* in November.

"Wonderful sweetcorn!" Tabitha tells her.

"And your asparagus sandwiches are yummy!" says Jenny.

Sam sent her great-granny's clock to a repair shop in Boston, and hopes it'll be returned in time to be Jenny's *Carousel* opening-night gift. The Wildrose Council appointed Lars to serve out Thaïs's term. He's seated next to Duffy, Tabitha, and Undine, who's peering between the strands of her beaded hair at Leah, who's filming the cookout.

Giles and his keyboard are on the porch with the Pasquins and their cellos and Henna on piccolo, playing Cole Porter. Later in the day Pierre will conduct the Founders Day Concert at the All Souls College band shell. He has little fear of the music being disrupted by traffic along Chipmunk Run toward the Turquoise Tower, as the vast complex's glamour has already peaked, and fewer vehicles are heading that way. The 1,007 shops are making money, but the hoopla has passed them by in favor of a more spectacular resort-and-retail gagaplex outside Walla Walla, Washington, which has an OctaBoard, twice as tall and four times as broad as the Turquoise Tower's QuadBoard.

At its August meeting the Wildrose Council—under Lars's, Cecil's, and Wanda's sway—voted to reinstate the Revised Noise Ordinance. Two more readings must clinch the matter, but it's clear that most Wildroseians are soul-sick of egregious vibes. For now at least the 70 dB limit that the Ashlars fought for will be the law in Wildrose. And fearing that another contagion of vehicular battles might overwhelm its many communities, the state legislature voted to expunge Statue 83 from the books.

Aaron Copland's *Fanfare for the Common Man* will open the concert, after Chief Truman announces that its performance will be dedicated to Olive Best, for whom the Village Commons will be named in a candlelight ceremony that evening. A bronze plaque is fixed to the sycamore tree by the Village Hall, inscribed:

How oft the Best of us
Give up their lives
To save the rest of us!

Truman told his friends he'll retire in a year or two, but for now he's enjoying the Cole Porter with Daisy and ruminating on Olive.

Leah is roving about, filming the cookout. Her documentary—retitled *The Days and Nights of the Moles Revolt*—has sold for $3,950,000 plus five percent of gross revenues and will premiere at All Souls College in January, with proceeds going to the Wildrose Wildlife Fund. Her VW sports a new windshield and rear window, installed by the Offmans. They did this in return for Leah's advice on starting an auto-rehabbing web show, elbowgreaseNOW, and the Offmans have taken over the lease on Tread on Us Retreads as their studio (keeping its aural outrages far away from Orchard Lane). Leah recommended camera and lighting equipment and urged them to seek their crew from the Elms' Sisters—a tactic she hopes will defuse any urges the Sisters may have to morph from windchimes to fireworks.

In a few days Leah will head to Knoxville to scout locations for a dramatic feature she's written, which she'll fund with her Moles Revolt film income. Although she's not especially vain, the scars on her shoulder are likely to dissuade her from ever again appearing in a shoulder-less dress. She rarely wears such garments anyway, so it doesn't matter very much to her. What does matter is that she'll miss Giles a good deal. She returned to his saltbox two or three times the last few weeks but gently refused his proposal to move in. She'll accept the occasional stab of loneliness in exchange for the joy of feeding her insatiable hunger for making films that tell a good story. For another 25 years or so Giles will be wedded to the Green Goose Café, whereas Leah will always be weighing anchor.

Except for the occasional car coming to the cookout, Orchard Lane is quiet, and the quietest spot of all is Mont-Obiston Manor. Its stalwart butler Gallifent is the caretaker of its vast and echoing rooms until it can be sold to a trophy house collector, or made into a retreat for detoxifying e-media stars. Petra has gone with Raffia and her stuffed giraffe to live with Raffia's several cousins in Milwaukee, where Zebulon's broken remains are resting beside Thaïs in the family crypt. The cousins have been appointed trustees of the Mont-Obiston fortune on Raffia's behalf, which one day will devolve onto her offspring. Raffia is looking much larger than expected and the doctor has arranged for a sonogram, thinking it might be another case of triplets.

The revelation that Thaïs had died a brief time before taking office as mayor and was so brilliantly impersonated for eight months by her reclusive brother had stunned Wildroseians, a sensation that turned to shock when it was learned that he'd also impregnated Raffia and instigated the attack on the Ashlars and murdered Olive Best. The Wildroseians most shocked by it were the first to claim they'd always suspected there was "something strange about them Mont-Obistons!"

But humankind being what it is, the shock is turning to forgetfulness as the Mont-Obiston scandal is overtaken by other, more grotesque events on the world stage. Meat, Brick Hakker, was buried in his hometown in Arkansas, and Oily, Jimbo Tavener, blinded permanently in one eye by Nightshade's laser, is behind bars in the Folkston jail, awaiting trial for assault and kidnapping. Conklin and Mum are sitting in their shanty at Orvis Alley in ankle-bracelet monitors by their TV, awaiting trial for harboring and abetting fugitives, as is Libretti at his double-wide trailer at Trade Wind Court.

Billy Umbo has gone underground and will doubtless emerge to plight his allegiance to another master. And the issue of the gem-laden ore is still being sorted out between the state's Bureau of Mines and Department of Parks.

This ever-changing scene is regarded tranquilly by Moleen. Her two moleetes have moved inside the cabin, to prevent them being hauled off by tourists who get lost on their way to the Green Goose Café or Woodsculptors Loft. At about 4,600 pounds Moleen is unlikely to become anyone's souvenir, and she keeps company with the bullfrog, the mourning doves, and the mockingbird (who at the moment is doubling with Henna on piccolo). New mole tunnels have formed around the yard, reminding us that although unseen and unheard, they're always underfoot.

Moleen's ivory complexion has acquired a green-tea patina since the Sunday in early June when the Ashlars brought her to life, which in time will turn ashen gray. And several fine cracks have appeared, the first of many that'll follow as the years come and go. In a decade or two, after Sam and Jenny have left the earth, the crevices will deepen and Moleen, overcome by abundant life, will waste away. After a century her gimlet eyes will sparkle one last time and she'll be gone forever.

"You oughta spray her down with a couple coats of KnokdaRot," Clovis said to Sam. "I can get you a dozen gallons at cost and she'll last forever and a day!"

"Naw," said Sol Silvertongs. "Ya gotta build a solarium for her. I got stacks and stacks of anti-UV glass left over from my custom window business!"

It occurred to Sam and Jenny that the library or All Souls College might want to adopt Moleen, to display in some corner as a relic of Wildrose's one moment of fame. A bronze tablet might entertain future generations with an account of the Moles Revolt, from back in the day. Or Moleen will stay where she is, to rejoin her natal soil.

Sam is restless from too much conviviality, and after pressing Jenny's hand he gets his cane and takes a turn in the frontyard. He pauses below the linden tree, whose summer green is turning autumn red. One of the fence rails has fallen from its mortises, a chore he'll attack tomorrow, along with what'll probably be the final lawn-mowing of the year. Then he'll wipe off the grass stains and oil the mower to have it ready for next summer. He hopes to fend off the sciatica for some years to come, but suspects the mower will outlast him. The Vietnamese-built chainsaw's recycled tooth-paste-tube manifold broke a few days ago and he tossed it in the recycle bin. But Growler is waiting in the shed. Sam hasn't drained the gas tank, as he wants Growler ready at a moment's notice, should a storm bring down another willow tree.

Sam goes to Moleen and runs his hand over the chisel marks on her mighty flank. He takes in the resin scent and shudders. Deep down, he hears the neighbors' rage and feels Growler's heft.

O reader! Put down your e-device and listen hard! The pines are summoning a breeze; the frogs and mourning doves a song! Mole End is beckoning!

CHARACTERS & LOCATIONS

~ Village of Wildrose ~

UPPER ORCHARD LANE

>Mont-Obiston Manor. The Mont-Obiston triplets: Thaïs, Zebulon & Raffia. Gallifent, butler. Petra, head housekeeper.

ORCHARD LANE

>Mole End. The Ashlars: Sam, Jenny & granddaughter Leah. Moleen & her 2 Molettes. Frogs, finches, barn owl, mourning dove, cardinals, foxes, & mockingbird.

>Middlemarsh Manse B&B. The Middlemarshes: Silt & Wanda; daughter Henna & twin sons.

>The Plinketts: Po, Pru & their 2 Chihuahuas.

>The Whingers: Clovis, Madge & their beloved swimming pool.

>The Offmans: Honus, Winney & their auto-rehab carriage-house.

>The Silvertongs: Sol, Figgie & their world-class sportplatz.

ORCHARD LANE BOTTOMS. West Side of the U-bend

>Dinsmore Farm: Dewey, Mynah, son Sparrow & numerous siblings.

ORCHARD LANE BOTTOMS. East Side of the U-bend

>The Elms. The Cosmic Sonic Sisterhood, LLC: Calliope, Pavana, et al.

WILDROSE VILLAGE CENTER

>Village Hall: Thaïs Mont-Obiston, Mayor; Duffy Nicklebob, Village Clerk; Vivian, Truman, Police Chief; Lieut. Reevas Conklin; Patrol Officer Olive Best.

>Green Goose Café: Giles McDrake, owner/pianist. Mable Flinn, chef. Rita, head server. Farting local diner & Shrinking World Tour Bus tourists.

>Woodsculptors Loft: Lars Anderson, owner, woodcarver & attorney.

>Spend & Loan Bank: Tabitha Tannenbach, Manager. Figgie Silvertongs, head teller.

>Whitlow Insurance: Buford Whitlow, owner/agent.

>Flinn Accounting: Cecil Flinn, CPA/owner.

>Knokdown Drugs: Clovis Whinger, Stock Manager.

>Cucumber Patch: Madge Whinger, Assistant Nursery Coordinator.

>2$ Duz It: Pru Plinkett, Assistant Sales Rep.

>Gas & Lube Boutique, pump attendant.

LOON LAKE ROAD:

>The Tannenbachs: Tabitha & wife Undine. Various parents, aunts & uncles.

CHIPMUNK RUN

>All Souls College: Pierre & Marie Pasquin, music professors & cello duo. Co-Principal hornist & other Symphonic Wind Band members.

CRABTREE DRAW:

>The Flinns: Cecil & Mabel & 2 college-age sons.

HATHAWAY HOLLOW:

>The Whitlows: Buford & wife. Teen daughter & son. Baseball coach & Okra TV Show fan.

OLD FARM RIDGE

>The Trumans. Police Chief Vivian & wife Daisy.

ORVIS ALLEY

>The Conklins. Reevas, Mum.& Rhode Island Red hens

SALAMANDER RIDGE ROAD

>Tread-On-Us Retreads Tires: Jimbo Tavener & Brick Hakker (AKA Oily & Meat), owner-operators.

PERSIMMON LANE

>Olive's encounter with the two fireworks bootleggers.

TUGBOAT INN

>Billy Umbo. Platinum LLC's Chief of Customer Persuasion.

TRADE WIND COURT TRAILER PARK

>Furrier Fashions Worldwide: Frederick Libretti, owner/taxidermist.

TURQUOISE TOWER

>Geoffrey Murgwynd, General Manager. Cornelius Flug, Chief Engineer.

>Lilly Pad Lotions & Notions. Po Plinkett, Manager.

>Sadie, CCTV monitor supervisor.

>Lucinda, Security Guard. Thousands of shoppers

WILDROSE BOARDING HOUSE

>Woman with parasol. Man with tortoiseshell glasses.

WILDROSE FOREST

>Moonlight Knob, Condor Lookout, Defunct Gemstone Mine.

PIONEER ACRES

>Nicklebob Dairy Farm: Granny Nicklebob.

~ Out-of-Towners ~

>ICEE (Internal Combustion Engine Enthusiasts) & other Supreme Saddle affiliates. Midnight Thunder Bikers. State Police Chief Adron Kroft & his officers & helicopter pilots. Goldenhawk, news chopper reporter & her pilot, Charley. Dr. Clara Duzzle & Dr. Reynolds Vey, dB experts. Jonas Norton, Captain, Coastguard Cutter *Maysville* & various crew members.

AFTERWORD

The seed of *Revolt of the Moles* was planted during the seven humid weeks the summer of 2012 when I filmed *And Paint the Sky*—an indie feature film I wrote, directed, and edited at my home in Bogota, NJ, with enormous help from my wife, Jo Ann, my lead actors Hannah Timmons, John Isgro, and Kali Morse, and with the company of our beloved dog, Puck. Eking out what eventually required 1,003 "Action!" and "Cut!" shots on a nano-budget, I avoided off-the-premises filming, the sole exception being the bucolic backyard of our good friends and next-door neighbors, John and Julie Meehan—whose comforting koi pond with its water fountain serenades were always welcome.

The film's many dialogue scenes that I shot indoors and outdoors were breached countless times by the roar of gas-powered leaf blowers, weed trimmers, and riding mowers: the loud braking and takeoffs of delivery trucks; the thundering airplanes from the Newark and Teterboro airports; the diesel-engine throttling and airbrake squeaking of the New Jersey Transit busses up the street from us; the vehicles hustling by with faulty mufflers; and the groaning of the six-lane I-81 interstate traffic, the length of a baseball diamond from us. I spent a good deal of time at my computer, looping dialogue!

Unwanted *indoor* noises were dealt with more easily: before calling "Action!" Jo Ann and I always shut the windows, turned off the AC units, unplugged the refrigerator, and muted all cellphones. By October 2013 this bedlam of noises had fermented in my head as the basis for a darkly comic satire.

ACKNOWLEDGEMENTS

My wife Jo Ann was my first and most ardent reader and critic during the several years I spent writing this novel, and I'm grateful for her loving but always frank comments as the story evolved. She's my ever-constant lighthouse.

After I finished the first draft (nearly twice its ultimate length) I had the good luck to receive the crisp and highly detailed comments of Phyllis Berk. Her sharp eye and penetrating mind—honed by her deep love of books and years of professional science journal editing—nudged me to see that I needed to make a number of judicious cuts and clarify areas that were puzzling.

Jean Dory, a family friend, scholar, and homemaker extraordinaire with a renaissance engagement of life, bucked up my spirits by pointing out the parts of the novel that were working well, at a time when all I could see were the parts that weren't working at all.

My colleague Lois Roma-Deeley, a highly respected college professor and multi-award winning poet, provided several key insights that helped me dig deeper into my novel's tropes and rhythms. She's a fellow writer's best friend.

James B. Nicola, a theatre professional, composer, musician, and prolific poet of breathtaking sensitivity, urged me to keep my core audience in mind. Thank you, James.

Another good friend, play director and university professor Graham Whitehead, urged me to level an eye on the novel's balance, the interplay of its light and dark aspects.

Arline Bronzaft, PhD., one of planet Earth's most highly respected experts on noises and their impact on humans, pets, and wildlife, kept me straight as to how sounds are measured, and urged me to include characters with expert testimony in the story. I'm most grateful to her!

My final reader was theatre pro Richard Leigh-Nilsen, whose multiple fine combings of my novel led to an encyclopedic list of helpful observations that ferreted out numerous errors, inconsistencies, and downright goofs. He also shepherded me through the convolutions of formatting my novel into Word in readiness for publication. A big handshake of thanks to him!

Now. I assure my readers that any typos, awkward punctuation, bad grammar, dangling modifiers, modified danglers or other errors, confusions, or shortcomings rest totally on my shoulders.

—ACT, Fallsington, PA

About the Author

ALAN TONGRET is the author of *The Inn of a Thousand Days: A Memoir of a Country B&B*. His plays that have been produced include *Memories of the Lost Acres*, *Child of the Kosmos*, *Brontë*, *The Ballad of Sam Pepys*, *Shakespeare and the Gospels—Primetime!*, *Poor Richard's Revolt,* and the Burge Sisters' Quintet: *Treasure at the Devil's Backbone*, *Birth of Venus*, *The Boughs of Folly*, *Aurora*, and *Arbor Day*. As a filmmaker via Tongret*ARTS* Alan produced and shot the indie feature, *And Paint the Sky*. Later this year he will release his next novel, *Diamonds in the Rough: The Greatest Ever Baseball Team.*

Born in Hancock County, Indiana, and raised mostly in farm country, Alan graduated from Boone County High School in Florence, KY. He earned a BA in Speech, Drama & English from Morehead State University, an MFA in acting from Ohio University, and an MFA in creative writing from Arizona State University. He was for many years in turn an actor with various companies around the USA, a theatre manager at the Brooklyn Academy of Music, and a tenured professor at Paradise Valley Community College in Phoenix, AZ., where he founded the Theatre

Program and oversaw the design and construction of its Center for the Performing Arts. He's a longtime supporter of the American Farmland Trust and The Thoreau Society. His most cherished union is with his wife, Jo Ann Yeoman, author, journalist, college professor, and multi-talented theater professional.

Made in the USA
Middletown, DE
13 February 2024